PHOENIXCRY

#1 IN THE ROGUE WITCH: A REVERSE HAREM ROMANCE

K.T. STRANGE

HEART *Candies*
PUBLISHING

For more information:

http://kstrange.com

hey@ktstrange.com

Book Design: Heart Candies Publishing

Cover design: Ciaran Strange

Photography: Curtis Noble curtisnoblephotography.com

Model: Becca Briggs beccabriggs.com

CONTENTS

STAY IN TOUCH!

KT's Newsletter

Be the first to know about my new releases, deleted scenes and other exclusive content, deals and my personal recommendations! Sign up for my newsletter here: http://pxlme.me/QPIZW4Ju

KT's Facebook Group

Come hang out with us in the KT's Beauties Facebook Group! We play games, we share hot gifs, and talk books! http://pxlme.me/rvGrrf8X

ONE

Darcy Llewellyn
@DarcyLuvsDonuts

 Follow

It's hot. We're hot. What happened to #fall?
C'mon, I want to get my #PSL on!

10 Retweets 30 Likes

♡ 14   ⟲ 10   ♡ 30   ✉

It's hot, sticky early-September days that made me wish I
was a better weather witch. As it was, I could barely spark
up my fingers with electric shocks, let alone bring the rains.
The truth is, I left the world of spells and potions behind
almost three years ago, and haven't looked back since. Even
if I could have conjured up a little rain-storm to break the
heat which had fallen over Seattle, I probably wouldn't
have. Suffering through the heat made me more of a
mundane, like a regular person, who didn't do magic and
didn't even know it existed. And as far as I was concerned,

putting as much distance between me and my past life in the magical world was a bigger priority than not melting.

Besides, it wasn't so bad. I was laying on the floor next to the lower bunk, with the fan pointed right at me, a hand-out from my earlier class in one hand, and a spray bottle in the other. The spray-bottle acted like a cooling mister when I pointed it at the fan and squirted. Who needed a wand and some fancy spell words when you had a cheap spray bottle from the Dollar Tree?

"Ugh. I hate leg day," my roommate commented as she kicked open the door to our dorm, and glared at the bunk beds that rested against the wall. "Why did I have to pick the top bunk?" she asked. "My glutes are screaming at me."

Max, or as she refused to be called, Mackenzie, had been my roommate for the last three years of my college experience at the private liberal arts school, Westerin Academy, and so far, the only person who knew of my abilities and a little bit of my background. She was the best friend a witch like me could ask for and I treasured her. Except when she was incessantly complaining over her choice of beds.

"Because you hate sleeping in a cave and it makes you think you're in a coffin," I reminded her as I flipped through the papers I was holding, not bothering to look up in time to see the grimace on Max's face. "You know I'm right," I said. She growled under her breath and proceeded to strip down to her underwear, rooting around one of the matching set of dressers for a fresh pair of pajama pants. Max lived for lounge wear. I did too. It's why we made such great roommates. There was a no-pants-required rule in our room that had gotten us labeled as 'dykes' for one semester, but considering the pantless freedom I had enjoyed that spring, I hadn't cared. Life was better without pants.

"You sound more chipper than you ought to. Did you get a new broomstick?" Max teased, and I could feel the hot gaze of her suspicion on me. She hadn't believed me, on the whole 'yo I'm a witch, for reals' thing, until I'd shot sparks out of my fingertips during a jump-scare at the freshman haunted house. Now she took almost every opportunity to tease me about it, especially because I wouldn't cast magic in front of her. I looked up with a smile.

"I got my internship placement today," I said, waving the papers in the air. Max's eyes lit up, and she proved once again, why she was the most awesome friend ever.

"Oh shit! Oh shit, did you score? Of course you scored, you're smiling. If you were frowning it would have meant you got your last choice—" Max babbled as she yanked open her top drawer. "This calls for a Terry's Chocolate Orange in celebration of such a momentous occasion." She pulled out the foil-wrapped globe and smashed it on the top of the dresser with a, "Ha!"

I couldn't contain my laughter as she peeled the foil back, and I shot her a mischievous grin.

"I thought those were your after-sex-snacks?" I didn't bother waiting for her response and grabbed a wedge of chocolate. The creamy flavor exploded on my tongue and I had to stop myself from groaning.

"Craig's busy and won't be coming up next weekend," Max answered with a shrug. Craig was her boyfriend, who was still living back in their home-town and refusing to answer the siren call of 'that money pit you guys call a school' while he worked as a mechanic's apprentice. "Plus when I tell him what I sacrificed it for, he'll understand. He likes you, Darce, so don't sweat it. He won't hold a grudge." She wrinkled her nose as the citrus-chocolate hit the back of her mouth, like she always did with anything that had the slightest hint of sour in it.

"He better not. I'm the one minding his girlfriend for Boozy Tuesdays at La Grille and Shot Study Nights," I pointed out, sneaking another segment of chocolate orange.

"I study better when indulging in alcohol," Max said, protesting my description of our educational existence which revolved around liquor. "It's not my fault you have to abstain cause of your finger wiggling."

I glared at her.

"Just for that," I said, scooping the rest of the chocolate out of the foil and into my hands. "I told you no teasing about the sobriety."

Max stared, her eyes wide as I scooted across the floor and out of her reach.

"I'm sorry," she said, not sounding it.

"Uh uh," I replied, another segment making its way to my mouth with no hesitation.

"I'm seriously sorry, Darcy, I swear," she insisted, holding out her hand. "C'mon. That's not fair. I didn't mean to mock your self-enforced sober stat—"

"If I drink what happens?" I picked up a segment and inspected it, as if considering how best to devour it.

"You lose control of yourself and fry every circuit in the

building," Max said, her eyes watching my hand. I swear, she was like a puppy when it came to food.

"Right. And it's crappy and I hate it, so please don't remind me. Besides, don't you want to hear about my internship placement?" I asked as I passed her a segment as a peace offering. She accepted it with a happy little moan and nodded.

"Tell me. Tell me. So was it? XO?" she asked around a mouthful of chocolate.

"No that's The Weeknd's label. This is XOhX Records, and yes they were my first choice, and I don't know how, but they accepted me." I stared down at the handout that lay discarded on the ground, a flutter of nervous excitement starting up in my belly.

Modern day witches were a lot more subtle than their medieval counterparts, but just because we're further removed from mundane society didn't mean we ignored it entirely. I'd spent my tween years bopping around to Paramore, Panic!, Blink, and other emo bands at least until my mother put a stop to it and fried all of my CDs when I wouldn't practice piano. Music had been a part of my life since I could remember, and once I was let loose in the world, my obsession had only grown. Max had helped in that area, scoring us tickets to the hottest local indie acts that rolled through campus. When it was time for me to declare my major, studying music marketing had been an obvious choice since I wasn't exactly going to pursue a career as a classical pianist. That would have thrilled my mother even if she was royally pissed I'd left the witch world behind.

"I know how they accepted you," Max said, slinging her arm around my shoulders and squeezing me in tight against her. At 5'8", and built like a pin-up girl with long, thick red hair and a perfectly adorable freckled complexion, Max dwarfed my much shorter and smaller frame. We couldn't share clothes (well not pants anyway), or shoes, but she was as close as I was going to get to having a sister-like relationship with anyone since bailing on my family. We had tried pretending we were real sisters once, at an arcade for a 'bring your fam-jam to play and get free credits' day, but they'd taken one look at her red hair and rockabilly figure and compared it to my dark waving hair and more girl-next-door look. Let's just say we didn't get our free-play credits that day. "They accepted you cause you're freaking smart, and organized, and dedicated, plus your TA has the hots for you and wrote you that wicked letter of recommendation." She smirked.

"Hey! I earned that letter of rec," I protested. I had, too. I'd volunteered, spending hours every weekend for a month straight, organizing the CD collection and documents of our professor, Doctor Wilde. The woman had multiple degrees and couldn't alphabetize to save her life.

"Yeah. You earned it with your ass in those yoga pants you like to wear," Max said, rolling her eyes, but the smile on her face told me she wasn't actually mad at me. She couldn't be or risk being a hypocrite. She'd used her boobs to get out of more than one citation for under-age drinking on campus. "But seriously, you should be totally proud of yourself and your accomplishments. Just think, three years ago, you were a tiny shrimp, unaware of the big wide human world—"

"I was not unaware—" I broke in but Max ignored me.

"Not even understanding how to do your own laundry—"

"We do laundry, we just have, uh, servants for that . . ."

"Uh huh. There you were, Little Miss Rich Witch, afraid and alone, and who was there to take you under her wing, introduce you to all the ins and outs of the real world, but your bestie, Maxy," Max said and gave me another tight squeeze before letting me go when I started to gasp for air.

Making a show of falling over and struggling to breathe, I crawled away from her and got up on my knees.

"You really gotta tone down the spell casting references," I said. "You used to be so good at not saying anything at all. What happened?"

Max started rubbing her long legs, working her thumbs into the tight muscles with a grumble.

"You're right. I'm sorry. I think I'm just getting a little . . . I dunno. It's our last year. I'm going to barely see you since you're interning at a record label, and I'm, well, not. Maybe because this is the only thing that we have that's special I'm kinda clinging onto it," Max's voice dipped and dropped off and I frowned. Max was anything but insecure, if anything, she could be a little over-the-top in love with herself but not in a *bad* way, because she loved everyone around her as much as she did herself. She'd never expressed any doubts about our friendship before, not even when I'd accidentally locked her out of the dorm and she'd had to sleep on the bench down the hall in our second year until the RA let her in.

"I'm not going anywhere," I said. The corners of Max's lips

tugged down as she finally met my eyes and shrugged. "Seriously, me interning isn't going to change anything."

"Except we won't have any classes together," she pointed out.

"We didn't have any classes together last year," I argued, feeling a well of panic opening up inside me. Max was my best friend, and pretty much the only person in the world that knew me in and out anymore. I couldn't say the same about my family since they'd been gone from my life from the night I snuck out of the Llewellyn compound and ran away to attend mundane college.

"I know I'm being selfish," Max admitted, "and I know you told me that your finger-twiddling is top secret, and there's dangers, and all that stuff and I get it. I'm used to keeping dangerous secrets. I'm just scared you'll get some super cool, fancy-pants rockstar buddies at the record label and then you'll forget all about Max and midnight chocolate chip cookie raids."

She looked so forlorn and small, which was a feat for her, that any bubbling anger which was building vanished.

"You're not selfish," I said, shifting across the carpet to envelop her in a hug. She hugged me back instantly. "I get it, and I promise, if I get any super cool rockstar buddies, I will totally invite you along to party."

"As long as you don't tell Craig," she mumbled into my wavy hair. It was probably doing a good job of suffocating her, but for once she didn't complain.

"Not a word to Craig about our exploits and shenanigans," I swore. "Witch's honor." I pulled back and offered her my pinkie. She stared at it and then narrowed her eyes at me.

"Is that even a thing?" she asked. I bit my lip, and she snorted. "Lying bitch. I love you." Her finger hooked around mine and we shook on it. "But whatever, even if it was a thing, you probably couldn't swear to it, since according to you, you're the 'worst witch in the world ever I swear Maxy and that's why I can't magic off that freshman fifteen from your ass'," she finished.

I rolled my eyes and got to my feet.

"Even if I was amazing, I promise you, there is no way I could magic away all those donuts you ate. That isn't a thing. I was a lightning witch. Electricity. If I tried to zap your ass, you'd probably end up in the hospital," I said as I gathered up my things into my backpack for my meeting with the internship coordinator in the morning.

"Hmmph," was all Max said for a long moment before she sighed. "You're probably right. I still haven't forgiven you for frying my last iPhone."

I shook my head.

"I warned you that I'm not very good, but you wanted me to try to charge it anyway."

"I was desperate. I didn't have my battery pack or my extra charging cable. And—and you'd charged it just the week before perfectly fine," she said, her voice plaintive. I lifted up some sheets on my desk.

"Yeah that was a fluke," I replied. "You want a real witch, you can go hang out with my mom and my sister. Except you don't want that. They'd hate you for not being magical and then ignore you for the rest of the evening while you had to choke down crappy hors d'oeuvres. Trust me, it's the worst. Have you seen—" I couldn't find my laptop charger anywhere.

Max sighed and fished it out of her bag without a second word.

"Sorry I forgot to tell you I borrowed it this morning," she said, her face sheepish. I rolled my eyes but smiled.

"You're going to need to be more organized. What happens when we graduate and you don't have me to rely on for chargers, and tissues and lip balm?" I asked. Max looked horrified.

"You mean we're not moving into a swanky two bedroom apartment in the heart of New York so you can pursue your music career and I can convince Craig to finally move to the big city?" She shook her head. "Never mind, don't answer that. We're going to get pancakes, and bacon. Bacon-pancakes. Right now, to celebrate your big internship win." She grabbed her coat and passed me mine.

"You just want to take the focus off your power-cable stealing ways," I said, but she cheerily ignored me with a wave of her hand.

"Pancakes, Llewellyn, pancakes. Stick to the topic at hand." She wrapped an arm through mine and dragged me physically out of the dorm. I couldn't help but laugh.

TWO

Darcy Llewellyn
@DarcyLuvsDonuts

(Follow)

You can't be fired for being late to an internship, right? #fml #solate

6 Retweets 17 Likes

♡ 5   ⟲ 6   ♡ 17   ✉

"Hey girl, you're gonna be mega late," Max's voice broke through my dreams and I sat upright with a gasp.

"Oh god, what time is it?" My heart was thundering in my chest and I flung myself from bed, my legs uncertain and threatening to give out under me at any moment.

"Uh, yeah, so it's like, almost noon," Max said. She glanced at the alarm clock on my desk that I purposefully kept far away from the bed to force myself up and out in the mornings. "I guess you slept in, huh?"

"Oh god," I whispered. Max pulled out her phone.

"I'll order an Uber, my treat," she said as she grabbed a pair of jeans out of my side of the wardrobe we shared. "Brush your teeth and put a bra on. Did you wanna wear that red sweater that makes your breasts look bombing?"

"It's an internship, not a nightclub," I said as I hopped around on one foot, trying to pull socks on and get out of my PJ pants at the same time. The clock kept ticking forward despite my most time-stopping thoughts and, for once, I wished I was one of those witches who could actually halt reality. Never mind that doing that kind of magic was just as likely to stop your heart and kill you as it would stop the world from turning, I figured today was worth the gamble.

"Your driver, Zeke, will be here in five," Max chirped as she passed me more clothes as I dressed.

"You're the best," I said as I grabbed my backpack and shoved my laptop in it and looked around for my phone. Max was down at my feet tying my shoes.

"You're damn right," she said as she held out my jacket and a granola bar. "Go kick ass. Break a wand."

"Seriously?" I asked her with a flat glare. She opened the door.

"You don't have time to sass me back. Get going!"

I didn't bother waiting for the elevator and instead bombed down the flights of stairs, getting outside the dorm just as Zeke pulled up. He stared at me as I flung myself into the back of the car and that's when I realized I hadn't had time to even do my hair.

As he drove and put on what he thought passed for 'sick club beats', I dug around in my bag for a hair tie and some mascara. I would have to do with a messy bun and minimal makeup. Whatever. Like I had told Max, this was an internship, not a blind date. Looks didn't matter, right? I tried to keep an eye on the clock but the sinking feeling in my gut told me that no way was I going to be on time. A brief pause at a stop light let me put on a few coats of mascara, before I was flicking through my paperwork to locate any phone number or e-mail for my intern manager.

Her name was Willa North, and no, I did not have her contact. It felt like I was back at home with my family, my mother standing over me as I tried again and again to cast some small, basic spell with a sick pit of dread boiling away in my stomach as I couldn't. Becoming a mundane had probably been a cop-out in some ways, because the demands of the mundane world weren't anything compared to how much was expected of me as a young witch of the Llewellyn family. While college hadn't been easy, at least I hadn't felt as out of place as I had at home, especially with Max at my side to guide me through the intricacies of daily life.

I sat, as ready as I could be with nothing left to distract me from my nerves, in the back of Zeke's car and sweated it out as the day ticked from AM to PM and I was officially late.

"You look nervous," Zeke commented, in a display of shrewd observation. It was probably the way I was gripping my backpack to my chest, or the lack of blood in my face.

"I'm late to my first day at an internship," I said with a shrug, as if I didn't care when I totally did. Zeke eyed me in the rear-view.

"I can speed it up . . ." he trailed off and I didn't encourage him. I'd noticed the way he'd nearly side-swiped another car as we pulled out of the dorm pick-up zone. I wanted to get to my internship in one piece more than I wanted to get there a little less late.

"Nah," I said with a flap of my hand and sank back down to text Max about the misery of life. She tried to comfort me and apologize because she'd gone out for her early class, but it's not like it was her job to wake me up. With dread clawing at the back of my throat and my stomach full of angry moths, Zeke pulled up in front of the label headquarters where I was going to meet Willa North, and be assigned my first duties as a new intern.

That was, of course, if she didn't fire me on the spot for being nearly thirty minutes late.

"Good luck," Zeke said over the last, gasping pumps of house music coming from his car sound system. Muttering a thank you, I scrambled out of the back of the car, and stared at the red brick building in front of me. It was low, only three stories, and sandwiched between glass-windowed condominium towers, and there wasn't even a sign on the outside, just a street number, a single black metal door, and an intercom.

Was I really doing this? I was really doing this. I slipped my arm through one backpack strap and walked up to the door. I pressed the intercom button. I heard static for a moment, and then,

"Hello?"

"Hi, I'm Darcy Llewellyn? I'm the new int—"

Bzzzt!

The door clicked and I grabbed the handle. As soon as I stepped inside I was inundated with cool, air-conditioned air, and the deep scent of incense from the few sticks smoldering away in a bamboo planter right inside the door. Stairs led up, and there was another door to my right.

Before I could wonder which direction to go, a tall, dark-haired young woman only a few years older than me appeared at the top of the steps. Her lips were pressed into a thin line.

"Llewellyn?" she asked and before I could answer, "You're late. Come on up. I only have a few more minutes before a licensing call with one of our partners in England, so we'll just have a few minutes to talk about what you'll be doing here."

All the air rushed back into my lungs and I felt like I could breathe again. So, not immediately fired then, that was great news. I jogged up the stairs as Willa, or the woman I presumed was Willa, turned on her heel and waved for me to follow her.

"Through this way," she said as we walked into a room that had a bunch of cubicles scattered across it. More than one person looked up at me as we walked by, and I tried not to stare in awe. Band posters were everywhere, along with gold and platinum record plaques on the walls. For such a small, independent label, XOhX had done amazing for themselves, churning out a steady parade of chart-toppers in the rock, alt-rock, and indie-pop scene. This was where I was working? I knew the label's reputation from being a fan, but they'd never come up in any of my music industry classes during case-studies. I tried not to make it obvious that I was gawking as I stumbled, zombie-like in Willa's wake.

One guy, who was sitting next to a quirky girl with thick orange glasses as she worked on what looked like some Facebook promo graphics, saw me staring at a set of triple platinum records on the wall above her desk. He winked at me when he caught my eye, and my cheeks went warm.

He was . . . to say he was hot, was probably an understatement. He radiated rockstar-cool vibes, with his ripped jeans and a white tank under a plaid shirt that snugged around bulging biceps. No thin-armed shoe-gaze guitarist then.

"Those're mine, you can look but don't touch," he said with a jerk of his head toward the triple platinum records.

"Llewellyn," Willa snapped, and I nearly tripped turning around to follow her. The guy laughed as I left him behind. Willa had opened up a glass french door that led into what looked like an informal meeting space. Low, dark leather couches were arranged for comfortable conversation. I put the laughing rockstar, and my embarrassment, behind me as she nodded to one couch, and collapsed onto the other.

"Look," she started with a sigh as I sat. "You were late, and nothing pisses me off more than people who are late, but you were recommended by your professor—"

I was? I stared at her, my fingers numb around my backpack as I tried to set it down and look at her at the same time.

"And he happened to be my professor when I went through the program, so you know, it's fine. Just don't let it happen again, okay? Especially not when you're dealing directly with the band. They can be late, they *will* be late, that's what musicians do, but if you're fifteen minutes early, then you're right on time, you got it?"

"I got it," I repeated, still trying to process the near-museum like walk I'd taken through the room where everyone appeared to work.

"That was the production floor, and you'll have your own desk there next week," she said, pointing at the glass doors we'd entered through. "Downstairs is the recording studio, don't go there unless you're accompanying the band or I'm bringing you. The equipment is worth more than your life. This is the meeting room." She gestured around us and I looked up. More records, so many of them, lined the walls, although at the far end a beautiful floral mural covered the entire thing from one side of the room to the other. "This is where we debrief after tours, big shows and media appearances. Also a lot of late-night drinking happens in here when it shouldn't, but don't be a part of that if you know what's good for you." Willa surveyed me, a tilt of her head indicating she wasn't sure about me.

"Um . . ." I cleared my throat, "so, what do you want me to start with?"

"I haven't figured you out yet, because my instincts are good, but not that good. I hope you're not a fangirl, because trust me, you'll burn out pretty fast. They say never meet your heroes and they mean it. Nothing like running into that rockstar that jangled your jimmies when you were fifteen to find out he's thirty-nine, and still interested in fifteen year olds." Willa's cheeks turned pink for a moment, and I wondered which rockstar had earned his place in her repertoire of war-stories.

"No, I mean, I love music—"

"That's sort of a given," she said, although there was a smile quirking at the corner of her mouth that made her words less mean than they should have sounded. "Anyway, the professor is never wrong about anyone he sends here. I would know, since I was the first one he sent here, and now I'm the management coordinator for all of the bands on our label," she said.

My lips parted in surprise. Seriously? She looked like she was maybe twenty-six, if that. Willa smirked a little, her face transforming, vixen-like.

"I don't want to brag, except I totally do, because I was the youngest intern ever taken on, and I moved up the ranks fast. They promote from within here as much as possible, and if you're good, not saying you are, there'll be a job for you at the end of the year," Willa finished, folding her fingers from one hand over the other, on top of her knees. She looked at me expectantly.

"Wow," I said, and she smiled, more genuinely this time.

"Before you meet your charges," she said, "which is, I mean, the new baby-band we just signed that you're going to manage—"

I coughed and she raised an eyebrow at me, as if daring me to say that I wasn't anywhere near qualified. Which, you know, I totally wasn't but it was obvious that admitting that was *not* a good idea.

"Anyway, before I take you in to the meet the guys, I

wanted to give you a few pieces of advice. Never turn off your phone, and I mean never. If you don't have a smartphone, we'll give you one, but we expect you to have it on all the time, and answer when it's label business. And, just to mention, any of the musicians on the label sexting you is not label business, so feel free to ignore that if it happens, because they're probably drunk and you should ignore them, if it gets serious beyond a few hey-babys' then let me know," she paused for a moment, and took a breath, as if she wanted to say something but then cleared her throat instead.

"Cellphone stays on and answer even when I'm in the shower," I said and she nodded.

"Right. The next rule is that in this industry there are broads, and there are bitches, okay? I'm talking about women. Bitches go out of their way to stab you in the back, take your accomplishments and claim them as their own, and look for any opportunity to cut you down or even get you fired if it makes them look good," Willa licked her lower lip and I felt a chill descend over me, raising up goosebumps on my skin. She didn't look happy, and I had to wonder what sort of run-ins she'd had with the bitchy kind of women.

"Then there are broads. They have your back instead of stabbing you in it. They don't fuck the talent, and if they do, they keep it on the down-low and don't make it everybody's problem. They share knowledge with you and don't hold anything back that could help you. They give you the heads up when a musician is running into trouble with girls or gangs or drugs, although those last two don't happen as much anymore—"

I gulped. The witching world was far removed from either gangs or drugs, and I'd avoided the seedier side of college campus life as much as possible. It's not that I was innocent or anything, I knew what went on, I just didn't know how I'd handle it from a, well, magical perspective. Last thing I needed was to toke up and start exploding people's laptops and power bars.

"You need to decide which one you are, Darcy," Willa said, using my name for the first time and dragging me back to the present and away from nightmare-inducing daydreams of being chased off campus by a mob with pitchforks screaming *witch!*

"Broad," I said without hesitation, "definitely, uh, not . . . not a bitch." Willa grinned.

"Well, you need to speak up when the situation calls for it, and stand up for yourself and fight for your band, but that's different," Willa replied. "There's a full welcome package in your desk on the run-down of your duties, but I'll be available at all times if you need anything. It shouldn't be too crazy, because these guys just got signed and like I said, they're still a baby-band and they won't be going on any world tours in the near future. They just wrapped up their debut album, and even though they aren't on a 360 deal, we're still managing their merchandising and a bunch of other things because Troy likes to have everything in-house and it's not like he needs the money anyway."

Troy as in Troy Granville. I recognized the name immediately. He was the half-owner of XOhX, and also had been a practicing entertainment lawyer before the label had taken off. There had been a few of his cases mentioned in my lectures since he'd been renowned for fighting for bands that had felt another artist ripped off their songs. No wonder he didn't need the money, because he'd probably gotten crazy rich off of those lawsuits.

"So who is the band?" I asked, way more timidly than I would have liked to.

"Phoenixcry," Willa said and grinned when my eyes widened. "You've heard of them."

"They do a lot of house shows," I said and she nodded.

"That's why we signed them, even though they don't have anything serviced to radio yet. Their fanbase is so ready to pop and make them huge, if the band has the right team behind them. Nobody else can be spared right now from our main roster of management since we had that one huge viral hit two months ago with Chelsea Sawyer—"

"Chelsea Sawyer is signed to XOhX?" I stammered out. Chelsea's single had been a break-away hit from the unknown indie-pop artist, taking over my summer semester, blaring from every car stereo and wireless speaker on campus. "I thought she was with Universal?"

"We upstreamed her there. As soon as they heard her single, they knew it was a hit, but we still take care of her entire career. It's just distribution and some promotion that runs through Universal, plus they have better reach around the globe, obviously," she said before looking at her watch. "Shit, okay, enough talk. I need to intro you to the guys, and then get on the phone. They're downstairs listening to the mastered tracks, but I'll bring them up here. You just sit tight, okay?" She buzzed out of the room without waiting for an answer from me, and I could hear the soft noises of people talking on the production floor filter in to me.

The weight of responsibility was keeping me glued to the couch. I'd been expecting to assist someone, not manage a whole band, especially not one like Phoenixcry. Maybe Willa saw them as a baby-band, and compared to someone like Chelsea Sawyer, they totally were since she'd gone from nobody to selling out arenas in sixty days. Still, Phoenixcry were a pretty big deal on campus and around town at the house-show level.

Calm thyself, I thought and took a deep breath of cool air. Willa'd said she'd be there for me if I had any questions, and it wasn't like I was being totally thrown to the wolves. I'd be fine. Right? Right.

The fidgets took over me after another few minutes, and the back of my neck itched from nerves. I was running hot and cold, so excited at the crazy turn today had taken in terms of where I was working and who I was working with. I was being struck by overwhelming nerves. I was just a senior year student, sure, graduating, but not an experienced music industry professional? The only thing keeping me in my seat (other than the debt I'd accumulated going to school and seeing that all go down the drain wasn't appealing) was the reminder that Troy Granville was a lawyer, and he probably did all the big negotiations for the band. I'd be doing lower-level, day-to-day stuff. Probably. Most likely.

Footsteps behind me, and low voices that rose in volume, told me the band was there. I felt it before I turned, the subtle hum of power that hit me and set my already crazed nerves further on edge. I got to my feet and turned as the room went from normal, mundane, expected to overwhelmingly *supernatural*.

I'd never seen Phoenixcry perform before. If I had I would

have known to run far, far away from XOhX as soon as Willa'd said their name.

Because it wasn't five members of a band that entered into the room, five seriously hot men that would have any girl tossing her panties at them, no. I would have been damn lucky if that's all they had been.

I stood there, my breath caught in my throat, my pulse slamming between my ears, and stared as the band stared back at me. Willa wasn't with them.

"*Witch*," one of them broke the silence with a low mutter. He had dark-brown hair, a scruff of five-o-clock shadow that crawled across his chiseled jaw despite it being just close to one in the afternoon, and piercing blue eyes that pinned me to the spot I was standing in. He crossed his arms over his chest, and for a moment my eyes dragged down the pinch of his shirt sleeves around his biceps. I had to yank my gaze away. He was built, and each of the other guys were all created along similar lines, some slightly more slender than others.

"Oh shit," said a second guy, his hair a dark sandy blond, with another pair of blue eyes that weren't narrowed like the first's. He was one of the shortest, and more slender, of the guys, his muscles long and lean. Even still, he filled out his shirt without an issue.

Phoenixcry were men, sure that was a word of truth, but they were also *werewolves*, and I bet that wasn't in their bio. Also not in their bio? That werewolves weren't supposed to be anywhere near witches.

I was so fucked.

THREE

"I think she's hyperventilating," said the second guy who'd spoken, the blond with the lean muscles who looked like he was the youngest out of them all, staring at me openly although his expression wasn't unkind.

"Heartbeat's up," said the first, his blue eyes narrowing further into something I would swear was a smoulder. He shook his head, dark hair falling into his face.

"Cash, Ace, be quiet for a minute," there was a taller, light-blond wolf at the back of the group, and I noticed he had a shadow of a guy behind him, exactly the same height as him with the same features, but slightly different style of hair . . . twins. *Well,* I thought without humor, *it's not like twins are all that unheard of with werewolves. Shit, werewolves.* They were werewolves, and the biggest crime of all, as they stared at me, I couldn't help but immediately feel my face flush. They were hot in a way that was criminal, especially for monsters. Was that how they trapped people? With—with their flexing forearms and devastatingly handsome faces?

"Where's Willa?" I asked, finding my voice, knowing that every second I shared a room with them I was in danger. They didn't know that, because they didn't know I was a crappy spell-caster, and barely had the most basic control over my powers. It's not like there was an all out war between witches and werewolves, because there wasn't, but we didn't as a general rule like each other, and we *never* fraternized. Bad things happened when wolves and witches hung out.

"Her phone call started early," said the tall, bossy blond wolf. He shouldered his way to the front of the group, their clear leader, as he surveyed me. I immediately tensed, and shivered as his eyes moved up and down my body. I tried not to do the same to him, because he was built, pounds of muscle that threatened to put a guy like Chris Hemsworth to shame. The blond wolf let out a soft whistle. "I didn't think they made witches in *hot*," he said. His words hit me like scalding water and I froze. Was he making a pass at me?

"Finn," snarled his twin, equally hot, equally muscled, but a lot more grouchy-looking. Finn held up a hand to hush his brother.

"I know, I know, just relax." Finn crossed his arms over his chest and gave me another once-over. While he did I averted my gaze, and found there was really no safe place to look—five pairs of eyes: one brown and four blue, met me wherever I glanced. I suddenly wished that there was another set of doors for me to escape through, but the only way out of the room was through those five sets of broad shoulders. "So what's a witch doing, posing as a mundane, at our record label? I'd swear this was a joke if it wasn't so damn serious," Finn said. He hitched his shoulder and one of two men with dark hair, the one that hadn't already spoken took a step forward.

"**Stay right there**," I said, harnessing the very thin control I had over my power to put *thunder* in my voice. The sound of it rolled out of me, and it had an immediate effect. Have you ever seen a wolf put up it's hackles? It was like that, in human form, times five. I did my best not to lose it and stood firm.

Cash or Ace, because I wasn't sure which was which, but it was the one with dark hair that had spoken first, growled at me.

"Oh is that how it's gonna be?" he asked, pushing past Finn. He would have walked toward me, except Finn grabbed him by the shoulder, and Finn had a good inch or two on him and a bit more muscle.

"We're in the goddamn label office, Cash," Finn growled low under his breath, solving the mystery of who was Cash and who was Ace, but not offering me any solution to my predicament.

"She's by herself," said the other dark-haired man, not Cash. "Why're you here by yourself? Are you helping hunters?"

I frowned. He said it with a look around the room as if the ancient order of men and women would leap from the shoulders to cut him down right then and there. Hunters had been humans trained and guided by witches back, oh, at least a few hundred years ago, to murder werewolves that stepped out of line and caused trouble with mundanes. But that practice had been quickly been abandoned as too barbaric, plus werewolves had become increasingly rare, so such incidences hadn't been so much of an issue anymore.

"Yeah, like that's a thing," I said with a roll of my eyes, trying to hide my nerves. If they wanted to fall on me and rip my throat out of my neck, they could, and I was pretty powerless to stop them. I had my binder in my backpack. I might, for a second, be able to beat one of them with it, or at least protect my face so my body could be identified.

Finn's twin moved, after standing stock still for long moments.

"You're going to answer his question, and if you're lying, we'll know," he said, his voice firmer than Finn's, so much that you couldn't mistake him for his twin even if their tone and pitch were similar. They were seriously worried about hunters? I shook my head.

"I'm not—I'm just here to do an internship," I said, figuring honesty was the best policy and if they were one of those paranoid packs of werewolves, that was the best bet. If I outright said that hunters didn't exist, they might not believe I was being truthful.

Finn's twin, and the rest of them, relaxed minutely. The hackles weren't quite down, but it was close enough that their shoulders relaxed out.

"What did we do to the universe to end up with a witch for our first label manager?" Finn asked. The dark-haired man who wasn't Cash snorted and asked,

"The better question is, why are they giving us an intern for a manager? That wasn't in the contract. I need to go talk to Troy." He turned on his heel, and without another word, left the room. I watched him go, my eyes popping wide. Had he seriously just... left? Just like that?

"Charlie manages the business end of things," Finn said, gesturing to the couches. "Along with playing rhythm guitar. You'll get to know him well if you're the one the label has assigned to us. Let's sit."

Slowly the other men approached the couches, and me. With each step they took, my nerves lit on fire again and again and I thought my heart was going to pound it's way right out of my chest.

"What are you doing?" I asked as they sat down on the couch across from me, their attitudes ranging from nonchalant to curious to vaguely hostile.

Cash's lips twisted up in a small smirk: his expression had been more on the hostile end of the spectrum.

"Having our first band meeting with our label-appointed manager," he said, sarcasm clinging to each word.

"Yeah that's not happening," I said, and grabbed my backpack. All four of the remaining guys froze, eyes on me and my bag. "It's got a laptop in it, my binder with handouts, and a granola bar," I said flatly. "No daggers made by the light of the moon to cut your hearts out. Trust me. That's the last thing I want to do right now. I'm going to go to Willa and tell her I can't work with you."

Ace, the sandy blond, frowned, and actually looked sad.

"What? You're not gonna . . . but we're great!" he protested. Cash let out a scoffing bark of laughter which was quelled when Finn's twin elbowed him, *hard*, in the side.

"Yeah, I heard about you guys, apparently you're amazing, but you're also werewolves, and I'm a witch. This?" I gestured from me to them. "This doesn't happen. Not even the slightest bit. Not ever."

Finn's eyebrow kicked up and he looked at each of the other werewolves in turn.

"You're here in the mundane world, right?" he asked. I knew he was leading me down a path I didn't want to travel but I couldn't help but answer him anyway. Werewolves, aside from being formidable in strength even in human form, able to shape-shift into large wolves among other things, were also incredible orators. If I had to guess at why they had enjoyed a meteoric rise from unknown band to signing to a good label in a short period of time, it would have been because of the innate powers they had, that was threaded through every fiber of their being. It wasn't like witches, where we had to call on our powers, do rituals, learn to harness it. For wolves, they *were* magic, every inch of them, and every time they opened up their mouths it was a siren call to any human or witch listening. It's why they were so dangerous and witches kept their distance. It was part of the reason that any association between a witch or a werewolf was forbidden.

My family was keeping tabs on me, I was sure, probably thinking that I was just out in the mundane world, sowing my wild oats, and that one day I'd come to my senses and come back to the fold. But if they found out I was fraternizing with werewolves? My freedom would be over. They bundle me up, wrap me in magic bindings so tight I'd never escape, and they'd drag me screaming back to the Council of Seven and the family hearth.

That couldn't happen. I'd worked too hard to establish my own life, a true life without the aid of an impressive magical lineage and more money than sense. I had *student debt*, something unheard of to witches, but a mark of pride that I carried showing that I'd left my old self and old life behind.

"Give her a minute, she's thinking," one of them muttered at the edge of my attention and I jerked.

"Yeah, thinking that every second I spend in this room is a bad idea," I said. "It . . . it was real, or whatever, but peace out," I said, and then bolted. It was over before it began, and I should have known better than to run from an apex predator, or four of them. Finn's twin was up and over the back of the couch in a split-second, shoving himself between me and the door. His hand reached out and wrapped around my hip, his other one grabbing onto my wrist. We spun, out of sight of the employees on the production floor, and then I was pinned up against the wall with probably two hundred pounds, or more, of muscled, angry werewolf.

His blue eyes were hot as he stared down at me. I'd never been near a werewolf. I'd never even imagined what it would be like to be this close to one. The wall was firm and cold against my back, but the wolf in front of me was firm but not anything close to cold. His heat would radiate off of him into me. My skin screamed, and I swallowed reflexively. His scent was thick, the hint of smoke at the back of my tongue as I inhaled it, smoke and the wet, crushed smell of pine-needles.

"You're going to hear us out," he said, and I felt the weight of his presence press down on me, demanding that I listen, probably the same feeling he'd felt when I'd told them all to stay where they were. I struggled to breathe, the power in him too strong for me and my feeble, underdeveloped willpower.

Deep down though, it was there, a small spark of molten gold inside me, the source of the thunder and lightning that made up my being. With unsteady mental fingers, I reached for it and held on.

"**Back off**," I gasped, the words crackling with power. With a low snarl, he shoved away, but only a few feet. I shuddered as the pull of what he'd asked of me still raced through my veins, demanding that I sit down on the couch, and listen to them, as if that was a perfectly normal thing for a witch to do with a pack of werewolves.

There was no way I was going to give him what he wanted, especially if he thought pushing me around and bullying me was going to be how he accomplish his desires. The other wolves had gotten to their feet, unsteadiness and uncertainty on their faces and in their body language.

"Let me make this clear to you, and listen up, because I'm only going to say it once," I started off, my words slow as I had to drag them from within myself. The men all stiffened, Finn's twin most of all. "I was a witch, but I'm not one now, I'm a mundane."

"Bullsh—" One of them started to say, Cash, and I jerked my gaze over at him. He shut up, and I felt powerful for one moment before I remembered I was writing checks with my tongue and eyes that my powers couldn't cash. Better not push them too far.

"You know I'm here, at the label. I know you're here, at the label. I'm going to go ask Willa to be reassigned to something else, anything else, and we are going to leave each other alone. I'm not working with hunters, and I want to be left *alone*. I'm not any more of a witch than any of you are." I watched them carefully as I spoke, glad that the door was at my back and I could slip right out of it when I was ready. One of the blonds, Ace, looked almost crestfallen at my proclamation, his shoulders rounded. *No*, I thought, *you are not going to feel bad just cause some werewolf is giving you puppy-eyes. That's . . . that shouldn't even be a thing.*

My eyebrows pulled together and glowered at them all.

"But I want you to know, if I hear even the smallest whisper that you've been pushing around any other girl here at the label, I'm gonna forget that I'm a mundane and do everything in my power to make your lives living hell, **do you understand me**?" I didn't need to use that last touch of power, and I felt my legs twitch as they threatened to give out on me. Magic is like a muscle. Use it or lose it. And I hadn't been using it for three years. I felt exhausted from my little show of dominance, but I needed to put the fear in these werewolves if I was even going to have a hope at finishing my internship. And even that idea was seriously questionable. My every instinct was telling me to run back to Max and bury myself in a blanket burrito, letting Max push cookies in through one end of my self-created nest.

I took a breath, about to unleash more on them, to let go of all the pent up fear and stress that their sudden appearance in my life had caused, but thought better of it.

"Thanks," I said, and turned on my heel and bolted out of the meeting room. *Thanks? Thanks?! You threaten a pack of werewolves and end it off with a super-scary 'Thanks'!?* I tried not to give myself too hard of a time, as I booked it to the stairs that would lead outside. I needed to go grab a coffee. Willa would be on her call for awhile yet, so I had some time, plus one of the wolves would be talking to her. I probably had ten minutes. It was stupid, to leave without telling anyone, but on the list of crappy things I had done or had done to me that day, it was near the bottom.

Time. I just needed a little bit of time to figure out my next move, and if I would ask Willa for other work, or have to go back to my internship coordinator at school and ask for a whole new internship. Putting as much distance as possible between myself and the singing werewolf pack was my only goal. Determined that everything would look a little more rosy after some caffeine, I shoved thoughts of wolves out of my mind, and ducked out the front door of the label office.

FOUR

**XOhXRecords**
@XOhXRecordssssss

Follow

They're the hottest thing off the block, and we just signed them! Please welcome @PhoenixcryMusic to the XOhX fam!!!! #newmusic #hotguys #srslylookattheseguys #totallypinchablebutts #plsdontpinchtheirbutts #supportindiemusic

6 Retweets 16 Likes

♡ 6   ⟲ 6   ♡ 16   ✉

"No. Not happening," Willa stared at me flatly as I flailed through a reason I couldn't work with Phoenixcry. Obviously she hadn't bought my lame excuse of *I'm seriously too much of a fangirl, please don't make me work with them, I'll vom.*

"Please," I said, "I'll do anything. Sort demo tapes. I'll listen through demos. I'll—please." I'd run out of good reasons for her to let me off the hook in terms of managing Phoenixcry, not that I'd had any good reasons to begin with anyway. I'd texted Max during my quick coffee run that something seriously crazy had gone down, like magic crazy. She was in class, because she hadn't texted me back yet.

I needed my best friend at my side right then and there, but couldn't have her. I'd have to deal with the situation myself. I'd gotten myself out of my family's home and away from the life I'd known just fine, why was I having so much trouble now with this whole adulting thing?

Willa sighed and rubbed her temples for a moment and muttered something that sounded like a request for patience.

"Look, you were seriously, really, highly recommended to me, Darcy. You seem nice. I can overlook the lateness on your first day, because it happens, but I'm not going to reassign you from Phoenixcry mostly because I don't have anyone to replace you with. Please don't make me be a bitch about this and tell your professor that you were useless, because if you keep pushing this issue, that's what's going to happen here." She gave me a kind, almost sympathetic smile. "Please, also, I wasn't born yesterday, and I know you're not a crazy fangirl. What's going on? I know, they're super hot and that can be kind of intimidating. That's okay."

I stared at her and swallowed, trying not to let myself spiral down into a miserable ball of self pity.

"But . . ." I started and fell quiet when I saw the expression on Willa's face. I was inches from getting a blistering lecture at best, or a phone call to my professor about how I'd utterly failed at my placement. Caught between the danger I was putting myself in by staying, and possibly flunking out of my internship year at college, I folded.

I'd just have to stay smart, and do whatever it took to keep my family from finding out who I was working with. Just because there were werewolves in the building didn't mean I had anything to do with them, and as their manager, the only times I would have to be in public with them was at shows, and I could always just stay backstage.

It was a pretty pack of lies, but I wrapped it up in a bow and gave it to myself. Whatever it took to finish off my degree, I was going to do. I'd fought so hard for freedom, I wasn't going to let the fear of my family taking me back home stop me when I'd come so close.

At least for now, until I could go back to school and throw myself down at my professor's feet and beg to be reassigned.

"Now, do you need me to come back up with you to talk to the band, or can I deal with the sixty-five other fires I have burning right now?" Willa asked. I knew better than to try her patience further.

"I'm sorry," I said.

"You're an idiot, and you're forgiven," she said, reaching for her phone. "Do you know how many students we turned down for this internship? Don't waste it, Llewellyn, and don't make me look stupid for picking you."

I nodded and ushered myself out of her cubicle, my ears burning. The office was mercifully mostly empty, so I didn't think too many people overheard our conversation. I steeled myself and walked toward the ominous glass French doors in the far wall. A shadow popped up beside me, and then I realized it was the hot rockstar guy from earlier.

"Hey," he said, putting a hand out to stop me in my tracks. Hot or not, I was annoyed at being stopped for a second time that day by a guy trying to get into my way. What was it with extremely attractive men and their belief that ladies needed to screech to a halt for them? I was nervous enough, and unsure about what I was walking into since the band hadn't left the meeting room after I bolted. They would be there, waiting for me, all five of them since Charlie had rejoined them.

"Uh, hey," I said, glancing past him to look at the door I needed to be walking through, like, yesterday. There was something disconcerting with how hot the guy in front of me was but at the same time I really wasn't into it. He just gave off a vibe that made me uncomfortable.

"Look," he said with a slow shake of his head. His hair was cut shaggy, and drooped in his eyes, his head dipping in what had to be a practiced move he used on fangirls. "I know it's tough, being at the label for the first time, but it's okay. Do you want a signed CD?" he asked, his words dripping with assured confidence and pride, like he just *knew* I'd be grateful for him offering that.

"Uh," I said, queen of verbosity, as I tried to figure out a way to let him know that I had no idea who he was without offending him. He stood in front of me like he owned the room. He probably thought that my silence was some fannish embarrassment, because his lips split into a handsome smile that grew wider by the moment. Not wanting to risk pissing off someone who was a big enough name to think I knew him on sight, I nodded without another word.

"So you're Darcy Llewellyn," he said, reaching over to a nearby desk and plucking a CD off the top of a stack. "I heard we were getting a new intern," he continued as he split the wrapping on the CD with practiced ease of someone who'd done it a thousand times. He probably had. Although, given how he was acting, he probably had someone to strip the plastic wrap off of his CDs for him at signings. He produced a Sharpie from mid-air it felt like, and he'd flicked out the CD insert.

"Yeah, that's me, Darcy," I replied, painfully aware that any moment Willa could stand up at her desk and see me acting like a total amateur instead of the professional I was supposed to be.

"Hey, it's okay, baby, no one is gonna give you shit while you're with Jake Tupper," he said with a playful wink.

"Right." I knew the name, of course, because Jake Tupper had been all over college radio with a massive summer indie hit, but his stuff wasn't the style of music I liked. Too much harmonizing gang vocals and a lot of 'Hey! Ho!' in a song wasn't my thing. I wanted driving guitars, and a heavy drum beat that I could feel in my blood, not some guy with a man-bun crooning over his mandolin about the rust flaking off of society or whatever. Plus the rumor on the street was he was a dirtbag who'd dumped a loyal girlfriend as soon as his career had started taking off. Also, he'd just called me *baby*. Ew.

"There you go. The prize of your collection now," he said as he tucked the insert in and snapped the CD case close. He held it out to me, and I took a breath before wrapping my fingers around it and gave him what I hoped was a happy smile.

"Thanks, that's so thoughtful," I lied, "but I really gotta get to my meeting." I pointed at the French doors to the meeting room. Jake Tupper made my skin itch in a way that made me think that even facing down a pack of werewolves was a better option than staying in his presence for a moment longer.

Jake gave me another once-over like he had earlier, his eyes lingering on me in a way that made me wish I had enough power left in me to spark him, hard. Some men looked at you like they wanted to eat you alive, possess you in a way that would consume you, like you'd be yanked in by their gravitational pull and never emerge the same, if you got out at all. I took an involuntary deep breath as a moment passed between us where all of *that* hung in the air and my gut instinct was telling me to get away, and fast.

Was it weird that I was having a more eerie response to a normal human like Jake Tupper than I had to the werewolves waiting for me in the meeting room? I tried not to parse that thought, and ducked around him.

Jake gave a low chuckle that set the hair on the back of my neck standing straight up, but he didn't say anything else. I made a beeline for the doors and opened it, feeling the weight of his gaze on me the entire way.

As I entered, the wolf pack as I was starting to think of them in my head, looked up as one. They were ranged on the couches, out of direct-line-of-sight out the door. It hit me again as I stood there, door clicking shut behind me, that they were werewolves, and I was an enemy of theirs, a witch. I waited for the same fear to rise up in me that Jake Tupper had inspired, but it never came.

"So you get reassigned to sorting old cassette tapes?" Cash asked, a hint of irritation in his voice and something else I couldn't quite place.

"Nah, Willa wouldn't do it. She thinks that Darcy here is a good match for us, seems to like her spunk," Charlie drawled, and when Cash's shoulders fell, relaxing minutely, I realized that he'd been *afraid*. Afraid I'd be reassigned, that they'd get someone else as a manager. Why he would even want me managing his band, when like Charlie said I was just an intern, was confusing. I pushed the thought away.

"Yeah, well, this is apparently going to be a thing, so we're going to have to set some ground rules on working together," I said, picking a small armchair to settle in. Five sets of intense eyes across two couches stared at me, and I felt the weight of their attention settle over me like a wave of heat rising from an oven.

"Ground rules?" Finn asked, leaning forward where he sat. He'd had his ankle slung over one knee, but he dropped his foot to the ground, his elbows pressing into his thighs as he clasped his hands. "What kinda ground rules? We already signed a no-harassment policy."

Finn's twin grunted in agreement.

I took a breath to steady myself.

"Yeah, that's not really enough for my comfort," I said. "This internship is pretty time-intensive, but I still have other school obligations, so outside of when I'm here at the label or attending your events, I'm going to ask you to not seek me out. Text me if you have to, but no coffee-shop meetings, or anything like that. We meet here, in the office, or we don't meet at all."

Ace was nodding before any of the others.

"Sounds good to—" he started, but Finn's twin interrupted him.

"You wanna give us a reason why?" He asked, and I was struck again by the flare of power I felt whenever he spoke. Of all of them, he gave off the air of being the oldest, and being in command, something like an alpha wolf, if such a thing existed in werewolf pack dynamics. I didn't know, it wasn't really something they covered in the short chapter on werewolves in my schooling.

"I don't really think I need to explain—"

"Hell yes you do," he said, "because if you're managing us, you're managing us. We're a team, and we work together." He looked at the other guys, although I couldn't take my eyes off of him. My cheeks were flushing, although I didn't know why. "If you're gonna set limits on when we can and can't see our manager, you need to tell us why."

My lips parted to speak but he pushed on.

"I think you're not as far out of the magic world as you'd like to be," he said, accurately pinpointing my feelings with no regard at all to my privacy. I exhaled a breath.

"Eli," Finn muttered, a warning. The air in the room was tense, and I could feel the crackle of electricity humming right under my skin, a sure sign that my own stress levels were through the roof. It usually took effort to call on my power, but when it came unbidden, I knew that things had gotten more heated than I could deal with.

"Llewellyn, right?" Eli, Finn's twin, asked. "Like the council Llewellyn's?"

My stomach dropped.

"I think we're good here, I'll see you guys tomorrow," I said as I stood up, picking up my bag. Eli was on his feet and over to me in a second. My breath caught in my chest as I looked up at him. Close up he was even more intimidating, towering over me like he had earlier in that day, and I nearly broke.

"Your family's council, aren't they?" he asked, and beneath the surface of his words was that current of power, demanding I answer, demanding I give in.

"Leave her alone, Elias," Ace's voice cut through the haze and he stepped into Eli's space, pushing him aside. "Forgive him. He's used to bossing us around and us listening," he said turning to me with an apologetic smile. "Let me walk you out."

Ace's arm came around my shoulders, but it had the opposite effect from Eli's presence. Ace was warm and comforting and relief flooded through me.

"Sounds good," I said, with a quick glance back at the other guys. Cash's face was stormy, Finn's amused, and Charlie looked thoughtful. I didn't look at Eli.

When we stepped out onto the production floor, there was no sign of Jake Tupper which further relaxed me. Ace walked me to the top of the stairs. Of all the wolves, he was the least intimidating, and I wondered if I would actually become friends with him.

No, it wasn't possible. It was just too dangerous. I'd have to keep myself at an arm's length, emotionally, with the band and not let our relationship develop past cool professionalism.

"I'm really sorry about that," he said, his voice low so that no one walking by would hear. He huffed out a breath and scratched the back of his head, an act that was so basely canine, that I couldn't help but grin. "What?" he asked, attitude turning self conscious.

Now that I was away from Eli, I could breathe again.

"He's pretty intense," I said, finding my tongue.

"I can tell him to lay off." Ace looked over his shoulder to where we'd come from. "He doesn't always listen, but he's got a good heart." He glanced back at me and bit his lip, an almost sweetly nervous gesture. "He just looks out for us, and I think that pressure makes him . . . yeah, anyway, we can talk about it later. We'll see you tomorrow?" His eyes searched my face as if he was worried I'd suddenly say no. If all I'd had to go on in terms of werewolf experiences was him and his behavior, Ace would have made me think they were all adorable, earnest, and puppy-like.

"Yeah, I'll see you guys tomorrow," I reassured him. I couldn't say no and hurt his feelings. He was too nice, and just because Eli had a stick up his ass, didn't mean I wouldn't do my job. I'd grit my teeth and get through the internship however I needed to.

"Great, cause we're going over the final masters tomorrow

after they make the tweaks our producer asked for," Ace said with a wide grin, all his nerves melting away. "You'll love it. The tracks are killer."

"You don't even know what kind of music I like," I replied, tilting my head to the side to give him a funny look. His grin never faltered.

"I know your type, Darcy Llewellyn," he said, with a subtle buzz of heat in his tone that made my heart give a weird squeeze. "You're gonna die for our music."

FIVE

Darcy Llewellyn
@DarcyLuvsDonuts

Follow

I feel like I need a do-over on today. Is that possible? #timetravelisitreal

8 Retweets 22 Likes

14 8 22

When I got back to the dorms after meeting my band of werewolves, I found a note from Max (along with a Snickers bar because she felt that bad news should always be accompanied by a sweet treat) saying that her dad had called her home. Apparently he needed her for an emergency Talk About Something Serious so she'd taken the train. Her note finished off that saying she would text me when she got to her town and had service again. I spent the evening binge watching videos on Youtube of Irish people eating food from the around the world, and fell asleep in a messy cocoon of blankets without hearing from Max.

It wasn't the most unusual thing, but I sent her a text message the next morning when I woke up, just in case, before heading off to the XOhX offices. My stomach was fluttering on the bus ride over. This time I hadn't slept in, so I didn't need to take a ride-hail. I'd thought that I would have wolfy dreams or nightmares all night, but my sleep had been surprisingly peaceful. It was only when I got off the bus on the street where the label's offices sat, that my tummy butterflies turned into hornets.

Leaning against the building outside was Eli, leather jacket draped over his shoulder, one foot propped up on the brick wall so his knee stuck out. He looked the picture of 1950's bad boy and, for a moment, it was all I could do to simply take in how *good* he looked. His hair was roughly tousled. It swooped low across his forehead in a way that made my fingers ache to brush it behind his ear, like when you need to fix a painting that's crooked.

"Dick," I muttered under my breath. He had no right looking so sexy when he was a pushy asshole. I'd given it a bit of thought and I'd decided that even if he was used to bossing his band members around, he wasn't going to get a free pass from me. Even if he was a werewolf and capable of literally putting me in my place if he so desired. He didn't know that, and he wouldn't if I had any say in the matter.

He lifted his head as if he heard me and I stopped still in my tracks. Could he have heard me? Did he have enhanced hearing? Crap. I took a breath, pulled up my invisible big-girl pants in my mind, and made a beeline for the door, pretending he wasn't there.

He stepped in my way again, and moved to grab my arm, but he let his hand fall as if he thought better of it. I looked up at him.

"Yes?"

"I'm sorry," he said, without hesitation, his voice low. "I behaved like an animal yesterday."

I snorted and bit my lip. His cheeks went pink and he looked away. Was he... flustered?

"Go on," I said, crossing my arms over my chest. He took a deep breath and glanced back at me.

"I treated you without the respect you deserve," he said, "and I'm sorry. I overstepped. I'm used to... a certain amount of—"

"Obedience?" I asked with a raised brow. His eyes tracked the movement of my eyebrow before he met my eyes again.

"You could say that," he said. "I don't have time to talk about it now, but if you're with us for a year—"

"Did you remember when I said no meetings outside the label office?" I asked and gestured around us. "Where are we?"

His pink cheeks went red.

"This isn't easy," he said. I glared at him.

"Apologizing shouldn't be. And hello, we're still outside," I retorted. He grabbed the door and opened it, holding it for me.

"After you," his voice was barely above a low growl and I

felt a small pang of guilt as we took two steps forward and one step back. Well, he hadn't listened, and if he was going to be in the business of apologizing for his mistakes, then he also needed to work at not making them in the first place. The mere thought of my family catching me fraternizing with a werewolf... or a whole pack of them...

My shoulders gave an involuntary shiver as I stepped into the office. Behind me, I heard Eli close the door.

"You going to meet us down in the studio?" he asked. "We're all there now..."

I turned, making up my mind to forget the events of the day before.

"You're forgiven," I said to him. "I just... have things I'm sensitive about I guess and, yeah..." I trailed off as he looked at me, an understanding in his eyes.

"You running from who you are?" he asked. That hit way too close for me and I didn't answer. I stared back at him, trying to let him know with non-verbal cues not to push it. He didn't know me well enough to be allowed to ask that. He surveyed me for a long moment before looking away with a heavy sigh. "You're not the only one. You coming?" He gestured to the studio door.

I shook my head.

"I'm going to put my stuff down at my desk first and check in with Willa. She texted me and said my office space was ready early, so I'll get set up there and then come down, if that's alright with you."

"You're the boss," Eli said although he had a small, wry

smile on his face. "Whatever you say... goes." Was he being sarcastic? I decided I wasn't going to ask.

"Good, glad we have that sorted out then," I replied. "I'll be down in a bit." I turned and walked up the stairs, and when I got to the top I felt the heat of his gaze still on me. I looked down to the bottom of the stairs but he was already gone. Shaking off the uncertainty of his apology and our talk, I entered the production floor only to be immediately stopped by Jake Tupper.

"Darcy, hey," he said casually, a grin on his face. "Willa is out with the big boss for a quick meeting, but I overheard her telling Chrissy where your desk was so I thought, maybe —" He pointed in the direction of the far corner of the room. "Let me show you."

I looked around for a brief moment and wondered if it was worth offending him by trying to find Willa myself. Besides, he wouldn't lie, would he? Like, there was no point to that. I gave him a brief smile.

"Sure, then I have to get down to studio," I said, carefully giving myself an out to escape him as soon as possible.

"Uh huh," he replied, not listening to me as he walked me to my desk. There were more people in the office this time than there had been yesterday and a few of them eyed me as we walked. While their presence took the edge off of my discomfort at Jake's sudden appearance by my side, I wasn't sure if it was going to hurt my reputation to have him paying me special attention. I really didn't want to become 'that' girl.

"Thanks," I said as I turned around the corner of my cubicle wall and stopped short. On my desk was a small, flowering cactus. The rest of the desk was clear except for a dock for my laptop, along with a phone and a pad of paper. I looked over my shoulder at Jake.

"You like it?" he asked. "I figured it was more original than flowers."

I looked back at the cactus. I was really bad with plants, mostly out of spite since my sister was so gifted with them.

"It's great," I managed. I reached to pick it up and immediately stabbed my hand on one long spine. "Fu—dge," I saved the curse word and Jake laughed.

"You can swear here, nobody gives a fuck," he said, not seeming to mind at all that I'd just injured myself on his 'thoughtful' present. I cradled my hand against my chest.

"Thanks for filling me in on that," I replied. My hand throbbed; the spine had thrust in deep to the fleshy pad at the base of my thumb and I hoped the thing was clean. If I'd stuck with my studies, I would have learnt how to instantly purify and cauterize wounds with my powers, something that was probably more useful to witches on the battlefields during the Napoleonic wars. Now I wished I'd stuck with it long enough to heal paper-cuts and other low level, day-to-day annoying injuries. "Well," I said, painfully awkward. "Thanks for the cactus. I'm gonna get settled and head down to the studio."

"Really?" he asked, his eyebrows hiking up. "I heard what they got going on down there. Nothing that's a smash, honestly. You'll have your work cut out for you until they figure out how to write a chorus."

Instantly I felt defensive. Sure, they were werewolves. Sure, we'd gotten off on the wrong foot. But they were my band.

"Well if they got signed as fast as they did, I'm sure they've got something special in their writing," I said. "Didn't you take like, eight years of demo submissions before anyone would even look at you?" I asked. I'd done a little research the night before on Jake Tupper in between laughing at Irish people eating poutine.

Jake's face clouded for a moment and he smirked.

"I just didn't want to sell out. I didn't change my sound; I just waited for the industry to change and then they finally figured out what a hit sounds like," he shot back.

"Right, well congrats on that," I said as I set my backpack down on the edge of my desk, creating as much of a barrier between him and me as possible.

"I went to number one on my first single on the hot indies," he insisted, the thread of wounded-male-ego in his words.

"That's great," I tried to adopt a soothing tone. "Like really, amazing."

He seemed to buy it.

"You're going to learn so much while you're here," he said. "If you have any questions—" He held out his hand, palm up. I stared at it and then looked at him quizzically. "Gimme your phone, I'll program my number into it."

My gut didn't even have time to flare with alarm.

"Tupper, why are you monopolizing our manager?" Finn had appeared behind Jake, startling him. Jake made a show of laughing loudly and pointing at Finn with both index fingers, as if he hadn't just crapped his pants.

"Hey there Finn Gunner, right? Just having a friendly chat, that's all," he said before glancing back at me. "Darcy here doesn't mind. She likes it."

My hand was aching and I pressed my fingers along the line of fire where his crappy cactus had stabbed me. Finn met my gaze over Jake's shoulder and tilted his chin down in a light nod.

"Well that's nice but she's gotta be downstairs right now. We wouldn't want to have to complain to Willa that Darcy here's not doing her job, right?" Finn said, and Jake stepped back in surprise.

"Well I think that would be a pretty dick move, Gunner," he said. I knew that Finn didn't mean a word of his threat though. He'd probably gotten the same vibe off of Jake that I did: if he'd told Jake to back off because I was their manager, Jake would have pushed back and taken it as a man-to-man challenge. But if he threatened my job, then Jake would think that Finn was an ass and back off on his own so that he seemed like the 'good guy' in the situation.

Finn's esteem grew ten times in my eyes right then.

"I know all the dick moves," Finn said, but he was looking at me and not at Jake. "You gonna come do your job?" He sounded so stern he could have been a dead ringer for his twin. I grabbed my laptop and shut my backpack in the locking drawer of my desk.

"Coming," I said, breezing by Jake. "Later, Jake." Behind me I could hear Jake murmur something to Finn, but I couldn't exactly make out what. I made tracks for the stairs, where Finn caught up to me.

"Sorry," he said as we took the stairs together. "I wasn't really—"

"I know," I said, "but it worked and that's all I care about."

"Just so you know, I'm helping you dodge a bullet. He's not a great person. Or even a good person," Finn commented, voice pitched low as he opened the studio door for me.

"That message I got loud and clear yesterday," I replied.

"Yesterday?" he asked. We'd entered into a sound buffering vestibule, where there was a door in front of us, inlaid with thick glass. I could see the band inside the control room, and the muffled beat of music barely reached us. The lights were dimmer in here, and I could feel the weight of the sound proofing press in all around me. It could have been claustrophobic, but it was comforting instead. Finn waited for the main door to shut before he put a hand on the glass door's handle. "Yesterday?" he asked again, concern etched around his eyes.

"He's the kind of guy who thinks everyone is a fan, until proven otherwise, and sometimes that's not even enough evidence for him," I said. Finn nodded slowly.

"If he gives you trouble..."

"I can take care of myself," I lied. Finn had no idea that I could maybe give out a few static shocks and his level of knowledge was going to stay that way.

"I know," he said, his voice almost cracking. "I know you can. Trust me, if there's anyone who knows just how much a girl like you can take care of herself, it's me. But even so, I don't give a fuck how high up on the label ladder he is, if he even breathes in your direction funny, you tell me and we'll deal with it."

His words took me by surprise. First his admission which sounded raw and almost angry, and second, his threat toward Jake. I swallowed my questions when I looked at him better in the dim light that filtered through the door to us. His expression was shuttered and entirely closed off.

"Alright," I agreed. He let out a breath.

"Good, let's listen to some rockin' tunes," he said, and ushered me into the studio.

SIX

**Phoenixcry**
@PhoenixcryMusic

Follow ⌄

We're almost done producing our new album with @RoryGriffBeats and can't wait for you to hear it. We've come a long way since our bathroom demos... #tincandrums #newmusic #newrelease #justwait #meltingfaces #andpanties

6 Retweets 18 Likes

♡ 13   ⟲ 6   ♡ 18   ✉

The rest of the band turned to see us enter, and another person, a guy a few years older than the band-members who was tapping furiously at his keyboard to save a file as he twisted his body to look.

I felt Finn's presence behind me, but as opposed to feeling loomed-over it was comforting. He had neatly slid himself in between me and Jake upstairs, giving me an out that I was grateful to take.

"Hey guys," I gave a little half-wave to the band before eyeing up the man in a swivel chair at the recording console.

"Rory, this is Darcy, our new manager," Finn said, putting a heavy hand on my shoulder. His fingers lingered there for a long moment before he pulled away, moving around me to get himself settled on the couch next to Charlie.

"Rory Griffin," Rory said by way of greeting as he got out of his chair and held out his hand, grabbing my un-injured hand to shake it firmly. I nearly squeaked but stomped on my inner fangirl. Rory Griffin had produced five of my favorite recent indie rock records, and I was amazed that he had worked with Phoenixcry at all. He had his pick of acts and, probably, turned down five times as much work as he took on.

"Darcy Llewellyn," I said. "Nice to meet you."

"Pretty name," he said, and winked playfully. "Pretty girl." Eli made a low noise, and Rory looked guilty. He held up his hands. "I'm sorry. I'm not sexually harassing you, I just— some of the older producers I worked with were, uh, older. And old school. You know. Anyway, now that I've made a total ass of myself," he pointed at a primo seat near the console. "Let's wow you with what these guys have put together."

I glanced at Eli in confusion. Had he actually growled? He was staring steadily at Rory's screen, ignoring my gaze, if he was even aware of it. But I saw his jaw clench, the slightest tensing of his muscles. He was totally aware of the fact I was staring at him and he probably didn't miss a single thing in the room. I needed to find out more about werewolves and their senses. What should have been a fun but challenging internship at a label had become suddenly difficult bordering on dangerous. *Don't worry about your internship, they said, it'll be fine, they said. You'll get to work with all kinds of people, and also supernatural beings. Oh wait, that wasn't in the brochure.* I took a breath and my seat, as Rory clicked around on his computer.

A roar of music burst out of the speakers and I tried not to jump in my seat. Guitars immediately filled my senses, and a drum-beat thundered into my heart as the first song played. I felt, rather than saw, the five guys looking at me, gauging me for my reaction. Normally I would have tapped my foot along to the beat, but I felt instantly self conscious. What if I was off-time? Finn's raw voice, the perfect mix of honesty and grit, reached right into my chest and wrapped tight around my heart. When the sound of a triple-kick drum-line opened up the chorus, I realized I was dealing with not only werewolf musicians, but *talented* werewolf musicians. It was one thing to know abstractly they should have had to be good in order to get signed, but bad acts got signed all the time.

By the time the post-chorus bass riff shivered up my spine, I turned to stare back at the band that I was now in charge of with a sinking sense that there was no way I could ask to be reassigned. Phoenixcry was too good, and it was only enhanced by the fact that their innate magical existence imbued every note sung and chord played. Breathing was difficult. I loved music on a bad day, and this was more than music, it was an experience. The lyrics were thrumming along through my veins, the drumbeat taking over my heartbeat. It was too much. I gazed at the floor, not wanting to meet the eyes of any of them because I knew they'd see how much their music had affected me. There was no way I was going to be vulnerable in front of them, even if they were a band I was managing.

The song ended on a drum crash, and Rory sat back in his chair with a sigh, one arm cast over his eyes, so he could better enjoy the music I guess.

"That's like good sex. Or amazing pizza," he said. He rocked forward. "What did you think?"

There was a tight feeling in the air, and it was definitely because a bunch of werewolves were staring at me intently. It wasn't easy to put aside a lifetime of fearing someone in order to work with them and be in enclosed spaces with them. But I needed to focus on my career and my future. That meant dealing with creatures I'd long believed to be a witch's natural enemy. So far it seemed like they were more interested in their music than ripping my throat out, so that was a bonus I guess.

"Well I wouldn't say it was amazing pizza," I replied, and saw Cash tense up out of the corner of my eye. His fingers had been drumming on his knees but they stopped when I spoke. I glanced up at the rest of the band: Eli looked like he didn't give a shit what I thought; Finn was gazing at me with a half-smirk tugging at his lips; Charlie was on his phone; Ace was as tense as Cash although, where Cash radiated irritation, Ace looked nervous. "But it was really, really good," I finished, transferring my attention back to Rory. "Honestly I think if the rest of the tracks are like that one, it's going to be one of the best albums to come out of XOhX in a long time."

I meant it too. Sure, they had a huge hand-up based on the fact they were werewolves and that musical ability pulsed through their veins, but the song was flat-out great.

Charlie lifted his head from his phone.

"Glad to know we've got your good opinion, Darcy, and now that we've got it we don't want to lose it," he said with a playful grin and I paused and wondered if he'd ever read *Pride and Prejudice*. Did werewolves even read? I really needed to know more about the band if I was going to manage them but that seemed like a dangerous road to go down. Eli cleared his throat and Charlie rolled his eyes, but fell quiet. *The master commands,* I thought as Rory made some humming noises and tapped up another track.

"Let's listen to—" he cut-off as Eli interrupted him by standing and clearing his throat.

"No, I think we're good on the listening party," he said. "She can hear the rest of it at the show."

"Show?" I asked, straining to look way, way up at him. He and Finn were strikingly tall, broad across the shoulders although Eli seemed to take up more room despite the fact they were both obviously identical twins. How long was it going to take before I got used to their overwhelming presence? Shaking myself out of my reverie, I couldn't help but frown. Why hadn't I been told about the show? I was their manager, wasn't I?

"Yeah," Finn said as he stood as well, kicking Charlie in the shoe as the other werewolf was staring at his phone again. Charlie jerked his head up and glared at Finn and I swore for a moment that Charlie actually bared his teeth in a silent snarl. "We've got a private house show tonight. We didn't tell the label about it because," Finn paused and shrugged, "It was booked before they signed us and it's not really their business because it's not like they can promote it."

Rory turned back to his computer.

"Troy's going to kill you if he finds out," he sing-songed under his breath but the wolves ignored him although I knew they could hear it.

"Why don't we take this to Sparrow's Coffee down the street," Charlie offered with an easy smile at me. He'd forgotten my no-outside-contact rule. I wasn't sure if I should call him out on it. Worrying my family was stalking me and would find out I was working with a band of werewolves was pretty paranoid, right? "That way Rory doesn't have to feel bad about overhearing things he can't run his mouth about."

Rory snorted.

"Thanks, asshole," he said with affection, throwing up the bird at him without looking. Cash was on his feet without a word, and out the door. Finn glanced after him before looking at me.

"Do you want me to go with you to get your stuff from your desk?" he asked. I licked my lips and shook my head. He obviously was thinking that Jake would be lurking around my desk. The indie star probably had better things to do but I didn't want to test that theory.

"No, I'm good. We'll go for coffee, and talk and then come back, right?" I asked. One cup of coffee at a cafe wasn't going to be the end of me. Eli gave a brief nod and nudged Ace up. The shorter wolf bounded to his feet.

"Sounds great. I could use a caffeine hit right about now," Ace said.

"If Willa or Troy comes hunting you guys down?" Rory didn't bother turning around in his seat as he spoke, his fingers flying over the keyboard. From the looks of it, he'd already pulled up another project and was setting up a new session to record.

"Tell them we took our new manager out for celebratory espresso shots," Eli said, his voice flat. "Come on, Miss Llewellyn." He gestured to the door. Finn's eyebrows shot up and then back down again when Eli glowered at him. Ace's lips parted in surprise, but he quickly went to the door and held it open for me.

"Oh it's *Miss* Llewellyn, now?" Finn hissed to Eli out of my hearing as I walked out of the room.

"Just reminding everyone of who she is, and what that means to us," Eli shot back. "Just in case some of you..." His words died away as I beat it out of the studio part of the XOhX offices and took a sharp left to go outside the building.

Cash was there, talking on his phone although when he saw me, he ended his call with an abrupt,"I'll call you back later." He shoved his phone in his pocket and jerked his head toward the door behind me. "Where's everyone else?"

"Finn and Eli are being twin buttheads, Charlie is eating invisible popcorn and enjoying the fireworks," Ace said from behind me as he came out into the light. He squinted hard. It was bright outside, enough that I'd been uncomfortable for a moment from the change of the softly-lit studio. Was it worse for a werewolf? His senses, like eyesight, should have been better theoretically, right?

"Great," Cash muttered as he shoved his hands into his jacket pockets. "Idiots."

"Well," Ace shrugged and looked at me. "Sorry, I just want you to know that I'm excited to work with you even if you're a, uh, y'know—"

"Ace," Cash growled, "Could you not be a complete fucking pleb for at least one moment of your life?"

"What? She needs to know it's fine. I'm fine with it, even if Eli's got a stick up where the sun doesn't shine and you're grumpy because you're old school. Charlie doesn't care, and neither does Finn."

"Charlie doesn't care because the band is more important to him than anything else, and Finn's too busy checking out—" Cash stopped short and fell quiet as he glared at me, seeming to remember I was still standing there.

"Well this has been educational," I commented to a leafy tree that stretched out its branches to shade half the street. Ace edged closer to me and playfully punched me in the shoulder, a light tap that was more of a brush than a hit.

"You seem like good people, even if you come from bad people," he said and Cash inhaled hard. He looked like he wanted to smash his face into his hand and hold it there. What the hell did that mean, bad people?

"What?" I asked, eyes narrowing. Okay, sure, my family were stuck up and thought themselves to be better than everyone, including the other members of the council, but that was just *them*. That was their deal, and most of their friends were the same.

"Ignore him," Cash interrupted, "he doesn't know anything."

"That's not true," Ace protested, "just cause I'm younger than you doesn't mean you're hot—"

"Stop it," Cash said and Ace's jaw snapped shut, his lips pressed together in a tight line. He looked pissed, his shoulders hunching, and I realized there'd been a thread of *command* in Cash's voice. He might not have been Eli, who seemed to be the alpha wolf of their ragtag little pack, but as Cash stared down Ace, it became clear that Cash was higher up on the pecking order.

Younger? Did Ace mean... a lot younger? Werewolves lived for centuries, going from a few decades of puppy-hood into young-adult and staying there for a good century or a century and a half. I had no idea how old any of them really were, because they all seemed my age or a little older, maybe mid-twenties or around there. I glanced between the two of them before Rory interrupted the tableau, blowing out of the building with a groan.

"Cash, you need to go deal with Finn and Eli. If they wreck the studio again, I'm not going to be able to cover for them and Troy is going to have all of our asses," he said as he fished out a pack of cigarettes from his pocket. A cigarette was at his lips and lit up before I could blink. Cash growled, low under his breath.

"Ace, take Darcy for coffee. I'll deal with those punks, Rory," he said and disappeared into the building. Rory waved his hand in the air to disperse the smoke, shooting me an apologetic look.

"Bands. Too much testosterone, not enough sense," he said with another drag on his cigarette.

"Hey," Ace protested, but grinned at me. "Well, more coffee for us. Plus Sparrow's has the most freaking delicious lemon bars I've ever had in my life. I'll get you one. C'mon, let's go."

"If the guys are arguing, shouldn't I—" I looked over my shoulder at the door, a shiver of fear running through me.

"Cash'll deal with it. And Charlie's there. He'll talk sense into them once they're calmed down enough to listen," Ace said, wrapping a hand around my wrist. "C'mon, let's go. You can pretend to be my girlfriend. Cabe is always giving me shit about never bringing in girls. Please?" His request startled a laugh out of me and I let him take me down the street.

"Cabe?" I asked.

"The coffee guy. Best coffee in the city, I swear to god, but he's a real asshole about my lonely heart status," Ace said, letting my wrist go when we were half a block away and he was sure I wasn't going to turn back.

"You're in a band, signed to XOhX, and it's not like you're bad to look at," I said, "how the hell are you single?"

Ace snickered.

"I'm not bad to look at huh? Thanks. Uh, well, when you've got four other pack brothers hovering around you all the time? And we're sorta focused on the band, music and stuff, before anything else," he said, and his voice dropped down low. "It'd have to be a pretty special girl to *understand* that I'm not like a regular guy." I shivered again, not from fear this time, my skin breaking out into goose flesh as he looked up at the sky. We'd come to a stop at the end of the block. "When you live a long time," he continued, "you don't want to fall in love with someone who's just going to fade away in a few decades and leave you." He let out a gusty breath. "It's nice to be able to talk about this with someone who gets it. I mean, you're a witch, sure, whatever, but you know what I am." He gave me a warm, even smile that melted the wall I'd been keeping up around the band, just a little bit.

"You could fall in love again," I said, "right? I mean it would hurt, but..." He shook his head and gave me a funny look.

"Wolves mate for life," he replied as he glanced up and down the street for cars. We crossed to the other side.

"Oh, I didn't know..." I trailed off and felt the yawning hole of my not-knowledge gaping inside of me. I had no idea wolves mated for life. The thought made me sad for Ace, until— "What about a female werewolf? You know? You could scratch each other's backs... chase rabbits together..."

Ace let out a bark of a laugh. He was cute, and almost sweet, I decided, the way his sandy blond hair shagged across his forehead where he'd tousled it at some point, and hadn't bothered to fix it. That and his blue eyes. I knew that guys in bands were usually attractive, maybe not model-hot or anything, but even still, the guys in Phoenixcry looked like they'd been plucked out of the pages of some fashion spread in a magazine. If they weren't so dangerous and my new clients, I would've been crushing on them. Did that make me seriously unprofessional? I didn't want to think about it.

"I never thought a witch could have a sense of humor," he said with a grin, which turned sad in another moment. "It'd be pretty hard to find a female who wasn't into one of the older guys," he said with a huff. "They're... older. I'm a millennial baby, but just barely. And also, there's really not a lot of packs left. Most of the females are older—much older. Werewolves tend to have more males born than females," he hesitated for a moment and pointed to a doorway. "There's Sparrow's. Let's get coffee for the rest of the guys. They'll be pissed their little fist-fight meant they had to go without."

"Fist-fight?" I asked, stopping in my tracks. Ace turned and rolled his eyes.

"C'mon Llewellyn. You're running with wolves now. Our blood runs hot and our tempers hotter, so what's a little fisticuffs among pack-mates? Not much. Coffee, and donuts. That'll make everything better," he said. I stayed put, so he stomped back to me and wrapped an arm around my shoulders. "It's no big deal. We heal fast. You won't even see a shadow of a bruise on Finn's face by the time we get back."

My mouth opened to protest but he hushed me, and I gave in. What was I going to do, anyway? Interrupt their brawl? Then they'd really know how powerless I was, and that wasn't information I was going to give up to them, under any circumstances.

SEVEN

Ace was right about one thing: I didn't notice a single bruise on any of the guys, although their clothes were rumpled and there was a broad scowl on Eli's face that wouldn't budge even when Ace offered him a chocolate smothered donut. I left them to patch things up and spent the rest of the day at my desk, going over my on-boarding package that Willa had sent to my new XOhX email address. There was a lot of information to absorb. The band wasn't big enough yet to have a dedicated booking agent, so a lot of those duties were going to be falling to me, although Willa said it was fairly straight-forward.

Finn stopped by my desk again, grabbed the cactus, and gave me the address for the house show. *Dress nice*, he'd said, but he didn't specify what he meant by that. My budget over the last few years been pretty skinny; nothing like what I was used to living with my family where there hadn't really been anything off limits to me.

When I walked into our dorm-room, I found that Max still wasn't back from her emergency visit with her father, so she wasn't there to help me cycle through my three 'fancy' outfits. In the end I picked some dark-wash tight jeans that made my butt look like I worked out harder than I did (thanks Lycra!), and a loose, off-one-shoulder black sweater shot with silver thread. For a moment I went to put on silver earrings but paused and thought better of it. What if silver made the guys uncomfortable? I needed to spend more time with Ace. Of all the guys, he seemed the most open to sharing information without judging me too badly. He'd said he was younger than the rest of the guys, so I guessed he was anywhere from his mid-twenties to mid-thirties in actual solar years, although in werewolf years, he was barely into adulthood. Maybe that was why he was so open with me, because of all of them, he was closest to me in age.

I got an Uber over to the condominium tower where the show was being held, and stared up at it. The glass building was one of the tallest I'd ever seen and, as I pushed open the front door, I saw an actual concierge standing behind a desk. The woman smiled at me as I approached.

"Um, hey," I said as I fished my phone out of my purse and squinted at it. "I'm here for the Liu... I'm trying to get to the Liu apartment. It says PH4 on the invite I was sent..." I trailed off as the woman smiled again.

"What's your name, please?" she asked.

"Darcy, Darcy Llewellyn," I replied. She looked at a tablet and tapped the screen.

"Final elevator at the end of the hall. It will take you directly to Penthouse Four," she said, gesturing down the hall behind her. The marble floors stretched out all around me, and I took a breath to keep certain memories at bay.

The council chambers were lined in marble, black though, not white like it was in the condo's lobby. Still, the echo of my shoes on the stone flooring reminded me too much of the last time I'd seen my father, scowling down at me from his council seat. The elevator couldn't arrive quickly enough, and I watched headline news on a small TV in one corner of it's small space as the floors beeped by softly.

My stomach gave an uncomfortable turn and my ears popped. The doors opened with a soft *woosh* and a *ping*. The sun hadn't set yet; Finn had given me instruction to arrive long before the guests would be coming. I stepped out of the elevator, eyes wide at the sight in front of me. A massive, soaring great room spread across the width of the entire building, and at the far end, back-dropped by a dominating scene of the city below, was a low stage with black curtains hanging on either side of it.

My idea of a house party was nothing in comparison to this. House parties were usually in frat houses, with a lot of drunk people stumbling over rotten couches, with solo cups littering the floor. At the Liu residence on penthouse level four, there was a crew of stage hands setting up, and even a portable sound booth toward the back of the room, tucked beside what looked like a bar and... possibly a catering table. I looked around for a friendly face but the guys weren't in the room, and the event crew ignored me.

The click of heels on the custom engineered wood floor made me turn. A girl, definitely not of drinking age, walked toward me, her mouth drawn tight. The clicking was from what I was certain were a pair of Valentino rockstuds because nothing about her screamed a girl who wore knock-offs. Her long, black hair hung straight to her waist and she was so thin I felt self conscious about the slight food-baby I had from a hastily scarfed microwave burrito before I'd left the dorms.

"Darcy Llewellyn?" the girl asked, holding out a slender hand to me. Her wrist dripped with Tiffany bracelets and, as I shook her hand and met her eyes, it was like looking into the gaze of one of the other young witches at our coming-of-age party; challenge, dismissal and derision all warred with one another in her expression.

I did the only thing I could do to fight back: I smiled.

"Are you Candy Liu?" I asked. She flicked her gaze down my body and her lips pressed together for a moment before she broke into an easy, faux smile.

"That's right. Thanks for coming. Cash told me all about you. You're so lucky to land an internship assisting them," she said. "They asked me to bring you back to their change room, so if you'd follow me," she said, turning on one, thousand dollar sole, and walking in the direction she'd come from. I took a few long strides to catch up to her.

"I'm not really assisting them—"

"Tonight is going to be epic. I've invited half my grade, and also the best people from the other private schools as well," she said, "the food and drink is usually off limits to the help, but since you're with the band..."

I'm with the band... That seemed like a phrase I was going to be using a lot in future. It was work not to roll my eyes as she referred to me as the 'help', but given the size of the penthouse she was living in and the opulent furnishings, I supposed I should have been grateful I hadn't needed to come up in the service elevator.

"That's nice of you, thanks," I lied as we turned the corner into a smaller hallway and she knocked on a carved, wooden door.

It swung open into what had to be a library or study. Eli was right there inside the doorway, blocking our view in. His gaze moved from Candy to me immediately, and pinned me to where I stood.

"Elias," Candy gushed, and it felt like she was about to vibrate right out of her skin. That was right, his full name was *Elias* Gunner. I'd read it in his bio but forgotten like an idiot. "I brought Darcy right to you like you asked."

"Miss Llewellyn," he said, practically breathing my name. My cheeks pinked. He really needed to get over bringing up my family name all the time. I couldn't help that we were on the council, and he didn't need to make such a big deal over it.

"Thanks Candy," I said as I stepped past Eli, trying to ignore the frisson of energy that I felt as Eli watched me go. Behind me I heard him say a few words to Candy, and then the door shut again.

"Thanks for taking that one for me, man," Cash said from where he was sprawled on one couch. "If she paws at me again, I swear I won't be responsible for my actions."

"Awwwww, is the big bad wolf afraid of a little eighteen-year-old girl," Charlie mocked from another couch, although he was staring at his phone as he spoke. Cash growled at him.

"More like I'm worried how I'm going to explain the blood stains on the floor," he snarled. I should have been alarmed by the threat of violence against Candy, but I felt certain that Cash had better control over his wolf-tendencies than that.

My view of the room, and its floor-to-ceiling windows and walls lined with books, was blotted out as Ace slipped up in front of me and enveloped me in a sudden hug.

I squeaked in surprise as his big arms wrapped around me and I was crushed into his chest.

"I'm so glad you're here," he murmured into my hair before he let me go when I squirmed. "Sorry," he apologized with a little shrug. "I just like to hug people I like."

"Thanks," I said, catching my breath again, my heart thudding away in my chest at his closeness. It was still hard to not react with fear, but bit-by-bit I was losing the baked-in dread from a lifetime of hearing the worst of werewolves. My family would have been freaking out to see me so relaxed around a wolf. Maybe it was a good thing I was spending time with them. My family had been wrong about a lot of things, as I'd learned.

"You want a Redbull? We have like a hundred. Candy went all out," Ace said as he crossed the library to where a mini-fridge had been set up against one of the walls of books.

"No, I'm good," I said, as I sat down on one of the couches. "So did you guys need me to do anything?"

Finn looked at Eli before shaking his head.

"We've got this. We've done a hundred of these things."

"Eighty-nine," Charlie interrupted before going back to his phone. He was going to need it surgically implanted in his hand if he wanted to get any more attached to it. "It was eighty-nine. This is our ninetieth house-show."

I let out a soft whistle and all five of them snapped their heads to look at me before going back to what they were doing. Cash was drumming his fingers on his thighs again, like he had in the recording studio, and I could see he had an ear-bud in as he played along to a track.

"That's a lot of shows," I commented. Charlie lifted his head from his phone and locked it, tucking it in his pocket before he answered.

"Well, we want this," he said, glancing at his pack and band-mates. "There's always going to be someone out there who's working harder, and is hungrier than you. Someone who wants it worse than you do. We want to be that someone. We're starving," he said, the last word nearly cracking in his throat with such intensity that I felt my own breath catch in my throat. He gave me a brief smile. "I need to go talk to Candy about the stage set-up for the opening act. You can come along, but she'll listen better if a competing female is not in the room," he said with a roll of his eyes.

Cash chuckled as Charlie left.

"What he means is that Candy'll get jealous if you're there, and he likes her attention too much to want her to split her focus between admiring him and being mad at you." He winked at me and I looked at the door where Charlie had gone.

"Does he, um, does he have a thing for her?"

"Fuck no," Finn piped up from across the room where he was squirting honey into his mouth from a squeezable honey bear. "Charlie just likes to be admired, that's all. If you ever want him to do what you want, just flutter your eyelashes at him and compliment him on something stupid, like the shape of his nose or something. He falls for it every time."

"Finn," Eli called from a table that was set up with a few laptops on it. "Can you come finalize the set list with me and stop gossiping." Finn twitched for a moment before he went, leaving me with Ace and Cash. Ace toyed with the pull-ring on his Redbull as his eyes tracked between Finn and Eli then me and Cash.

"You all right, kid?" Cash asked him. "Too much caffeine?" Ace shook his head.

"Just hoping tonight goes good. We have a lot of merch to shift, and I think Troy heard about the show so if we don't sell well, he'll be pissed that we gambled and lost on a stupid house show."

"Candy's paying us three thou' to be here. That's huge for us," Cash pointed out. "Troy can't be mad at us for something we set up before we ever signed to the label."

I felt like I had been dropped right into some sort of private scene where I didn't belong. Half of what they said made no sense.

"You guys really want it bad, huh?" I asked, looking from one to the other. "Most artists are worried about selling out period, not selling out of merchandise."

Cash gave me an even, flat look.

"Well maybe they have mommies and daddies to run back to," he said, his voice clipped. "We don't. Excuse me." He got to his feet and went to Finn and Eli. He said something, too low for me to hear, and left the room. My cheeks were hot with embarrassment, although Ace was purposefully not looking at me.

"Don't be mad at him," Ace finally said after a few moments of awkward silence.

"Mad? He's the one who's mad at me, not the other way around," I countered, my voice rough. "I know I said the wrong thing, but I don't know why it was wrong." I gave Ace an expectant look. He squirmed and shook his head.

"Later," he said. My fountain of knowledge had just run dry. Great.

"I'm really flying blind here, Ace," I whispered. He shifted even more in his seat and, for a moment, I thought he might crack and tell me.

"I gotta go re-string my, uh, my bass," he said and bolted out of the room. A second later he came back and grabbed his bass in its case, gave me a weak smile, and disappeared again.

Eli turned around from the table, shooting me a disdainful look. I held up my hands to stop him from making any snap judgements.

"Look, if you guys don't give me the info I need to not piss you off or chase you away, I'm not going to be able to do anything but that," I said. Eli's eyes narrowed but Finn chuckled and elbowed him.

"She's got a point," Finn said. "It's not like any witch we've

ever met knew enough about us unless they were, y'know..."
He trailed off and didn't elaborate what he *y'knowed*. I
made a noise of frustration.

"I'm going to go see Charlie." Getting to my feet, I leveled
Eli with a heated glare to match his. "I'm gonna tell you, in
case no one else has or you've forgotten, there's no other
person at the label who has time to manage your little wolf
pack project here. I'm all you've got. I can't get reassigned to
anything and you can't have someone else. So can we please
stop posturing and growling at each other and actually work
together?"

Finn froze, but Eli crossed his arms over his chest, looking
more amused than mad for the first time. I don't think I'd
seen that expression on his face yet.

"Is that what you want, little witch?" he asked, his voice
almost a purr. The urge to take a step away from him
fluttered in my belly but I fought it and stood my ground.

"Yes, that's what I want, you heard me the first time, unless
you don't have super hearing after all," I replied, refusing to
take the bait on his 'little witch' comment. He tilted his
head to the side, a smile still on his face as he gazed at me
searchingly.

"Good to have you on board. It's about time you made up
your mind if you were staying or going," he said, before
looking back at the set list. "Let's perform *Falling Down*
right after that extended outro here," he said to Finn,
ignoring me completely.

"Is that it?" I asked, incredulous at his instant dismissal.
Who the hell did he think he was?

"That's all." He didn't even look at me; instead, he scribbled on a sheet of paper with a sharpie. Now it was my turn to narrow my eyes as I stared two holes into his back.

"Was that a *Devil Wear's Prada* reference?" I asked. Finn laughed but turned it into a hasty cough when Eli glowered at him before looking at me again.

"We're not stuck in the 18th century," he commented. "We watch movies, just like you do. It's as if you don't know anything about werewolves at all."

I went still and his pupils dilated for a moment in realization. Finn was also looking at me. Shit, they knew. I waited for them to come down on me like a pile of bricks, to somehow take instant advantage of my lack of knowledge.

"Well, that's interesting then," was all Eli said, before looking at Finn with a measured, meaningful look. "Go see Charlie, Miss Llewellyn."

Confusion, aborted-panic, and what was left of my pre-show burrito boiled around in my stomach. I opened my mouth to speak again, but Finn just raised his hand an inch, a clear sign telling me to shut up. My face tomato-red, I left the room in search of Charlie.

C-C-C-Candy
@Candy2Shoes

Follow

Bet u wish u were me. lol #concertprivee #uwishuwereinvited #thxdaddy

12 Retweets **34** Likes

♡ 14   ⟲ 12   ♡ 34

EIGHT

The opening band kinda sucked. The lighting crew was doing their best to make the band better than they were, but there were only so many strobe lights that could be packed onto a stage before it became a fire hazard. Candy Liu hadn't been lying either about her invite list. The penthouse was packed, wall-to-wall with bodies, mostly girls, who were milling around and getting drinks from the bartender.

I was nursing a soda, feeling vulnerable and out of place. Charlie hadn't needed me, so I'd spent some time hiding out in a fancy bathroom that had marble walls and a little low sink that sprayed water upwards. I think it was to wash my ass, but didn't dare try it.

Fast-forward a few hours. The sun had set, the stage was lit up, sound-check had been done, and a horde of sweaty, well-heeled music fans were crowding into the great room of Penthouse Four. I'd lost sight of Candy earlier in the night, and the guys of Phoenixcry were holed up in their dressing room, taking quiet time before their set.

I leaned against a marble pillar that held the roof up, and watched the opening band tune their guitars after one song, barely even looking at the crowd as they did so. Rookie mistake, big time.

"You look like you're having fun," Cash's voice rumbled in my ear and I dropped my soda with a yelp, splashing us both. He jumped out of the way, and yanked me with him, his arm wrapping around my waist and hauling me off the ground. The breath was still shuddering out of my lungs when he set me down on dry ground with a grumble. "You're easily scared."

"You're forgiven," I said with a glare. If he'd been Ace, he would've smiled sheepishly and scratched at the back of his head. I was starting to recognize a few of Ace's tells. But Cash was different, and his slow smirk told me he wasn't at all sorry, and I shouldn't hold my breath for an apology.

"So, what do you think?" he asked, nodding at the stage.

"Could be better," I said, trying to be diplomatic. He snorted.

"Understatement of the year. But you've got good taste," he said. "Want me to get you another drink? That'd probably be the right thing to do since I made you spill your last one." It was probably as close to an apology as I was gonna get, so I took it.

"Just a soda, maybe root beer?" I asked. He disappeared in the crowd without a word, and I wiped a few droplets of soda from my jeans. A song passed, and then another, and Cash still hadn't returned. My anticipation melted into irritation, and I walked over to the bar, where I spotted Cash, and then Candy hanging off of his arm. She was staring up at him with adoration in her eyes, even as it was obvious that Cash was not into it. He reached up to put a hand on her shoulder and push her away gently.

Nope, he wasn't into it at all. A spark of fury lit in my chest at the sight. Candy was taking advantage of her position of power as the person booking Phoenixcry in order to hit on Cash.

"Hey," I said as I walked over, grabbing Cash's hand. "I was looking all over for you, I was really worried." I didn't bother looking at Candy as I stood up on my tiptoes and brushed a kiss across Cash's cheek. My heart beat slowed as the world around us melted away and he turned his head slowly to stare at me. Beyond the fuzz of noise, I could hear Candy's gasp. Cash shook her off, his eyes narrowing at me before his arm slid up, up, around my shoulder. He pulled me in tight to his side. The press of his body, every muscle, molded against mine and I could smell the fresh linen-scent of clean laundry on his shirt, and beneath that something earthy, like water hitting heated rocks, on his skin.

"Oh my god, seriously?" Candy looked at Cash, then me, then Cash again. She took a step back. "Well, now I know how you got your job," she spat.

"Not okay, Candy." Cash held me tighter still, his fingers squeezing around the top of my shoulder. Candy shot me a venomous glare and turned with a scoffing sound, stomping off through the press of bodies. I felt Cash turn his face into the top of my head, and his words warmed me through my hair. "You okay?" he asked.

No, I was not okay. My body felt flushed and trembly, and not because of Candy's nasty implication I'd slept my way into my internship position. Cash's closeness, the way he'd instantly protected me, was making my blood run wild and all I wanted to do was soak up the affection, even if it was a ruse to chase Candy away from him.

How long had it been since I'd felt truly safe? Max was my best friend, and she'd held my hand through a lot of tough times over the last few years, but there was a marked difference from how Cash's body wrapping around mine made me feel. I got my hand up between us and pushed, gently, against his chest.

"I'm good. You good?" Precious inches opened up as he unwound his arm from my shoulders with a low rumbling noise, deep in his chest.

"I never got you your root beer," he sounded remorseful, but as he looked at me I felt my cheeks warming, a heat flaring deep in my belly. Getting away from him was suddenly priority number one.

"It's fine, I'm not thirsty anymore." I licked my lips and stepped back. His gaze dropped from my eyes to my mouth and he inhaled deeply. His chest pressed against his shirt, and I was very aware of how good he made a cotton Henley look. His eyes tracked the movement of my gaze and his lips spread in a slow smirk.

"You sure about that?"

My cheeks went from warm to hot at his implication that I wanted him. The grip of his shirt around his biceps was the last thing on my mind.

"I'm sure you've got a show to get ready for," I said, turning back to the stage where the opener was trying to get the audience to give them an encore. Cash stepped up behind me, and I could feel the heat radiating off of him, his hand lifting to hover over my shoulder. I couldn't breathe, my body screaming at me as I waited for his fingers to make contact, for him to touch me. He was a wolf. I was a witch. Whatever was happening? It needed to not.

His hand brushed over my shoulder, only once, briefly, and he leaned in, to whisper in my ear,

"Thanks for saving me from the kraken."

Then he was gone and I could breathe again. My eyes slid shut and I tried to control the shiver that his touch, his nearness, was waking up in me. It'd been so long since anyone had been that close to me in a way that was intimate. Cash was different from Creston, the guy that'd tried to take things further than I'd wanted, back at our coming-of-age party. Creston was the reason I'd been happily single for the last few years and hidden myself under layers of sweaters and knit beanie hats to avoid male attention. Jake Tupper reminded me of Creston.

Cash should have scared the crap out of me just based on who he was, and the bad blood between us as witch and werewolf. So why hadn't I run screaming away from him? Why had I even kissed his cheek in the first place? Questioning my judgement took up the crappy opener encore and when the lights went down again. About thirty girls near the front of the stage started screaming and I reached into my pocket for the earplugs that I always took with me to shows. I wanted to work in the music industry forever, and losing my hearing wouldn't help with that.

The first strains of the song I'd heard earlier that day in

studio rang out in the darkened room, and the corresponding scream rocked me. The lights on the stage came up, and four of the guys were there. Immediately I sought out Cash with my eyes, wondering if the moment we'd shared earlier had changed him like I'd felt it change me. White and blue lights glinted off the curves of his shoulders, and down his arms as he powered into a thudding intro for the first song. His eyes were half-closed, but his head was tilted upward, as if he was feeling the music more than hearing it. I tore my gaze away from him and tried to focus on the band as a whole.

In my on-boarding package, it had emphasized taking performance notes to the band after shows. We'd done a lot of critiquing throughout my music business program. I wasn't going to let Willa down by coming away from this show without notes for the guys, especially since the label was probably already going to be mad that there was a show and no label reps there except me.

Then Finn came on stage, reaching out to the crowd with one hand, and reaching back for his mic-stand with the other. He dragged the mic in front of his face, and I had to grab onto the pillar.

If their power had overwhelmed me through the recorded track in studio, it was tripled in force when they were performing live. I could hear the drum-beat right inside my heart as if Cash was demanding I keep up with the kick on his bass drum. My skin tingled and I couldn't look anywhere but at them. Finn demanded most of my attention, as he worked the front of the audience. I saw hands reaching up from the crowd, touching his arms, his belly, his chest. He didn't seem to mind it, playing right into their hands, almost literally. For some reason, an edge of frustration was rising in my chest every time some girl grabbed onto his shirt.

I looked away from him, because I knew if I saw one more person touch him, I'd march to the front of the crowd and... and...

Eli, so serious normally, was transformed, his face light and happy, the first time I'd seen him really look like he was enjoying himself. He was pressed up against Charlie, back to back as they played, their guitar lines weaving around one another. I could feel every shred of the rhythm pulse, and I pushed away from the pillar, drawn by the music and the raw waves of power coming from the five men on stage. They soared into the bridge, the hook coming fast. Ace let out a whoop and jumped up on top of his bass stack, and the girls shrieked as he bent almost backwards, his back arching, bass pointing to the sky as he played.

They were pure, unfiltered talent, and the overwhelming joy coming off of them as Finn's vocals jumped up a step in the final chorus. I found myself holding my breath every time he caught his, and suddenly I was in the middle of the crowd, staring up at the five of them. Hands reached all around me, for the band.

They were monsters, I had to remember that, but it was so hard when all they were doing was performing their hearts out.

Finn grabbed the front of his own shirt and pulled, nearly ripping it. A girl next to me covered her mouth with both hands, gasping for breath. My head was pounding with blood and sound, and I reached up and tugged out my ear plugs against my better judgement. It was like I was compelled to make myself vulnerable to them. Was this how they seduced witches and ripped their throats out? A thought came to me, a memory that had been lost to time; the memory of being little and my older sister telling me whispered stories of werewolves and the dangers they presented.

The song ended in a clatter of drums, and cymbals, shaking me free of my thoughts. My chest expanded and I breathed for what felt like the first time in four minutes.

"They're fucking amazing, huh?" A girl next to me said, since we were pressed shoulder-to-shoulder. "I go to all their shows, but I haven't seen you at one before." She eyed me up. "You a band-wagon hopper?" She tilted her head and wrinkled her nose.

"I—I... no," I said with a swallow. "I'm from their label..." I trailed off as her eyes widened.

"Oh shit, seriously? You're with the band? Can you get me into their dressing room?" She stood up on her tiptoes, almost nose to nose with me and I pressed back and away from her. Opening my mouth to shut her down right then and there, I was drowned out as Finn hollered into his microphone, and the girl turned away from me to cry out in response.

"How's everybody doing tonight?" He asked, and the screams around me were deafening. He threw back his head and laughed, looking at the other guys. Eli was furiously tuning his guitar, his pedal muted so the audience wouldn't hear it. Trying to focus on the small aspects of their performance was going to keep me sane.

"We're Phoenixcry," Finn said, and grinned when someone yelled out "we know!" in the back of the room. "And we're so fucking happy to be here with you tonight. Thanks to Candy for throwing a crazy party, and don't forget to tip your bartender. Now, let's jam!"

Cash stuck his hand up in the air, fingers wrapped tight around a drumstick.

"And one, and two," he yelled, voice carrying despite the fact he didn't have a mic. His arm came down, striking one of a set of toms hard. The band jumped into another song, Eli taking the front of the stage as he picked fast through a rising and falling guitar line. Caught in the magic he was making, I stared at him with my fingers clutching hard at the neckline of my shirt. His eyes shut tight as his left hand fretted up and down the neck of this guitar, until Charlie shoved him out of the way with a laugh as the intro solo wrapped up. Eli shoved him back, a matching grin on his face. The girls around me cried out, clearly loving the play-fighting.

Finn burst in between the two of them, racing forward and standing on his toes right at the edge of the stage. He loomed so far forward I thought he was going to tumble straight into the crowd.

"*I've got a dirty little secret,*" he sang, his hand out in front of him. A girl grabbed for it, and he hauled her right up on stage. His arm came around her waist, and he held her close as he sang.

She looked like she was going to faint, and that's when I felt the loosening of my shirt at the neck. I looked down. My fingers were still wrapped around fabric tight.

I'd ripped my shirt.

Fuck.

It was warm enough out that I hadn't brought a jacket to the party, and now I was stuck with a ripped neckline. The panic was enough to break the tight hold the guys' music had on me, and I swallowed down the impulse to flat-out cry (why were my emotions so haywire?). Instead I turned and worked my way out of the crowd, as it filled in the gap behind me instantly. The air was so cold when I emerged on the other end of the mass of people that I shivered.

"You gonna be my dirty little secret, baby?" Finn's voice tugged at me, so insistent, and I turned to watch them from the pillar I'd been leaning on at the beginning of their set. His hand was raking through his hair, and he pointed behind him. "Cash Legend, on drums, everybody!"

The guitars cut out, and Finn stepped to the side as the lights flooded on Cash. His arms blurred they moved so fast, glimmers of light sparking off the edges of the cymbals as they shuddered and shook with each hit. Ace was playing along with him, changing the tone of the beat with his bass, and I was caught again. The music had me, the drum beat in my head, in my heart, filling every inch of my body with thrumming heat. The song ended, and immediately raced into another one, and I breathed along with Finn, my fingers clenched tight and aching to hang onto each lick of the guitars and the raging beat of the drums behind them. One song melted into another, until Cash was throwing his drum-sticks into the crowd and the boys were gone from the stage. I gulped and shook my head, and edged around the crowd, ducking behind the curtain to the backstage area.

There was a bouncer there, one of Candy's crew, but he recognized me and let me pass.

"We gonna do an encore?" Finn was wiping his face off with a towel. Cash had his shirt off, and I had to look away. It was too much. My skin was humming, and I felt like my whole body was electricity, fluid and crackling. Their set had left me reeling, and I was still struggling to catch my breath.

Ace saw me and stopped in his tracks.

"What happened to your shirt?" he asked, and the rest of the guys looked over at me as they realized I was standing there.

"I—"

"Did someone rip your shirt?" Eli was the first to speak, clouds forming on his face. "Did someone hurt you?" He took a step toward me and I shook my head hard, not able to answer. "Darcy?" He'd dropped the *Miss Llewellyn* thing he'd been sticking to as his voice dipped low and quiet. "Did someone touch you?"

"N—no," I said, and managed a brief smile. "You know, it was pretty crazy out there, it just got snagged in the crowd," I lied. Eli's eyes half-lidded as he looked at me through ridiculously long lashes (Max would be jealous when she finally met him), and said gruffly,

"If someone touches you again, tell me. I'll deal with it." He looked over his shoulder. "One of you assholes going to give me something for her, or are you just gonna stand there?"

Charlie passed me a hoodie with a playful wink.

"Getting crazy in the mosh pit, huh?"

"There was no mosh pit," I countered as I shrugged into it and zipped it up over my top. It wasn't his, I knew right away, the subtle scent of heated rocks and water hitting my senses. My eyes flicked up and I saw Cash staring me down. He was still shirtless. I averted my gaze.

"Let's do an encore for them," Finn said. "C'mon, they'll love it and Candy might be a bit on the crazy side, but she's paying us bank."

"Acoustic," I heard Cash say. I didn't look at him, but sat down on a couch that pressed up against one of the floor-to-ceiling windows. "Ace has that new acoustic bass of his, you guys have your acoustics too. Strip it down. They'll eat it up."

"Sounds good," Finn said without arguing. "C'mon, idiots." There was a shuffling of feet, and Ace patted me on the head before the crowd outside cried, greeting the reappearance of four out of five members of Phoenixcry.

The music started, the lights dimmer backstage than they had been out in front. I sat there, half-listening, and played with the ties on Cash's hoodie. The couch dipped beside me and he was right there.

I looked up at him, not sure what he wanted.

"You okay?" he asked. His eyes were so blue. How had I not seen that before?

"A little overwhelmed," I admitted, being more honest than I wanted to be. But something about his presence, and the floating, trembling notes off the acoustic guitars was doing something to me.

"It does that to people. The music, I mean." He looked down at his hands and chuckled, shaking his head. "We knew it would happen, cause of what we are, but I was watching you. It hit you harder than anyone."

"Huh?" He was going somewhere that I couldn't follow. "What was hitting me harder?"

"The music. I always had a hunch, why witches wanted nothing to do with us, why they want us dead—"

"What?" He wasn't making any sense. Witches didn't want werewolves dead. They just didn't, couldn't, associate with them or be anywhere near them.

Cash gave me a slow, sad smile.

"The music is affecting you. It does to all humans, but... you looked—you looked entranced out there. Like the building could have come down around you and you wouldn't have noticed. I was watching," he said again.

"How? The stage lights—" I felt defensive. He put a finger to my lips, and hushed me. That sparking feeling shivered out along my mouth, down my neck, from where he touched me.

"You think a wolf can't see through some stage lights?" he asked. "It hurts to look through them, but that's not the worst pain I've felt. You looked like you were drugged out there, and..." He dropped his hand from my mouth and I lifted my own fingers to touch my lips, to stop the tingling. His eyes followed my movements. "You're still feeling it?"

"Feeling what?" I asked, but I knew what he meant. "Yeah," I admitted. He sighed and reached over beside the couch to an ice-bucket and pulled out a can of soda, popping the top.

"Drink this," he said, passing it to me. I took a long sip, the cold, sugary liquid sliding down my throat. As it did, I felt the fog of the music's power break, like a cracking egg, and peel away from me. I cleared my throat and closed my eyes for a moment before opening them to look at him again.

"Thanks," I said, feeling shy and embarrassed. "I had no idea that... that your music would do that to me."

"We knew, but didn't think it would be that strong." His lips pressed into a thin line. "Makes a lot of sense though. Most werewolves play some sort of instrument, and if we can do *that* to you with a few songs, it's pretty clear why witches and wolves have been enemies since the beginning."

"Yeah," I breathed the word out. "That... that weirdly makes sense. I don't know any witch who'd want to be controlled like that."

"You sure you feel better?" he asked abruptly.

"Yeah, I'm good. Back to myself, fully. I don't feel foggy anymore. Why?" I looked up at him. I did feel better, surprisingly. Maybe it was the caffeine.

"I don't think I could live with myself if you weren't in full control of yourself when I did this," he said. His fingers tucked up under my chin and his mouth covered mine. For a moment, I froze, and then melted up into him, my eyes sliding shut.

Every instinct in me should have been screaming to pull away, to slap him, to run. Instead, his mouth moved over mine, softly, so softly, and a moan rose in my throat. His arm slipped around the small of my back, and he pulled me against him. My hands splayed flat against his chest, and I kissed him back. The breath stopped in my lungs, and the blood was thudding in my ears. He tasted *good*, the soft scent of him overwhelming me.

"Oh," I whispered when he pulled away. He was breathing faster, slightly, his eyes half-closed as he looked down at me like he wanted to consume me entirely.

"I shouldn't have done that, but I wanted to from the first moment I saw you," he said, licking his lower lip. "You... you okay?"

"Y-yeah," I stuttered, and he chuckled, cupping my chin in one hand. He gave me one, brief soft kiss that left me more foggy than the music had.

"C'mon," he said, standing and pulling me up with him, his arm still wrapped around my back. "Let's go."

NINE

In the dark of the crowded room, no-one noticed us as we slipped from the backstage area and made our way along the edge of the crowd. Cash kept his head bowed, as he led me from the room. We were in the hallway outside the dressing room. All I could hear was the music, and the rapid flutter of my heart in my ears. What had happened? He'd kissed me. My lips were tingling, and my breath came in soft puffs.

"Come here," he whispered as he pulled me in for another kiss, this one hungry. His hands ran over my shoulders and down my back. In return, I stood on my toes, tongue slipping out to slide over his lower lip. That made him growl and his fingers dug into my hips. "Why do I want you so badly?" His eyes searched my face and I didn't have an answer for him. He kicked the door to the dressing room open and tugged me inside. Before I could take a breath he had me pushed up against the door and he was kissing me again. This time the full press of his body held me firm against the wood, and I grabbed at his shoulders to get some sort of leverage.

"Cash. Cash, what are we doing?" I peered up at him from beneath my eyelashes, feeling like I should push him away but not wanting to. Was the music still affecting me? My head was more clear that it had been in days.

"Making mistakes," he whispered throatily, bending down to kiss me again. This time, his lips travelled to the corner of my mouth, and over my jaw. He brushed kisses right up to the soft spot beneath my ear, and I was breathing so hard and fast that I felt faint. I'd had a boyfriend, back when I'd lived with my parents. Creston Hailward. Tall, dark, and handsome enough. He'd never sparked a fire in me like Cash was, and he'd even pushed my boundaries, forcing me to tell him to stop more than once.

Cash was different, his kisses burning on my skin but sweet at the same time. His hips cradled against mine, insistent but not inescapable. I could've gotten away if I wanted and I knew, deep down, if I told Cash to stop, he would in an instant.

The problem was I didn't want him to.

"Ace is usually the king of bad ideas," he muttered between kisses. "They told me not to, to stay away from you, that you were dangerous to us, and you are dangerous to us, Darcy, you're so... damn... dangerous." His tongue licked up the shell of my ear and I shuddered, fingers flexing into his back as I wrapped my arms around him.

"I'm not," the words came out in a soft squeak and he pulled away to gaze down at me, a smile curling up one corner of his mouth.

"That noise you made, that was cute." He chuckled and pulled me away from the door. I followed him, legs wobbly like a baby deer's. A baby deer being led by a wolf to its doom.

"Why am I dangerous?" I asked. They were the ones who were violent werewolves, able to rip me to pieces in a heartbeat. A fully powered witch was a match for one werewolf or two, but not a pack of them. And I wasn't fully powered, not even close, not that he knew that. Cash shook his head and pulled me down on the couch. I went without argument, my body deciding that what was best for me was to follow him, and curl up against him as he wrapped one thick arm around me.

"C'mere and hush, I can't—" He kissed me again, silencing any more questions. Even if I wanted to know what he was talking about, it was more important to be on the receiving end of his heated embrace, and I let my apprehensions go. There was an ache in my chest, a loneliness that had been there for years I realized, as it unfolded and melted away in the face of Cash's open affection. We broke for air after a moment, and his fingers slid down the side of my face as he stared at me, confusion on his face. "I can't have you, but I don't give a fuck," he growled, and he rolled me underneath him.

A gasp escaped my lips as the full press of his body on mine took me by surprise, and my fingers tightened around his biceps, sparking with power. He jerked back for a moment, shocked, literally, and stared at me.

"Oh shit, I'm sorry, I didn't..." My face flushed, and mortification settled under my breast bone, making a home there. I'd lost control of myself, and *shocked* him. His surprise gave way to amusement as his brow pulled together.

"You're a storm witch, huh?" he asked.

"Uh, yeah," I didn't bother correcting him, because it was close enough to lightning, really, and what did it matter when the most I could do was spark people anyway?

"Knew you were a firecracker," he said as he bent down.

"That's fire, it's not the same—"

He cut me off with a kiss, all tongue and heat, his teeth scraping over my lip, pulling a groan out of me.

"Spark me again and I'll bite you," he threatened, but there was no anger in his voice, only blatant arousal.

"Are you getting off on... it?" My own voice was hushed, a mixture of shame and confusion.

"If you only knew how good you smell, how good you look, sweetheart, there's nothing about you that I don't get off to. I shouldn't. It's fucked up and wrong and I should know better, but I gave up caring about the rules a long damn time ago." He paused for a moment, pushing away to look down my body. "You don't know any better. You're too young to know better, so I shouldn't be doing this, for your sake."

"I'm twenty-one," I protested. He snorted and for a moment I thought he was going to pull away. *Please don't,* I begged with my eyes. I needed this, needed him, more than anything I'd ever felt. I was breaking all the rules, both witch and musical, but my heart was aching for the attention, relishing in the way he looked at me like I was the most beautiful thing he'd ever seen.

"God, you're amazing," he said. His hands were on my stomach, slipping up under the hoodie I was wearing, his hoodie. "And you're wearing this, my scent all over you, like you're mine—

He fell quiet as he shifted down and I pressed my hand over my mouth when he kissed the bare skin of my belly. When his tongue flicked out to trail over my stomach, good sense and any other reason to tell him to stop vanished. My eyes closed as he kissed and licked up my belly, hands cupping my ribs right under my breasts as he pushed the hoodie up.

"You smell good, like me, like *pack*, like power." He mouthed at the edge of the hoodie and I felt the shift of my bra as it moved over my skin. My nipples were pebbling hard underneath the lacy fabric. One of his hands slid down over my hip, along my thigh, to wrap around my knee. Fire traced after his touch, and I moaned, letting my hand fall away. I wanted him to know how good it felt. I didn't want to hide it.

"Mine," the word was guttural, in the back of his throat, and when I glanced down at him, his blue eyes were almost glowing in the dim light of the dressing room.

"Yours," I agreed, because there was no other choice for me. His hand lifted up and he dragged the edge of his hoodie, and my sweater, up, up over my breasts. My breath was just barely moving in my lungs, my whole body still. A small shiver shook me when his hands held the sides of my breasts almost reverently.

Cash's fingers curled into the edge of each cup, and pulled them down. I let out a long breath as his head bent and his mouth wrapped around the peak of one breast. A cry ripped from my throat; electric fire raced along my skin, and his tongue lashed against the sensitive nipple.

"I've got you," he murmured when he moved to the other breast, his hand slipping under my arched back. He held me up for him, supporting me as he mouthed at my other breast. "I've got you," he whispered into my skin. Each breath that raced out of my lips was a soft gasp. Nothing had ever felt this good, and I was half convinced that nothing would *ever* feel this good again but each second that passed Cash proved me wrong.

There was a soft rumbling sound in the distance and, after a few moments, I realized that it was him. The low noise was emanating from what seemed like his breast-bone, and it was soothing and arousing at the same time.

He let me down gently, easing me onto the couch, his hands resting on my hips. His thumbs traced across my hip-bones, and I watched them stroke back and forth. My whole body was aching, and I wanted to ask him why he was hesitating.

His head jerked up and he reached up, yanking the hoodie down my body.

The door burst open, and Ace tumbled in, followed closely by the rest of the band.

"Hey, there you—oh shit." Ace stopped still, and Charlie bumped into him from behind. I sat up, arm crossing across my body despite the fact I was fully dressed. Eli and Finn bracketed the other two men, wearing murderous glares.

Except their glares weren't aimed at me. The twins were looking at Cash. He glared back, leaning forward to half-hide me from their view.

Eli was the first to speak.

"Thanks for coming out tonight, Miss Llewellyn. Charlie, would you drive her home?"

My lips parted to protest but Eli slashed his hand through the air to silence me. Cash growled and Eli's head snapped to look at him. Cash fell quiet, although his shoulders were tense and I could feel how angry he was without him even saying anything.

"Excuse me? Don't I get a say in this? I don't need a ride, Charlie, but thanks," I said after a moment as I gathered my courage. I stood up. Cash stood up in tandem with me, his hand out, as if he wanted to push me behind him. Finn was oddly quiet, no hint of his normal smiling self.

"We've got band business to talk about. Non-label related band business," Eli bit out each word like they were hurting him, as if he knew what I would say before I said it. "And it's late. Take the ride from Charlie. Please," he growled the last word. Cash's hand twitched and he turned to me.

"You should go with Charlie," he said, eyes searching my face. He was seriously backing down? We hadn't been doing anything wrong—

Making out with a band member that you're managing, at their first show, and he's your sworn enemy, Darcy, and you think you weren't doing anything wrong? I could practically hear what Max would say to me when I told her. Maybe I just wouldn't tell her.

"Cash, please," I whispered. I didn't want to be by myself. Something had happened between us, something special, and I felt it slipping away, sliding through my fingers with each passing second. I needed to grab it tight, hold it close, or it was going to vanish forever.

"This doesn't concern you," Cash answered, a coolness shuttering in his eyes, shutting me out. I stepped back, hurt exploding in my chest.

"Fine," I snapped, and I was across the room before I knew it. The guys parted for me as one, and Charlie held the door open for me. I stormed through it, leaving him to catch up with me. There was a DJ on the stage, and beats were thudding through the room, but the music was empty and dull compared to what Phoenixcry had played. That bit at me harder, feeling betrayal, hurt, and loss swirling in my stomach.

I shouldn't have been so attached so quickly, it didn't make sense. I always kept people at arm's length, and this was exactly why. Charlie caught up to me, and touched me on the shoulder as I waited for the elevator.

"Hey," he said, although the words were half-lost under the shaking noise of the DJ.

"I can't hear you," I shouted at him. His mouth snapped shut and we waited, not speaking, for the elevator car to arrive.

The doors of it closed in front of us and we were halfway to the ground floor when he tried talking to me again.

"You okay?" he asked. I glared at him and shoved my hands into Cash's hoodie pockets, stirring up a waft of his scent, linen and evaporating water, all around me. Charlie whistled softly and decided that silence was the better part of valor.

He was right. If he'd tried to talk, I was probably going to give into the very unreasonable desire I had to punch him in the nose. He led me down to the parking lot and into a sleek, black van, the kind bands used for touring in before they hit the big-time.

I had misjudged him. He hadn't decided to not talk. He only decided to wait until I was belted in and we were rumbling down the freeway to ask,

"So you and Cash, huh?"

I hunched my shoulders in response.

"Don't be like that, kid," he said, and I felt my cheeks flush dark at the nickname. Cash had said I was too young. Too young compared to him?

"I'm not a kid," I spat. Charlie held up one hand in apology.

"You're right, you're not. You're... powerful. We all sensed it, and I guess it got the better of Cash even though Eli warned us all off of you—"

My head jerked up and I looked at him, properly, instead of just glaring at him out of the corner of my eye. Up until then I'd felt like a naughty child being sent to her room for getting her hands all up in Cash's cookie jar.

"Warned you all off of me?"

Charlie let out a sheepish, hesitant chuckle.

"Well uh... you know, right?"

"Charlie, do I sound or look like someone who *knows* what the hell you're talking about?"

"Cash shouldn't have made a move on you, and don't tell me otherwise, cause I know it was him who pulled the trigger. He's got no self-control, for all he tells me I have none. We're a small group, Darcy. We're all that's left of our pack. There's no... females like us, for us. We wouldn't want a human, she wouldn't understand, and we might hurt her... but a witch..." he let his words die in his throat and laughed softly. "I shouldn't say anything."

"Too late, Charlie," I growled. "Spill, right now. I don't get what you're saying." He sighed, sounding frustrated.

"Don't freak out. I don't think you know about this, because as far as I'm aware, witches aren't exactly well versed in how pack dynamics work, or about how werewolves breed except the big stuff. Like how small packs are usually a group of males and a single female mate." Charlie's hands were steady on the steering wheel, but he was holding his breath.

I stared at him as the math added up in my head, and I felt my cheeks turn hot, red-hot.

"All of you?" I squeaked, a noise I'd made twice that night now, "At once?" The image clouded my mind, taking me back to the hot kisses Cash had given me on the couch in the dressing room, but this time Finn crowded beside me at the same time. I inhaled sharply.

"Well not all the time..." he snapped his mouth shut. "See this is why I shouldn't have said anything. You're a witch, for all that you're playing at being a mundane, and witches are the most stuffy, stuffed up, puritanical—"

"I'm not a damned witch," I cut him off, still reeling with the image of Cash's fingers wrapping around my jaw, turning my face so that he could capture my mouth in a searing kiss.

"Uh, evidence would suggest otherwise," he said, wiggling his fingers at me. I glowered.

"I gave that life up."

"That's sweet. But that's not something you can give up. It's baked into you, blood and bone. Just like I can turn into a howling, very large and friendly wolf. It doesn't matter what kind of fancy smartwatch I wear, or that I like to shower twice a day, I'm still a wolf, deep down," Charlie said, sounding perfectly reasonable like he argued with people all the time about their magical heritage. I eyed him, silent.

"So this whole... thing, the pack, taking a single mate between you, were you guys planning—I mean, with me?" My voice came out in a squeak, but Charlie smiled instead of laughing at me like he probably wanted to. I felt dumb, like I was fumbling around in a situation that was way over my head. Hell, the idea of me, and the guys? It was *way* over my head.

"Eli said no, and we all listened, although if you ask me, he's just protecting himself because I've never seen him so attracted to anyone." Charlie took the exit for my university as I sat in the passenger seat and tried to make sense of what he was saying. Eli? Eli was attracted to me? Like hell he was. Charlie was smoking something. "Here you are, kid," Charlie said as he pulled up in front of my dorm.

"I didn't tell you where I lived," I said, my voice sounding faded and dreamy to even my ears. Charlie gave me a smile and shook his head.

"You've got a lot to learn, witch-child," he said. "Go to bed."

I took a gulp of air and nodded.

"You okay?" he asked.

"It's a lot to take in."

"Yeah well, five guys is a lot to take in."

"Charlie!" I stared at him, shocked, and appalled, and for some inexplicable horrific reason, also really turned on. He smirked at me, his eyes sparkling with mischief.

"If you stay, I'll have to take you back, and trust me, if you thought the fight they had in the recording studio was bad..."

I unbuckled myself and slipped out of the car.

"Oh, wait," I said, unzipping Cash's hoodie.

"Keep it," Charlie said. "Serves him right for getting hot and heavy with our manager. Idiot. Plus it'll smell like you when you finally give it back to him, and that'll drive him crazy." He smirked and waved at me as I shut the door, the window rolled down. "Be good. See you tomorrow?"

"Right. Tomorrow," I said, and took a step back, then another. I turned and ran to my dorm, confusion, hurt, and hormones pushing my every step. I hoped Max was back. I desperately needed to talk to her.

TEN

Max Mmmmm
@Maxamillionilicious

(Follow) ⌄

Missing my @DarcyLuvsDonuts rn :(

12 Retweets **34** Likes

💬 14   ⇄ 12   ♡ 34   ✉

Max still wasn't back when I got in, and for a moment I pushed aside everything that had happened at the party and actually called her.

"Hey you've reached Max. Don't bother leaving me a message, I don't check them. Yes, even for you, Craig."

I stared at my phone in my hand. How many days had it been now since I'd even seen Max? Other than weekends when she went home, or holidays, I'd never seen her gone for so long before.

A knock at the door startled me, and I went up, pulling it open.

Zahrah Varma, our floor's RA was standing there, a worried look on her face.

"Hey Darcy, have you seen Max at all? I'm friends with one of her professors and she's been missing all her classes for the last two days. She's usually so on top of everything," Zahrah said, playing with the loose ends of her headscarf out of nerves. Dread came roaring up inside of me.

"She went to visit her dad, some sorta emergency. I just called her because she hasn't been answering my texts, and the call went straight to voicemail. I've got her boyfriend's number though, he lives back in her town..." I fished out my phone and found him in my contact list.

"Craig's Auto Repair and Improved Performance. Leave a message and I'll get back to you same day or next business day."

Zahrah stared at me blankly as I cancelled the call and bit my lip.

"I can call her dad," I said, and turned, searching through the pile of papers on my desk. I had his number somewhere...

"She's not in trouble, but if she needs a leave of absence," Zahrah paused.

"I don't think it's that serious, just you know, her dad's like a cop or whatever, so if he said it was urgent, it probably was."

"Isn't he a sheriff?" Zahrah stood just inside the door as I dialed Mr. Morgan's number.

It rang once.

"Hello?" Max sounded groggy and stuffed up.

"Max, oh my god, finally. Where have you been?" Relief flooded through me as her voice came on the other end of the line, and a small amount of annoyance that she hadn't called.

"Darcy, I... I can't talk right now. I was sleeping." There was a hitch in her voice, and I turned away from where Zahrah stared at me with curious eyes.

"Are you okay? You sound like you've been crying."

"No I was sleeping, I'm—Craig got arrested."

"Arr—hang on. Are you sure you can't talk? One sec." I turned around and smiled at Zahrah, putting the call on mute. "She's fine. I'll see when she's coming back to class and get her to email her professors."

"Uh huh," Zahrah said, looking suspicious and not at all like she believed me. I took a deep breath, and decided to risk it. Using my powers of persuasion, which was the most basic skill, sometimes backfired on witches like me who weren't that good at it.

"**It's fine,**" I said, and Zahrah blinked once, slowly, and nodded. My gamble paid off, and I tried not to let guilt eat at me for using a hint of power on a mundane. It wasn't that it was against the rules, only that I felt like a bag of assholes for doing it. It was sort of against my personal values, but it was harmless and whatever was going on with Max was none of Zahrah's business.

"Alright, sounds good. Tell her I miss the strawberry

popcorn she makes, and hope she's back soon." Zahrah closed the door behind her and I unmuted the call.

"Sorry I had to get rid of Zahrah. What's happening?"

"She's nice, but she likes to gossip too much, so thanks." Max sighed heavily and I could hear her taking a sip of water. *"Craig tried to break into my dad's place, and my dad was home, and he arrested him."*

"What the hell? Seriously?"

"Yeah, so I've been dealing with that, and Craig won't talk to me to tell me why, but he's not an idiot, and it's not like he's hurting for money, his garage has been doing really well the last few months... so it's not like he was trying to rob us... but I've been trying to convince my dad to drop the charges and just say it was a mistake cause Craig thought I was home and forgot to answer the door." She let out a long, slow, shaking breath and I heard her burst into tears. *"I'm just terrified..."*

"No shit, oh Max... do you want me to—"

"To come? No. Stay there. I've almost got my dad convinced and then I'm telling Craig to stay the hell away from my house. My dad hates him so much, Darce," her voice dropped down low and I heard her hiccup a sob. *"He wants me to dump Craig."*

"What?" My knees gave out and I thumped down onto the edge of my bed in shock. "What? Why? You guys are like, high school sweethearts. If he'd had a problem with Craig, he'd have said something way before this? Or is the whole cat-burglar thing?"

"He never did like Craig much but I figured it was that old

macho 'that's my baby girl' kind of crap, and he pushed me to date other people, but I love Craig, I love him so much and I don't know what I'll do without him—" she broke into another sob and all thoughts of my problems fled.

"Max, come on, without him? You aren't going to be without him."

"I have to do it, Darcy, I have to, or Dad's—he's seriously, he's losing his fucking mind, and I have to save Craig. He doesn't need a record."

"But... but... you can't, I mean, you love him, you'd be a mess without him, Max, and I'm sure your dad will come to his senses," I said. My phone buzzed against my ear signaling an incoming text message but I ignored it.

"You don't know him, oh—" She paused and whispered, "I gotta go. I'll text you later."

The line went dead and I sat there for a moment, wondering if I should call her back or just let her be. My instincts were screaming at me to go visit her, but I was pretty sure she'd be upset if I did that.

I shot her a quick text, *I'm here if you need me, anything, anytime,* and left it at that. She'd message me if she needed something, and I'm sure Willa would understand if I had to take off for a day. I hoped she would, anyway.

Willa, *fuck.* The show had been a disaster, at least in terms of me as a manager. I'd crossed so many lines. Curling up on my bed, I tugged the blankets over my head. It was probably best to hide from the world. What had I been thinking? That's right, I hadn't been. It's not like I asked for werewolves to sing and turn me into some fourteen-year-old mess of hormones and bad attitude.

"Oh god, I'm an idiot." The room was empty, but saying the words out loud felt like it was bleeding the poison a little. A creeping sense of loneliness overcame me as my memories from earlier that night came rushing back. I'd been counting on Max being at the dorm when I got back. The world seemed like such a vast, scary place, and I was lost in it. Would watching the band perform be like that every time? Swamping me with feelings and desires I could barely fight, and honestly didn't want to fight?

This was a path that was too dangerous for me to go down. It had been one thing to make peace with working with werewolves, it was only for a few months before it'd be over. Graduation wasn't that far away, really. Sticking it out would have been possible but not if...

Not if I wanted to rip the clothes right off my body and have Cash's hands all over me, or worse...

My face reddened and I felt the building heat between my thighs, a subtle ache of need pulsing there.

There was no way I was considering all *five* of them, like Charlie had lewdly suggested. The answer came to me, rushing through the fog of my confusion.

I picked up my phone. There was a text message from Cash. I didn't bother opening it, but instead sent off a short email to Willa.

I MUST RESIGN from my internship at XOhX immediately.

Thank you for the opportunity,

Darcy Llewellyn

ELEVEN

The ghost of Cash's hands haunted my dreams, and I woke up feeling overheated and uncomfortable. I dragged myself to my professor's office as soon as he had opening hours to plead my case and ask for a reassignment.

I used Jake Tupper and his blatant interest as my excuse. My professor was immediately sympathetic, and thanked me for telling him but there was nothing he could do other than mention it to Willa if that's what I wanted.

I didn't want that, I said. I'd left abruptly after two days and that was enough to give me a bad rep in the indie label scene. I didn't need any whispers about my *other* reputation starting up. My professor assured me he would look to finding me another placement, and in the meantime, I could help him with some office work to prepare for the first year program students' first major projects.

Every time I stayed still for too long, I remembered the press of Cash's body into mine. To shake it off, I went to the campus gym, and panted out my frustrations on the treadmill for half an hour.

It didn't help that when I left the gym, I had to pull on Cash's hoodie. I'd grabbed it first thing in the morning without thinking. The sweet, hot petrichor scent lifting off of it chased me back across the campus to my dorm. My fingers touched the front door and I heard my name.

Turning, I nearly dropped my backpack when I saw who was standing there.

"Was it Cash?" Ace stood there, looking angry. I'd never seen him mad before. "Did he hurt you?" He stalked up to me, his shoulders stiff under his denim jacket. He looked me up and down.

"What are you doing here?" I asked. "How do you know where I live?"

"Charlie told me," he answered and that should have been obvious. "Why did you leave? Cash? Want me to deck him? He's older but I can take him." His eyes narrowed. "Did you... did you not want... that? Him?"

"This really isn't... I don't want to talk about it," I said, looking around me as a few students going into the dorm eyed us both up. Ace followed my gaze and his cheeks pinked up.

"Right, I guess, this isn't the place," he said.

"There won't ever be a place. I'm sorry, Ace, but it's not like I'm some big-name manager. I'm just an intern. You guys don't need me," I swiped my fob at the entrance.

"Please," Ace said, stopping me in my tracks. I heard the

door click to unlock, but I didn't open it. Something in his voice, not command, or his natural power, made me feel like I needed to listen to him.

"What?" I asked, not looking at him.

"There's something about you—"

"Yeah, you know what it is about me," I interrupted. "And that's an even better reason for us to never see each other again, professionally or personally."

Ace growled, low, sounding irritated.

"Just give me twenty minutes of your time," he said, "please. And if you still don't want... us, then I'll go. I'll go without argument."

Turning to look at him, I eyed him suspiciously.

"You promise?"

"I swear. Please, Darcy, let me get you a coffee or something." He pulled out his wallet. "We got paid bank last night and it's the least I can do. Just coffee between acquaintances. Not even friends. We don't have to call it friends."

My better judgement vanished. He was so unassumingly sweet, and I couldn't help the smile that crept across my face.

"We can be friends, but just for now, for coffee, all right?" What compelled me to even offer him that small crack in my armor? The relief that flooded onto his face warmed my heart, and even though I knew my answer would still be 'no' after coffee, it felt like I was doing the right thing to hear him out. "There's a coffee place around the corner," I offered. "Let's go there."

SITTING across from Ace reminded me of last night's show, but everything was reminding me of last night's show. Like an infectious song, it was stuck in my head on repeat, over and over again. I shut down the memories as fast as they cropped up, but it didn't seem to be enough. My skin itched, aching to be touched. Cash had woken something up in me, something dangerous and dark that wouldn't be put back to sleep now that it had gotten a taste of freedom. Not thinking about it was the only way I was going to get through coffee. Ace set two cups down on the table.

"Two sugars, one cream," he said, as he sat down as well.

"Thanks," I said, taking a long, slow sip. "So talk."

Ace swallowed a mouthful of coffee, turning his head to cough.

"Burns," he gasped and I had to work hard not to smile. It was obvious he really was just out of his puppy phase, and he might have been old enough chronologically, but I could see the *hapless baby* in him.

No, you are not going to feel bad for him just because he's adorable and bites his lower lip and worries it all the time in that way that's super cute, ugh, Darcy, get ahold of yourself.

"You okay? Want some water?"

"No I'm fine." He shook his head. "I'm not fine actually. You don't get it. We *need* you."

"I'm nobody, Ace, you don't need me."

"Yes we do. Listen, the guys? They're not going to listen to just any manager, not even a big name music manager. Seriously, you could get someone from Universal or Sony and still they wouldn't listen because those people don't have the same power as you do." Ace's eyes glittered as he stared at me intently, the determination coming off of him in waves. He wanted me to come back to managing the band, so badly.

"I managed you guys for like a minute," I protested weakly. "I didn't even do anything. I caused fights."

"Yeah, because they don't know what's good for them, but I do. Charlie does. Finn does. It's just Eli and Cash fucking everything up, and we're dealing with them."

How the pack worked together, or how I thought it worked, was quickly changing as Ace spoke.

"I thought that Eli was like, your alpha-wolf, or however that goes," I said. He snorted, and shook his head.

"Alpha isn't just something you are, it's something you earn, and you have to keep earning it, if you know what I mean."

"Not really, on the council, the power passes down from one headship to the next, as long as it's a male son in the family line. You can't lose your council seat."

Ace was looking at me funny, his upper lip curled, teeth bared.

"What?" I asked, self-conscious.

"I forgot your family was *council*," he spat the word out like it burnt, making me want to physically recoil from how angry he sounded.

"Well, I'm not my family," I reminded him. Gesturing around us, I asked, "Do you think they'd let someone who was still in the flock go to a mundane university? Not on your life."

He frowned and swished his coffee around in his cup for a moment.

"Tell me about them," he said.

"No thanks," I shut that line of questioning down right away. "Look, you're really nice, and not like the other guys..."

Ace perked up for a moment and frowned as he realized where my point was going.

"You're not coming back are you," his voice was flat, the hint of disappointment and hurt in it.

"Can you blame me?" I whispered, staring down at my coffee. "All I wanted when I left home was a normal life, to be *normal*. I'm happy here, with my friends who don't know anything about the other world or way of life. Then you guys explode into my life—"

"And Cash blows your mind," Ace sounded so smug that my jaw dropped as I looked up at him. He immediately bit his lip and muttered, "Sorry, that was rude."

"Yeah, no shit." The conversation was over. I grabbed my bag and stood. "Thanks for the coffee."

"Darcy, please," Ace stood up. "It doesn't have to be like your old life, I promise."

I stared at him.

"What would you know about my life before?" I asked. "What would you know about it at all? You and your pack have made it pretty obvious, multiple times, that we come from very opposite ends of the spectrum in that world, and every time I try to just be *me* it seems like there's this gulf opening up inside me, one that you guys insist on cracking open."

"It was the music, wasn't it?" Ace took a step toward me, and I remembered suddenly how tall he was. Maybe a few inches shorter than the other members of the band (other than Charlie), but Ace was still imposing in his own way. He had broad shoulders, and lean muscle flexed under his skin. "The music got you. I told them, I told them to warn you, because you might not know." Memories came rushing back in, of the cool surface of the pillar under my hand in the venue, the way I'd felt compelled to watch them, compelled to walk toward them. Werewolves were magic when it came to music, and it had drawn me in like a spider reeling in a fly caught in its web.

"What about the music, Ace?" I asked, not able to help the shiver in my body come out in my voice. Anger at myself, embarrassment at being so powerless during their set, shame for what had happened after; the emotions all swirled in my chest, making it hard to breathe.

"Some witches," he swallowed hard, "most witches can't resist it. That's why... that's why..." he paused and the weight of the band's betrayal sank onto my shoulders.

"You knew," I whispered, "you knew what would happen to me, that I'd... that I'd *fall* for you guys, that I wouldn't—"

"No, no, Darcy, no, I had no idea that you and Cash would, that it would, do whatever it did, but I knew that witches, you guys are susceptible, more than mundanes, and they said it wouldn't matter, that you had been out in mundane society for too long, that you'd feel maybe like, a mild buzz, or something," he was panicking, his voice raising as he spoke, and I felt the hot stares of other coffee shop patrons on us.

I grabbed his wrist and he shut up.

"Outside," I hissed.

"Okay," he nodded, eyes wide in his face, his skin gone pale during our heated conversation. I turned on my heel and left, and he was dogging my footsteps, grabbing the door for me. I didn't thank him. Had Cash known that the music would knock me for six? There had been something so special, so tender in the way he'd held me and touched me. Had what we shared been a violation?

I felt sick.

There was a bench a few strides away from the entrance to the coffee shop and I collapsed onto it, putting my coffee cup down on the wood and bending forward to put my head between my knees before I fainted.

Ace trailed after me, standing right in front of me. I could see his shoes, a pair of purple Converse, and the frayed hem of his jeans.

"I don't think any of us knew," he said, "but it seemed to affect you, and I think it affecting you? The fact you wanted us so badly because of our music? That affected us, and Cash, I guess... I guess he just went with it."

"Went with it?" A hollow laugh erupted from my chest to follow his words.

"Look, I'm not stupid, I know what you're thinking, and if you think for a minute that Cash would ever, *ever* take advantage of you then you don't know him—"

"No, I don't know him, Ace!" Fury propelled me and I stood up. Ace took a step back, his face even paler than before. "I don't know any of you! And you don't know me, not one bit. You think you do, maybe you know more about witches than I know about werewolves, but you still don't know me!" I pointed a finger at him, poking him in the chest hard.

"Darcy—"

"Shut up. I don't want to hear it." I poked him again, harder. My finger ached.

"But you're sparking." Ace was staring down at my hand. I looked down. Sure enough, small sparks were flickering at the edges of my fingers, dying out along the lines of my fingernails only to flare up again. I cursed and yanked my hand back, pulling my sleeves down over my hands. We stood there, in silence for a moment until Ace spoke. "He didn't mean to hurt you. He really... I think something happened to him to, because he's not like that. I mean, he likes women, sure, but he hasn't done that with anyone in a long time, not in a long time, Darcy, I swear it, and never without them wanting it as bad as he wanted it too."

I didn't answer him and his voice got more urgent.

"Please believe me."

My shoulders trembled.

"I have to go," I said, and pushed away from him. "Don't call me, and don't show up at my dorm again."

"Darcy—"

"**Don't!**" I whirled on him, breathing coming rapid in and out of my throat. He took a step back at the command in my voice.

"We need you," Ace said softly. "Please. *Please.*"

"No," I said, shaking my head, "I can't... I barely know you and I already know that's enough. I know *enough.*"

Ace reached out for me with one hand, but his hand fell far short as I took another step back, then another. I turned and ran, hot tears streaking down my cheeks, the salt-wet stinging in the corners of my eyes.

TWELVE

Sleep took me for the rest of the day. I crawled into my bottom bunk and exhaustion washed over me, pulling me down into a dreamless world until I woke up at 3:00 AM, groggy and disoriented. My face hurt, eyes itchy from crying. I dragged myself to the shared bathroom down the hall, washed up in the sink, and then went back to bed. The darkness cradled me, but in the quiet Ace's words played over and over in my head.

They knew.

They probably had no idea.

They knew a little bit.

They couldn't have seen it coming.

*Cash took **advantage** of me.*

The thoughts chased after each other, contradicting one another and drawing swords to do battle in my brain until I wished I could drink to chase them away. Given how I'd lost control and started sparking up in the middle of public campus space earlier that day, alcohol was definitely off the menu.

Sleep was elusive, hiding at the edges of my consciousness, and it refused to tug me back down into sweet relief.

Cash didn't seem all that in control of himself either.

That thought took root around 4:30 AM and refused to let go. The hot press of his body, the wild look in his eyes, his murmurs... he didn't seem like a Jake Tupper. He wasn't a Creston. He'd protected me, and that memory warmed me, spreading a feeling of calm through my muscles.

He'd protected me. Maybe it wasn't true, maybe he hadn't thought I'd be so weakened and vulnerable. Maybe he hadn't...

BZZT. Bzzt. Bzzt.

Light fell across my face. It was morning. I'd slept.

Bzzt. Bzzt. Bzzt.

My hand shot out to grab my phone. It was vibrating, and had nearly fallen off the edge of the bed onto the floor.

"Hello?"

"You sound like crap. Are you at your dorm? It's Willa."

Dread clenched in my stomach.

"I'm..." I didn't have the energy to lie. "Yeah, I'm at my dorm."

"Mind if I come over? It's okay if now is a bad time. It can be

later, if you want. Just name a time and I'll be there." She didn't sound remotely mad. I hadn't heard back from her after my abrupt (and in hindsight, stupid) resignation email, and I had been terrified of the well-deserved tongue-lashing I'd get when I finally did hear from her.

"Uh I'm not—""

"I quit my first internship at XOhX after the band I was working with wanted to hire strippers for their music video and pay them in one dollar bills. That band isn't signed anymore. Let's talk. It's not as bad as you think, okay?" Willa's voice was filled with compassion and my eyes teared up. I missed Max. She would've made everything better. Or at least made me some crazy-good hot chocolate and queued up a night of good Netflix movies.

"Is an hour okay?"

"You bet. See you in an hour."

"Hey wait, where are we..."I stopped talking when I realized Willa had hung up. Laying in bed for forty-five minutes, staring at the ceiling uselessly seemed like the thing to do, so that's what I did. When there was five minutes to the hour, I rolled out of bed, glared at my messy curls and stuck them up in a bun. I shoved Cash's hoodie in a plastic bag, and got dressed in the first things I could lay my hands on.

As the minutes ticked to the hour, there was a knock at the door. I pulled it open and Willa was there, a white paper bag in one hand.

"Nutella croissant," she said as she came in without waiting to be invited. "It makes everything better." She held it out to me. Taking it without being able to help the suspicion from coloring my expression, she chuckled. "You look like a cat about to hiss. I'm not going to yell at you or tell you I'm disappointed in you. Mind if I sit?" She sat as she asked, on Max's desk chair.

I sat too, on the edge of the bed, and pulled out the croissant. If I was going to have a difficult conversation, I was going to do it with chocolate stuffed into my face. The pastry was the expensive kind, with sliced almonds sprinkled on top, and a generous shaking of icing sugar. I bit into it, and the buttery, sweet dough gave way to the thick, nutty chocolate spread inside.

"Cash talked to me."

I looked at her, mortified, a mouthful of pastry and nutella.

"Keep eating," she said with a wave. "He talked to me, he told me what happened between you guys, and honestly, it's not the first time, and it's not the last. I wanted to make sure you were okay. He can come on strong, in every aspect, not just sexually, and I wanted to know that he didn't take advantage of you." She crossed her arms over her chest. "Because Troy may love the band's music, and I may love the band's music, but I'm not putting up with any of that boys-will-be-boys shit."

If it had been any other kind of situation, if I hadn't been what I was and overpowered by the magic in the music, I would have said that Cash in no way took advantage of me. He was... a more than attractive guy, and I was a girl who'd been without that kind of physical, sexual contact in a really damn long time. It had felt good, so good, and the barest memory of it still gave me shivers.

But I'd batted my doubts back and forth until they're bruised and unrecognizable.

"No," I said, "he didn't take advantage of me. If anything, we sorta took advantage of each other. In a good way." My voice was small as I spoke. "I feel stupid about it though."

"Why?" Willa hitched one shoulder and pointed at the croissant. "That thing isn't going to eat itself. Sugar's good for you. One of the two food groups. Beer, and sugar." Her flippant comment couldn't help but make me smile. This was a different side to Willa that I hadn't seen before. "You think you're the first intern, or even first manager, to fall into bed with her client? Music is sexy, that's why we're all in it. It makes us feel things, and Phoenixcry is one of those bands that makes us feel more than most do. You know, not that I thought you were easy or anything, but I kinda... I kinda expected it?"

My lips parted in shock.

"What?"

"That's not a judgement on you, Darcy, not at all. But you're a pretty girl, and they're guys who are dedicated to their craft. They don't have a lot of time for women, and sometimes when you get a band like that, putting a girl in who's safe and not going to post their dick pics on Instagram, it's natural. Maybe it happens on tour, or after a big show, but it happens. You get caught up in the adrenaline and..." She bit her lip and looked away. "Let me tell you, from personal experience, don't beat yourself up about it. If he didn't take advantage, that's great, and I'm glad to hear it. You sure?"

"I'm sure," I said, my voice steadier this time.

"Good. So now you've had a few days to feel like a crap-bag, and I'll even give you another one to mope, but then I need you back at the office." Willa folded her fingers over her lap. It was all I could do to not stare at her.

"Um, yeah, I resigned?"

"Yeah, well, I don't accept," she said. "You sent that in the heat of the moment, and while we might have to have a talk about proper email etiquette and the art of *waiting* before you shoot from the hip, I'm more than willing to pretend you never sent in your resignation at all."

My brain stuttered over what she said for a few moments.

"But I meant it," my words were soft but firm. "And I still do."

Willa's brow furrowed.

"You don't want to come back?"

I shook my head. She sat back in Max's chair.

"Well, I didn't see that coming," she said. She worried her lower lip with her teeth before running a hand through her shoulder-length hair. "Look, I'm going to level with you. A big offer just came in for Phoenixcry, bigger than they could hope for at their level."

An offer? I couldn't help it, I wanted to know what it was.

"Okay... what kind of offer and what does that mean to me?"

"You've run into Tupper," Willa said, with a slight roll of her eyes.

"Uh, yeah, I have. He's..."

"You don't need to say it, and I don't need to hear it, because he's a real shit-stain, but he's signed to the label for now on a three disc deal and I can't get rid of him. I'm sorry about that. Anyway, he's friends with a pretty big act, bigger than he is, and they've offered to take him on tour and are letting him pull one of the smaller bands off our label's roster as an opener since their original opening band bailed on them."

"Ooookay," I stretched the word out, feeling like I wasn't going to be happy about what Willa said next. She gave me a grim smile.

"But there's a catch. Tupper's decided that he enjoys your company, and is only willing to take one band on the road, Phoenixcry, and only if you're managing them. He doesn't know that you quit on us, because otherwise, I don't think he would have ever offered the guys an opening slot on this tour, but he made it pretty clear that you're the reason he wants the band along. It's a full North American. Every major city, and Montreal, Toronto, and Vancouver as well up in Canada." She paused and I realized she was done talking. She was waiting on me.

I knew what my answer would be. Even if Cash hadn't taken advantage, it was just too much for me. It was too big of a risk. I should have stuck with my original gut feeling and asked to be reassigned and pushed Willa to give me some other work.

"I'm really sorry," I heard myself saying, the words echoing in my ears. "But I'm not taking back my resignation letter. I can't."

"Is it Tupper? Because he's a sleaze, but he's never going to make a move on you without your permission. He likes his record contract. He'll look and comment, but he won't touch. I know that's kinda gross to put up with but..." Willa sighed. "The music industry is still thirty years behind on equality and I fight for it every day, but I'm at the point I need to pick my battles."

I got it. I really did. There was only so much energy one person had, and you had to choose which people you were going to burn bridges with and piss off.

"It's not Jake Tupper, but yeah, his taste in office-warming gifts needs work," I said as I thought back to the cactus he had given me. "No it's just... I don't think XOhX is the place for me. I'm really sorry, I know you had high hopes for me and stuff." I shrugged.

Willa gave me a long, thoughtful look and dipped her chin in a slow nod.

"All right. I can respect that. If you're not feeling it, you're not feeling it. But just promise me, Darcy, that if you change your mind—"

"I won't."

"You're sure. Even if I told you the band they'd be opening for was Glory Revolution." Willa waited for my reaction. Inside I let out a yelp, but outside I kept quiet. GR were huge, that was for sure, on the indie scene? It would only help a band like Phoenixcry. But their big break would have to come another time, from someone else.

"Yup."

Willa got to her feet and sighed.

"I would have liked working with you," she said, her tone softening from hard and business-like. Guilt nipped at me but I shoved it away. I had to do what was best for me, and hanging around with a pack of wolves who could melt my defenses like butter in the sun with their music was *not* best for me. "If you ever want tickets to any of our shows, just shoot me an email." She gave me a thin smile and went to the door, pausing there. "You're really sure? It's thirty dates."

"Willa," I said, my exhaustion plain in my voice. "Could you take that plastic bag? It's got Cash's hoodie in it." Thankfully Willa picked it up without a second thought, and didn't ask me any questions about it.

"I'll see you around," she said as she opened the door.

"Maybe," I replied. The door clicked shut behind her, and I collapsed back on the bed.

Was I fucking my entire life up, or was I saving myself? The pillow that I curled around didn't have any answers.

THIRTEEN

Three days passed, and Max came back. She was red-eyed, and looked as exhausted as I felt. As soon as she stumbled in through the door we stared at one another, and we both burst into tears. I had my best friend back, but a hole in my chest the size and shape of five guys who could have possibly offered me a life experience that I'd never find anywhere else. The hole in her chest?

It was Craig Mackenzie-shaped.

"I dumped him," she whispered in the darkness of our room. She was down on my bunk with me, in a big blanket burrito we had both wrapped ourselves up in. Sometimes you needed a cuddle from a guy. Sometimes what you really needed? Was a good, long, platonic snuggle from your best friend. I tucked my head up under Max's chin, and she wrapped an arm around my back, holding me tight.

"You must be wrecked, I don't even know what to say..." Because what was there to say? She and Craig had been in love since he'd first shuffled into her 3rd period history class.

And apparently her dad had hated him throughout the whole thing.

"I feel like I'm dying, but at the same time, here I am, still breathing, my blood still pumping... everything physical is working, but my heart is like, wow. Yeah. It hurts so bad, I feel like I shouldn't be taking in air, but I am." Max buried her face in the top of my head. "Your hair tickles." She sounded so sad, like she was surprised that hair would tickle.

"Then don't stick your nose in it," I pointed out gently.

"That's what she said," Max whispered and burst into tears. "He used to make that stupid joke so many times when we were like, fifteen, that I punched him in the face. I gave him a black eye. God I was a crappy girlfriend."

"You were fifteen. And if any guy I was dating made that joke—how many times?"

"Like at least three times a day."

"That's definitely in the realm of face-punching land." I shifted and sat up. "Want some water? I'm thirsty."

"I never want to drink anything again. I want to fade away, waste into nothing," Max said morosely. I sighed.

"That's not happening. I'll get you a drink." I padded out into the hallway, stealing her slippers so I wouldn't have to find mine, and filled our water bottles. When I returned, she had curled up into as tight a ball as a tall girl could, and was crying.

"Oh Max," I said, stroking her cheek and pulling out a packet of tissues. "I'm so sorry."

"And I know shit went down with you," she said between hiccups. "And I can't... I haven't even asked. You haven't talked... I'm the worst friend, worst girlfriend, worst daughter, just bad, bad—"

"That's a pack of lies, you're not the worst anything," I said gently and wiped her tears, offering her a sip of water. She blinked at me, eyes bleary.

"Can I sleep in your bunk?"

My eyebrows rose.

"You hate my bunk."

"But it's got you in it, and I don't want, I don't want to be alone..." Her face crumpled and more tears sheeted down her cheeks.

"Okay, but if you kick me, I'm sleeping up top," I said. "You're like Bambi when you nap sometimes." It said a lot for how distressed she was that she didn't even laugh at my Disney reference. Max adored Disney movies. I settled in beside her as she made room for me.

"This is good," she said, sounding sleepy. "Chicks before dicks."

"Craig wasn't a dick though."

"Yeah but my dad is, so it makes sense in my head, please don't argue with me." She was fading fast, and I felt her body go loose and limp as she fell asleep. I pulled up the covers to her chin and snuggled in close. If she hadn't smelled like her lilac moisturizer and salty tears it was almost like what sleeping next to a guy would have been like. A very curvy, very snuggly guy.

I smiled as she burrowed against me in her sleep, and let the night take me.

I WOKE up alone in bed, to Max stretching and going through her morning yoga. I stretched my arms up in time with her downward dog and sighed.

"Good sleep?" she asked as she pulled herself back into a sitting position.

"Better than I've had in a few days," I admitted.

"So you wanna talk about it?"

"Not really."

"Alright." She got to her feet with a sigh. "Cause your phone has been going non-stop crazy for the last thirty minutes and while it wasn't exactly disturbing my zen because I don't have much inner peace to begin with right now, it was sort of annoying."

"Oh, shit, sorry." I grabbed it off the floor.

I had ten text messages, which might not have been unusual for someone else, but I didn't have a load of friends texting me all the time.

My heart dropped when I saw they were all from Cash. I'd deleted his first one without looking at it the other day.

"Is it that thing you don't wanna talk about?" Max mused sagely from across the room. "I'm right, aren't I? You're making the I-hate-you face."

"Good to know you're back to normal," I shot at her, and

immediately felt bad. I glanced at her. Her eyes were wet around the edges. "Shit, Max, I'm sorry."

She shook her head and held up her hand to stop me from talking.

"It's okay. I'm okay. I'm really okay. Just... it's hard. Every moment feels like I've got a knife twisting in my heart. But honestly, I don't want to talk about it anymore. You need to talk, or if we aren't gonna talk, you need to deal with that phone buzzing stuff and tell whoever's texting you to stop." While she was babbling at me, I'd unlocked my phone and scrolled through the messages.

I'm sorry.
I never meant to hurt you.
But I did.
I hurt you. I scared you. I just wanted you, and I thought you wanted me.
Willa says you won't come back, and I get it. I know it's my fault.
So when I ask you to reconsider, I want you to know that *I* know I don't deserve it.
But I'm asking you to reconsider.
Not for me. I don't deserve it.
But for the rest of the guys, especially Ace.
Message me back. I'd like to talk in person, if that's okay with you.

"You look freaked out," Max commented.

"I am a little freaked out," I admitted, my voice distant and feeling like it was coming from somewhere out of my body. Cash's text messages had raised the hair on the back of my neck, and it felt like so much more than a request to reconsider only because of a tour opportunity. Maybe I was giving him too much benefit of the doubt, but it felt like he was asking for more serious reasons.

I needed to trust my gut. I was done acting on impulse, but this felt like the right decision, the first right decision, that I'd made in a long time. I tapped out a response and waited not even thirty seconds when he replied.

You name the place and the time.

I closed my eyes, bit my lip, and opened them to give him the details. I hit send, and looked up at Max, before pleading,

"Can you help me do my makeup? I've been looking like death for the last few days..."

"And this is some guy you don't want to look like crap in front of? I got you girl. Get your makeup and we'll fix you right up."

HE WAS WAITING RIGHT where I'd told him to.

"Is this some kind of joke?" he asked me. I glanced up at the letters on the building. *CITY POUND.* I tried not to smile.

"No, I'm not turning you in. We're gonna go walk a dog and talk. My roommate and I volunteered here last year when they got overwhelmed with kittens." I said. "I figure maybe a furry animal would diffuse the tension between us."

I felt *it* as soon as I saw him, the flickering of desire in my stomach. Electricity ran up my back, and told me that what had happened between us the night of Candy's house show may not have felt consensual, but it definitely had been. Cash Legend was a five-alarm fire, and he was setting me alight. I was grateful that Max had let me borrow one of her low-cut, emerald green sweaters that showed off my curves, because Cash's eyes followed the neckline before he yanked his gaze back to my face with a red flush in his cheeks. He knew he shouldn't be looking, but he couldn't even help himself. That made me glad in a small, evil way.

I was flirting with danger, and it felt stupid, and the last thing I should be doing when I'd questioned him and his motives only days before but....

I couldn't help it. I wanted him to look, so badly, and worse than that, I wanted him to touch. What was wrong with me? I wasn't guy-crazy, not by a long shot.

"I like dogs," Cash said, and bit his lip. "Don't say I am one, because I already know I am."

"Can we not mention it? You said you wanted to talk, and I'm okay with talking as long as it's not about... that night."

"Maybe let's go get our dog first?" He opened the front door for me. A few signatures on release forms later, and we had an excitable mixed-breed pup on a leash. I'd offered Cash to take him first, and witnessed the transformation as Cash's normally broody attitude melt at the tail wagging of a new four-legged friend.

We ambled out, and across the street to a large park dotted with towering firs.

"So talk," I said. The dog tugged at his leash but Cash kept his grip firm.

"This tour means everything to us, but not for reasons you think. This tour means safety, it means freedom. How much do you know about the werewolf population?"

His question came out of left-field, even if the first thing he'd said hadn't surprised me all that much.

"Um... well, we didn't study it a lot or anything, just how werewolves were *forbidden* and to stay away from them, but we did learn that werewolf population has been declining over the last two centuries." The fresh air was crisp on my face, and I was grateful for Max's sweater. It was thick enough to be snuggly in the fall air.

"Did they ever tell you that werewolves are dying out because we're being hunted?" Cash's words were icy and I stopped still to look up at him.

"Hunted?"

"Yeah, as in human hunters. They're tracking us, killing us. Destroying pack after pack, systematically." His expression was serious enough that I didn't laugh at him even though I wanted to.

"Uh, human hunters? There haven't been human hunters in well over a century," I said. "Humans, mundanes, don't know anything about werewolves, or witches for that matter."

"Or vampires?" he asked, expression turning dark. The dog whined, and tugged at his leash, wanting the walk to continue. Cash gave in and moved, and I followed him.

"Well..." I tried to think it over. Back in the 'days of yore', things had been even less friendly between witches and werewolves, and I knew there'd been a bit of bloody war between them and that humans had been roped in to mop up some rogue werewolf packs here and there, by the witches. "I mean, I've never heard anything about hunters in recent years at all. I'm sorta out of the loop and all, but there wasn't any talk about it in anything other than the very past tense."

"Yeah, I'm pretty sure they don't tell their kids that human hunters are still out there, murdering werewolves. It goes against the whole 'benevolent to society' image that witches want to project to one another." Cash scratched the top of the dog's head when it came in close for a snuggle, his touch gentle despite the harshness of his words.

Maybe someone else wouldn't have agreed with him. But there was a reason I'd run from my family and the witching world, and it wasn't because they were fun and happy people who never did anything wrong.

"Well, okay, so there's hunters... like modern day mundanes hunting werewolves. That's terrible, but I'm not sure what that has to do—"

"They're hunting us, Darcy," Cash turned to me as he dropped his voice down. "They don't know who we are, but they do know we're in the city, and they're coming for us. They got most of our pack almost thirty years ago. Ace was just a puppy, a kid, and me and the guys, we grabbed him and ran for it. We survived, raised him, and now we're all that's left. Now these bastards, they want us too."

"I don't understand," I said, the enormity of what he was explaining overwhelming me. "How do they know?"

"I don't know the answer to that, I just know they know, because we've got our own ears out on the street," he said.

The dog at our feet thumped his tail once, and nuzzled Cash's hand for more pets, shameless little beggar that he was. "They're tracking us, and for the most part we've been able to stay on the move, but that's getting harder to do."

"If you don't want to be found," I said because I had to point it out, "then why the hell are you guys in a band? Isn't getting up on stage and putting yourselves in the spotlight, literally, a bad idea if you're trying to avoid attention?"

Cash's mouth flattened into a thin line.

"They don't know what we look like, because honestly, this is probably the next generation of the hunters, offspring of the people who got our pack the first and second times."

"First and second? I thought you said—"

"Me and Eli, and Finn, were overseas when they hit us the first time," Cash said, and he looked so haunted, his eyes shadowed, that I didn't want to press for more information. "But this tour? It's safe. It's safe for us, and safe for Ace, especially Ace. We'll be moving around a lot, and from what I've heard, if we're not in any one place for more than a few days, they're going to have a hell of a time tracking us down. This is our chance to take the heat off, and get out of dodge fast." He measured my reaction, and huffed out a breath. He must've seen that I was bending.

"Really? It's that easy? Just take off in a tour bus?"

"We've done it before, just a lot lower budget, and we ran through our cash stores, what our pack had saved when they, well, were murdered. We don't have anything left of it to keep ourselves on the road. XOhX is advancing the costs of the tour, because they think it'll pay off big for them down the road, and that means we can go for almost a month and a half. Put some distance between us and the people who want us dead." He was serious. Completely serious. And if I was honest, my every instinct, witch and mundane alike, was shouting at me to trust him.

"It's a lot to think about," I said, stalling for time, even though I could feel the winds of fate stirring around me, preparing to pick me up and drag me along whether I wanted to go or not. Maybe it was time I stopped fighting the path I was on, and start running along it instead.

"Is it? I'm telling you that this is a life or death situation, and you have to think about it?" his voice was harsh, his blue eyes narrowed.

"No," I answered without hesitation, "you're right. I don't have to think about it." I swallowed hard. "Just one question. Why aren't you, like, fighting them? These hunters?"

Cash gave a humorless laugh.

"They really don't teach you shit about werewolves, do they?" He closed his eyes and let out a gusty breath. "We aren't fighting them because we can't. They wiped out our pack, almost entirely, and destroyed what makes us whole, so that we could never be strong enough again to recover."

"What?"

"Our heartstone," he said, "they stole it. They stole it and then they destroyed it. Without it, we're wolves... but, well, we can't shift anymore. We can't shift, and over time, we're getting weaker. One day we're going to be as strong as mundane, human men and when that happens, well you can pretty much just sign our death warrants then."

What the hell was a *heartstone*? I'd never even heard the word, but when Cash said it, he almost *sang* it, his voice lilting like it meant something special. I should have asked for more info, but I thought of Ace and his happy rambling talk about everything, of Charlie with his sarcastic little quips and obsession over his smartphone, even of Eli's glowers and low-murmured *Miss Lewellyn*'s. And Finn, raking his hand through his hair and grinning at the audience, making them swoon, making them his.

If what Cash said was true, and I knew in my heart he was telling the truth, they'd all die, die at the hands of men who had become the real monsters.

And of all of them, right then, I wanted Cash to suffer the least. He carried his guilt of our little make-out sesh around his neck like an albatross.

"I'll do it," I said. Cash's eyes lit up and he started toward me, one arm out as if he wanted to wrap it around me. The dog barked and Cash stopped short. I swallowed hard, and closed my eyes before I stepped forward, wrapping my arms around Cash's middle, hugging him tight. His free arm came around me and he held me close.

"Thank you," his voice was low and half-broken.

"You shouldn't have to thank me for doing the right thing," I whispered back.

"Well I'm gonna do it anyway," he argued. I kept my eyes shut tight. I knew I was making the right decision. Wasn't I?

Phoenixcry
@PhoenixcryMusic

When bae comes back to us we make this
face: http://t.com/V2S00ilAd2

5 Retweets **14** Likes

♡ 5   ⬆ 5   ♡ 14   ✉

Phoenixcry
@PhoenixcryMusic

We're hitting the road! Can't wait to see you on #tour with @GloryRevBand!

5 Retweets 14 Likes

  ♡ 14   ↻ 5   ♡ 14   ✉

When you read about preparing for tour, there's a lot of making lists of everything in the case studies. But that doesn't seem to really tell you how many lists you're gonna end up making. Lists of what everyone needs for gear. Lists of what everyone eats (meat, meat, and more meat, according to Charlie). Lists of the venues, their talent buyers, when to send in posters and to who, the local poster guys in every town, the names of street teams that were for hire, and everything in between.

The worst part of it had been telling Max, and seeing her

war between being happy for me and being devastated that I was going to be gone for long swaths of time with the tour.

"You're lucky that your supervising professor doesn't mind you doing your classwork from the road while you're interning. Also, we'll keep up by text, right? Add WhatsApp on your phone, you absolute peasant," was all she said about it, before bursting into tears and consoling herself with half a carton of Ben & Jerry's. Willa had welcomed me back into the fold with a brief nod and a smile. Jake Tupper was nowhere near my desk when I was at work because he was already on tour, and I could breathe easy without him and his stupid prickly gifts. My days were filled with doing social media blasts, checking in with my departmental professor at college, working with the street-team leaders in various cities where me and the guys would be in just a few weeks, low-key wondering if hunters were really after the boys, and not seeing much of the band.

They were hard at work with some performance coach the label had hired for them, getting their show road-worthy. Maybe I was biased, but they were already so good, what more could a coach do?

Finn appeared at my side one afternoon as I glared at a spreadsheet, hating life.

"Hey," he said, startling me. I yipped and my fingers skipped across the keys, destroying a few cells of data entry. "Sorry," he said, not sorry at all, when I glared up at him. It was hard to be angry when he looked so good in a simple gray t-shirt and a pair of well worn-in jeans, but I shoved the low-simmering attraction to the side. If I couldn't manage to keep the thought of touching all five of the guys, or them touching me, out of my mind for three seconds then the tour was going to be painful.

"What do you want, wolf-boy?" I smirked when his eyes flicked up and around us, but my words had been quiet enough that my voice wouldn't carry.

"So we're leaving early. Tomorrow, cause the next tour date is a few hours north. We'll meet up with them down in Eugene and join up for the show then. Willa's in a meeting with Troy, and the rest of the band, but I snuck out to get coffee so I could tell you before anyone else did."

"Manager's always the last to know," I groused, but it was something that I was getting used to. Decisions were made so fast in the business that things changed from hour to hour if an artist was hot and up-and-coming enough. Ugh, I'd need to let my professor know—the college was fine with me going out of state because most interns in music industry did, but I'd still have to keep him updated. Finn laughed and chucked me on the shoulder gently.

"Don't be grumpy. You should be happy. You told me yesterday when we were prepping that poster pack that you *liked* the work, and now you have more of it to do."

"Ugh, right. Well, that's great, but please go away now so I can get this stuff done in time for Willa to give me extra stuff on top of it, okay?"

Finn obliged and vanished, leaving the soft hint of mint and soap behind him when he went. I tried not to breathe it in, but couldn't help it. The few times I had seen them up close, I'd started noticing more that each of the guys had a unique, soft scent to them that wasn't after-shave. In fact, after-shave seemed almost choking in comparison, and I had slipped into more than one day-dream about what it would be like to be enfolded close into the mint scent that clung to Finn's clothes, or more of the heated rocks and water of Cash, Ace's curling paper and honey wax, or Charlie who was like worn in leather. The only one that I hadn't been able to suss out was Eli, and that was because he was either glowering at me (resting bastard face as Willa called it), or breezing by me with a low-murmured *Miss Lewellyn* too quickly for me to take a guilty deep breath of his trailing scent.

I asked Ace about it, the next morning when we were packing up the gear into the back of the trailer that would be towed by our tour-van.

"Scent?" He lifted his head from re-coiling a bunch of cables. "Shit, really, you're that sensitive to it?" I blinked.

"Um, doesn't everyone smell it?"

"Nah. Only other wolves, or you know, I guess witches. I don't know, I've never been close enough to another witch to ask them if they can smell me." His grin was cheeky. "I guess this is like a first, right? We should write a book, submit it to your council for consideration under their educational program. *Witches and Wolves: An in-depth study of close proximal relationships.*"

A laugh burst out of me. Shaking my head at him, I zipped up Cash's drumstick case, making sure he had enough for the first show. The guys didn't have an official sponsorship yet, but one of the major brands had sent over a box of drumsticks anyway. Maybe Cash wouldn't even need to buy any on tour, but the way he splintered them during every show made me think we'd need to make a few Guitar Center trips.

"First of all, they're not my council. They stopped being my council when I fucked off at nineteen. Secondly, I'm pretty sure they don't care what any werewolf has to say, so if we're publishing this then it has to be under my name only." I shot Ace a cheeky grin right back and he wrinkled his nose in response.

"Would you two stop flirting and get the trailer packed?" Eli came around the corner, storm clouds on his face as he carried an acoustic guitar case.

"Sure thing, captain," Ace said, taking the case from him. "Maybe if you guys didn't leave all the heavy lifting to me and the girl, it would get done faster."

"I have a name," I protested. Eli didn't look at me, but sighed.

"Fine. I'll get Cash and Finn and we'll get this done."

"What's that, Eli?" Ace crossed his arms over his chest. Eli growled.

"What's what, Ace?"

"I think that's the sound of you being totally wrong, and me being right. So you're welcome, since you forgot to thank me," Ace said, and my eyes widened at the subtle challenge in the younger wolf's voice. That was something else I'd noticed. There was a subtle pack-dynamic change all the time. Like Eli was the alpha-wolf, but he didn't rule over the rest of them without question. They'd come to blows at least twice that I knew of (in the studio and at Candy's house show), but for the most part they settled disagreements with a few heated words and curses. And Eli wasn't always the one who had the last word either. He was less of a dick than I'd first thought, because he did seem to listen when the other guys countered his opinion with their own.

"You're right, Ace," Eli said, although it sounded as if his teeth were hurting from the way he was gritting them. "I should have gotten the much stronger, and faster members of the band to load the bus instead of leaving it to you. Why don't you call Finn and Cash over to help?"

Ace's face fell at Eli's insult and I quickly revised my opinion. Eli was a dick. Ace glared at him and stormed off, without another word.

Eli moved past me to grab a drum case as if it weighed nothing. He walked inside the trailer, his boots thumping on the metal floor.

"That was an asshole move," I said as he went.

"I didn't ask your opinion," he answered, voice flat as he came back out. "Either pass me something or go find Charlie."

"What's your problem, Gunner?" I got in his path, standing between him and the rest of the gear. "You're pissed off about something and you took it out on Ace. He's a good guy, and he had a point about you guys not helping."

"Miss Lewellyn," Eli started but I made a noise in my throat and he fell quiet.

"Yeah don't go all formal on me, okay? It's not as charming as you think it is—"

"Charming?!" Eli actually sputtered.

"Yeah, that old-timey-wimey-yes-ma'am-aw-schucks thing you and Cash do. Finn's your twin and he doesn't do it, so I'm guessing either he got with the times, or you two think it makes the ladies like you, but it doesn't cut it with me." Standing in front of 6'2" of heavily muscled, apex-predator in a man's body should have scared the crap out of me, but I'd been spending enough time with the band in a professional way to know that I could stand up for myself, and anyone else, if I needed to. Eli shifted his weight from one foot to the other, looking uncertain.

He cleared his throat.

"I call you that because it's polite," he said.

"Well that's the only thing about you that's polite right now."

He had the grace to flush with shame and sighed.

"I'm sorry, I just... I guess I want to get on the road." He looked away, and I had to take a moment to remember half the reason we were going on the road on the first place. The guys weren't twitchy, not very much that I'd noticed anyway, but it had to be weighing on their minds that they were running from a fight. Elias seemed to hear my thoughts. "It feels like I'm being a coward," he said. "But whoever they are, we can't face them down. It's my job to keep the pack safe, and until the day we get a heartstone of our own again, we won't be."

There was that heartstone again.

"A new heartstone?" I passed him another drum-case, a smaller one this time. "You guys can get a new one?"

"Yes," he said. I was interrupted from asking more questions by the arrival of the rest of the guys, sans Ace. Finn waltzed right up to me and wrapped an arm around my shoulder.

"Say cheese," he said, and held up his phone, smooshing me right against his chest as he took a picture of us both before I could argue. "Looks great." He held the phone out of my reach.

"What're you doing?" I asked, reaching for it. "Let me see."

"You look hot, don't worry," he said as he tapped on his phone, way above my head. "Just something for the band Instagram."

"Chrissy's going to be pissed at you," I said, "she told me that you guys aren't supposed to be posting on there without her approval after the ham-sandwich incident. She wouldn't tell me what the ham-sandwich thing was, but I'm assuming it has something to do with dicks." Chrissy, as I'd gotten to know her, managed all the social media strategy at the label, as well as worked with the radio trackers who pushed songs to music directors at radio stations around the country. She was older than Willa, liked to wear all black, and had an affection for calling me 'honeycakes'. I liked her and I didn't want her to get mad at me for the band dicking around on their Instagram.

"I'm offended you would think that," Charlie commented as he pushed his amp stack up the ramp into the back of the trailer. "We're more well-behaved than Jake Tupper."

"Shut it about Jake," Eli ordered with a grunt as he pushed up his own amp stack and Charlie grabbed the other end of it, pulling it inside. "We're lucky to be on this tour, and if we so much as look at him the wrong way, we could get kicked off."

"Nah, he won't do that. He just wants to stare at Darce's ass, not that I blame him—" Finn cut off with a yelp when Eli reached over and grabbed him by the arm, twisting it up and behind his back in a heartbeat. "I'm sorry, shit, I'm sorry, Eli, you asshole—"

The scent of petrichor engulfed me, and a hand covered my eyes. Cash. He pulled me back, against his chest, his other arm wrapping around my waist.

"You shouldn't watch this," Cash murmured, his lips near my ear. A shiver trembled through my muscles that I hoped he didn't notice. I swallowed hard. Cash had been keeping his distance from me, not in a rude way, more of a cautious way, but each time he did get close... my body reacted like he was a live-wire.

From the trailer I heard Charlie laughing. There was more sounds of scuffling, and Finn's muffled cursing.

"Stop screwing around. You guys fight like you're brothers or something," Charlie joked. Above and behind me, Cash snorted. Prying at his hand on my eyes, my fingers bit into his skin.

"Let me see," I said.

"Yeah?" he asked, his voice so soft I knew it was meant for me. "You like the idea of two guys wrestling each other? Fighting over you, maybe?" At his words, a small puff of heat blossomed in my belly and I inhaled slow and quiet. "That's what I thought," he chuckled in my ear again, and this time I felt his lips close, brushing my skin. "We're never gonna fight over you, Darcy, I can promise you that. Maybe we'll fight over who's first, or who gets to fall asleep holding you, or who gets to wake you up in the morning, but fight each other? Never. So if you think for a minute you can make us jealous of each other, you can't."

His words hurt. Not as much as the elbow to his gut had to. I jerked my arm backward, driving the joint of my arm in to his stomach hard.

Cash grunted, and his hand fell away from my eyes, his arm away from my waist.

I spun and glared at him.

"Seriously, dude?" I spat. "What makes you think I'm trying to—"

"What's going on?" Finn was at my side in a moment, apparently free from Eli's clutches. Cash looked at me, his eyes half-lidded, a smirk on his face even as he had an arm wrapped around his gut.

"Girl's got a good strike on her," he commented. "You should watch out, Finn, just in case you get a little handsy."

"I have a *name*, Cash." I stared him down for a long moment, until he dropped his gaze and looked away, to the side. His words still confused me, waking up all sorts of thoughts, bringing back what Charlie had said, how they shared, how they were very much *okay* with sharing. As in sharing me. The idea was as scary as it was arousing.

"Well, unlike you, I only get handsy in the polite way," Finn said, his arm sneaking around my shoulders. I let him and he pulled me against him. "I'm thinking you were rude just now, and maybe you ought to apologize to our manager. Our—" his tongue tripped for a moment and Cash tilted his head, one eyebrow hiking up as if he knew something that I didn't.

"Our?"

"Our manager," Finn finished lamely, his fingers squeezing my shoulder gently. "Now say you're sorry. Or I'll make what Eli did to me look like a fucking picnic." I met Cash's eyes.

"I'm sorry for being rude," he said, and shrugged. "Let's get the rest of this gear packed."

Willa came out of the label office into the loading-bay to see us off when we were ready to go. She took a step back and surveyed the tour van. It was like the one we'd used the night of Candy's party but bigger. This one actually slept six people, although two of the guys would have to share the pop-up top area that turned into a queen bed and opened up over the front seat. It wasn't a luxury tour bus by any rate, but I still had excited butterflies in my stomach as I stored my duffel bag with a week's worth of clothes, and my backpack, in the back of the van.

"Is that all you're taking?" Willa asked me as she eyed my stuff.

"Well there's not a lot of space," I said with a shrug. "And we'll stop to do laundry, right?"

"Yeah, you will but still—" She shook her head and sighed, before passing me an envelope. "Here's your per diems for you and the guys. Don't spend them on clothes, or you're going to starve."

"Is that a thing?" I asked, opening up the manilla envelope. Neatly sealed envelopes were in there.

"You'll get another drop-off of per-diems in two weeks, so

that you guys don't run through the cash all at once. You already have your merch float, right?"

"Yup." I'd been loaded down with a box of merch stuff, not just t-shirts but all the paperwork and sales reporting sheets that went with it. XOhX was a vinyl-preferred label, so we'd have records waiting for us at each tour date stop in advance. I don't know how Troy had gotten them pressed so fast, since most of the wait times for vinyl records to be manufactured were six months to a year and half, but he'd done it somehow. Charlie had muttered about *'back-room blowjobs'* when I'd asked so I didn't question it further. I'd met Troy once, and I didn't want to think about him giving anyone a blowjob. Plus I was pretty sure he had a wife and kids, and the way he'd eyed up my breasts made me think he probably wasn't gay. Maybe bi, but definitely not gay.

Willa wrapped her arms around me in a quick hug. The first few weeks of my internship had whipped by, especially with her help. She hadn't held my initial quitting against me, and done her best to teach me everything she knew about road management before I left for tour. Still, it wasn't hard to feel underprepared.

"You need anything, you text me. My phone's always on," she offered.

"I know. We'll be okay."

"Are you two gonna make out?" Charlie asked as he came up beside us, heaving his own bag into the back of the tour van. Willa made an annoyed noise.

"If you weren't so talented," she left the threat up to his imagination but smiled anyway. Charlie had been working with her closely since the label first took interest in

Phoenixcry, and I was pretty sure out of all them, she was closest and fondest of Charlie.

"Thanks mom," he teased, and jerked out of the way when she went to punch his shoulder.

"All right," Eli shouted from near the front of the van. "Load up, everyone."

Willa grabbed me in tight for another hug.

"Don't forget to put your tour pass on the driver's seat at rest-stops if you're going to the bathroom," she said. "Or they might leave you behind."

"We'd never do that," Finn said firmly, he walked up to her and wrapped his arms around us both. "Can anybody get in on this, or is it a girl-club thing?"

I grumbled as his warmth seeped in through my hoodie, and the scent of him overwhelmed my senses. Willa squirmed, and ducked out from under his arm, seemingly unaffected by Finn's closeness or his scent. The guys all made me go a little trembly though. I needed to work through that before I melted all over myself in the tour van.

"Don't be weird, Gunner," Willa said.

"Weird's my brother," he quipped.

"I heard that," Eli called.

"Good." Finn winked at me, and bumped his hip against mine. "Wanna sit in the back of the bus and talk business? Chrissy emailed me the *actual* approved social media plan after she saw my Instagram photo go up."

"I told you not to put it up," I said with dismay, pulling out my phone to check out the feed. Willa watched us for a moment before she walked off. She was talking to Eli about the best route to take to avoid rush-hour when we got to the first tour stop we'd be on. Flicking my thumb through the feed I held my breath as the picture of us came up.

THE CAPTION READ:

Heading out on the road. This girl's gotta put up with us for over 45 days. Wish her luck.

"IT'S A GOOD PICTURE," Finn defended.

"You can't see my face," I said, and he laughed, making me realize how silly that was. The fans didn't need to see my face. I was supposed to be invisible, behind the scenes. Chrissy had given me a big talk about it, how the band needed to appear available and unattached so female fans could envision themselves as attached. *But they are unattached, Chrissy,* I'd said. She'd given me a look and sighed, *And they're going to seem to stay that way, no matter what.* Whatever she meant by that, I had no idea.

"C'mon, faceless wonder. Let's go grab our seats before Charlie sprawls out and takes them all with his crap."

"That's not physically possible, and all my stuff is in the back," Charlie argued mildly as we gave Willa one last hug each and piled into the van.

"Get in tight everybody," Ace said, sitting up in front with Eli. Apparently they'd patched up their argument from earlier. Ace held up his phone. "One picture for the road, of all of us in the tour van." Finn scooped me up and set me in his lap, squishing me forward. I laughed as Ace took the picture; I was nearly falling off Finn's lap.

Eli fired up the engine and I sat back, doing my seatbelt. My stomach gave a jolt as the parking brake released, and we rolled forward. Ace let out a sigh of relief as we turned out onto the road. All the guys seemed more relaxed to finally be moving, and I knew that it wasn't all just the excitement of going on a big tour. Part of it, I was sure, was them thinking of leaving behind the threat of being found by hunters. A shiver rolled down my back at that thought.

"Say goodbye to the present," Finn muttered as Willa waved to us and walked back inside the building.

"Say hello to the future," I whispered back, looking up at him. He swallowed hard and glanced away.

"Let's hope it's good."

FIFTEEN

DarcyLuvsDonuts
5 mins

♡ ⬡ ↱

♥ 11 likes
This is my life now. #bandlife #tourlife
#phoenixcry #touring4ever #arewethereyet

Being on tour was boring. Mostly. Or at least, the first few hours after Finn and I wrapped up our plans for the social media (lots of pictures of the guys goofing off, minimal or nothing of me) that would go out over the next few days. Eli put on Muse, and Finn sang along for a few songs before Charlie told him to save his voice for the show.

A few middle fingers flashed between the guys but they all settled down. Ace sat up high on his seat, staring at everything as it passed. Eli was steady behind the wheel, talking to Ace quietly as he drove. Charlie was on his phone, although I'd come to realize he spent a lot of time interacting with fans over the Facebook group. Finn was Snapchatting, a lot, and I had to dodge a few of his attempts to rope me into the pictures. Cash glared at him every time I grumbled and ducked out from under Finn's arm.

"You do that when we have a car-accident, and you'll break her neck." Cash was irritated, and I avoided his eyes. We hadn't interacted much since he'd grabbed me outside the tour van earlier.

"You're just sour you're not sitting next to her," Finn replied, his spirits undampened. My phone buzzed and I looked at it.

A text from Max.

HAVE FUN, peanut, and don't forget to text me when you get into Redding!

"THAT YOUR BOYFRIEND?" Finn asked, peering over my shoulder. A hand in his face, pushing him away, was all it took to get him to back off. I was getting a lot more comfortable, physically, especially around him. My sister had always been a perfect child and we'd never roughhoused like some of my friends with their siblings, so pushing Finn around, and even doing the same with Ace and Charlie was a little weird at first. One thing I'd noticed about the guys though? They were very physical. Constantly touching each other, punching, running a hand over someone's shoulder, hair, back. It made me think of the close way that other pack-animals lived, and I couldn't help, for a moment, to imagine them as wolves, tails up and nudging each other with their wet-cold noses.

"That's Max. I told you about her."

"Oh yeah. Max Morgan. That's such a cool name, like a super-hero."

"Her first name is actually Mackenzie, and her boyfriend's name, I mean, her ex-boyfriend's last name was Mackenzie, and so she always joked that she was gonna be Mackenzie Mackenzie when they got married..." I trailed off. I felt so bad leaving Max behind. I texted her back, a picture out the side window of the van.

"That's fucking terrible. Mackenzie Mackenzie? Her boyfriend should take on her last name. That'd be the fair thing to do," Finn said, stretching his front legs out. The tour van had captain chairs at the front, and another set of two chairs in the middle, then the kitchenette area, and a bench seat where Finn and I sat.

"I don't think most guys would be okay with taking their girlfriend's name," I said. He rolled his eyes.

"Then they're stupid," he said with a shrug. "We're, well, I mean, Eli's top dog or whatever, but we still listen to our women. Women first. We're mostly about the equality, but when it comes down to a final decision, it's lady's choice." He seemed so relaxed about it and matter-of-fact.

"You guys?" I asked, pointing at him and the rest of the band. "Lady's choice?" He grinned, lopsided.

"Yeah, does that seem weird to you?"

"Well, yeah." I sat back in my seat and looked out the window. Modern society still wasn't equal, but it was *nothing* compared to how the witching world was. How many times had I seen my father outright cut my mother down in front of us? Tell her she didn't know anything, and needed to be quiet. My sister Eva had told me that when I was born, our father didn't speak to my mother for a week because she'd committed the crime of having a second girl.

I should have been a son, after all. They'd 'procreated' or whatever on the dark of the moon to bless their future child with male genetics so that they'd have a kid to carry on the Llewellyn name and take on the seat at the council.

Except it hadn't worked. The whispered spells my mother had uttered each night of her pregnancy (ultrasounds were forbidden, for reasons I'll never understand now that I know they even exist) to make sure the babe in her belly was a boy? They hadn't worked either. I'd come into the world, Darcy Evangeline Llewellyn. Darcy was the name they'd picked out for me before I was born, because my mother was a big Jane Austen fan, but Evangeline was given to me. I was named after my mother since I wasn't the boy they'd wanted. I would have been Darcy Vail Llewellyn, named for my father, if that had been the case.

"You gone rabbiting?" Finn's voice was near my ear and I inhaled sharply, turning.

"Sorry I got lost in my thoughts. Rabbiting?"

"When you run after rabbits that don't exist," he said, and pitched his voice louder. "Ace does it all the time."

"What do I do?" Ace twisted in his seat, looking back at us, confused. His hair was all at odd ends where he'd run his fingers through it, and he'd gotten ink on his face from sticking a pen behind his ear. He held a Sudoku book in one hand. Finn shook his head and relaxed back into the seat, crossing one ankle over his knee.

"Rabbiting," he said with another shake of his head.

"That was mean, calling him out when he can't hear us."

"You think he can't hear us, sweetheart?" Finn asked, with a slow lilt to his voice that warmed me from the bottom up.

"I—"

"He's got young ears, and he didn't live through a war," he snickered. "He can hear better than any of us."

"War?"

Finn's eyes flicked forward to Cash, then Eli, at my question. The corner of his mouth lifted up.

"Later," he said. "While the guys are sound-checking and I'm off preening and saving my voice for the show."

The slow rock of the tour van on the road was getting to me anyway, and I closed my eyes.

A HAND on my shoulder woke me, and I sat up with a start.

"Guh," was the noise I made. Ace was peering down at me, grinning.

"You fell asleep, and napped the whole way. Eli made us all shut up so we wouldn't wake you."

"It was annoying," Charlie said, but he smiled at me in a

way that made me think it was more that Eli was annoying than me napping.

"Are we here?" We were stopped, and I looked outside. We were in the loading dock for the first venue. I recognized it from the picture on Google Maps when I'd looked it up. In person, The Clutch was imposing, rising high up off the ground.

"Yeah, and there's already a crowd but they aren't for us, obviously. I think some people even lined up overnight." Ace pointed out the window, and I could just see the tail end of a line-up, past a metal barricade that kept them out of the loading-bay. A bored security guard stood by the partition, ready to let more tour busses in, or keep people out.

"Holy crap." Not that I hadn't been that person standing in line. There'd been more than one show I'd lined up over night for, shivering beside Max through the whole cold and miserable event.

"They're waiting to get in on floor tickets, for the mosh pit, since it's not assigned seating they show up early to get right in front," Charlie said. I didn't bother telling him I knew. That I'd been one of those girls, pressed up into the security barrier right at the front of a stage before, a few hundred people crowded behind me.

"Where's Finn?" Eli was gone too, and Cash. I unbuckled my seat belt and sat up. Thankfully the tour van was werewolf-height (or full grown man-height), so I could stand properly. My back cracked and I rubbed it.

"He and Eli went to go talk to the stage manager. We're

loading in, then we're sound-checking last. We'll get some food before we sound-check. You hungry?"

I had to laugh when he looked at my backpack, that was on the floor in front of me with a manila envelope sticking out of it.

"Is that why you woke me up? You're hungry?"

"Well, you do have the per-diems," Ace said with a shrug. Charlie snickered and hopped out of the open side-door of the van.

"Good luck with her, Ace," he taunted as he sauntered off to the loading-bay doors. Another, larger, longer tour-bus was parked parallel to ours but further away.

Ace saw me looking.

"That's Glory Revolution's and Jake's bus," he said, and bit his lip. "One day we're gonna be in one of those. Just you wait, Darce."

"When did I give any of you permission to call me 'Darce'"? I asked, but I thought about him and the guys in a big tour bus like that, maybe with their faces on a wrap plastered across the outside of the bus. Would they be safe then, though, performing in stadiums around the world? They'd have bodyguards, right? That would deter any hunters. If they had a staff of humans meant to keep them away from possible threats in the form of fangirls, that would help.

"You didn't say it wasn't okay?" Ace blinked and brought me out of my daydream. "Do you mind?"

"Not really, but I thought I'd give you a hard time."

Ace eyed me up and down.

"You think it's a good idea to give me a hard time, *Darce?*" he asked, and there was a sudden purr in his voice, turning him from slightly hapless goofball to smouldering, six feet of man. I took a step back, and yelped when I tripped over my bag and nearly went down. "Oh shit!"

Ace dropped his swagger, and grabbed me, pulling me into his chest.

"I'm fine," I mumbled into the front of his shirt.

"Yeah, but if I killed you, Cash and the rest of the guys would murder me too." He let me go, setting me on my feet. "You're not klutzy are you?"

"Uh, not really. Only when I'm tired. You know, like most people," I explained. I reached for my bag. "We've gotta load in merch, and—"

"Hold up. We've got this. This isn't our first show," Ace said, jumping down from the van and holding out a hand for me.

"How long have you guys been playing anyway?" I asked as I slung my backpack over one shoulder. Ace grabbed one of the guitars and we headed to the loading bay doors into the theater.

"As soon as I was old enough." That made me laugh, and he rolled his eyes. "No, seriously. As soon as they knew I wasn't going to embarrass them anymore, and my playing was good enough. They'd been playing together already for years, writing songs, well, music's just really in our blood, isn't it?"

"Makes sense, yeah."

"It kept us together when things were the worst they'd ever been," his voice grew wistful. "Maybe it was scarier then, when we really weren't sure if we'd live to see another week, but the music kept us going. It gave me purpose anyway, I don't know about the rest of the guys." He smiled at me and shuffled his feet. I was hit with a sense of relief from him. This tour was more than just for their career. It was keeping them alive. My neck prickled. I wanted to take a closer eye on things as kids filtered into the venue. I didn't know what a hunter would look like, but it wouldn't hurt to keep an eye out, right?

"Did you bring earplugs?" Ace looked cautiously at me as we stepped into the cool air of the theatre. It was warm outside, but there was a fall of air conditioning pouring down on us from above as soon as we were in. Ace set down the guitar next to the rest of the gear that had already been loaded in.

"Yeah. Why?"

"Well," Ace shoved his hands in his pockets, "we were thinking that maybe if you could use those, like, protective ear covers that maybe it might stop you from..."

I felt my face turning hot and red. He didn't need to finish his sentence. I knew what he meant. They wanted to make sure I didn't end up throwing myself at one of them after the show because of the magic woven into every note of their music.

"I think I can probably manage," I said, "now that I know what to expect." Silence, tense and awkward, hung between and around us.

"None of us knew it was gonna do that." Ace broke first,

giving me a tentative, hopeful smile. "I mean, we've never performed for a witch before, so…"

"You should know better than to call our road manager a witch, Ace," Finn said as he strolled up, warning in his voice as a technician trailed along after him. "This is Paul, our gear tech."

"We get a gear tech?" Ace asked, eyes wide. I was trying not to panic that Paul had overheard something a mundane shouldn't. Paul gave him a brief smile before glancing at me with curiosity, and back to Ace again.

"I'm with the venue, so I'm just with you for this show. Can you show me your instruments for tonight?" he asked. Ace turned to the stack of cases. Finn stepped into my space, talking low as Paul and Ace started to speak about the gear for the night.

"Want to see the green room?"

"Is it nice?" I asked.

"It's got a couch," Finn said, and caught my hand in his. My heart skipped a beat as he tugged me along after him like a kite in the breeze.

"You implying something?" The bad, wrong, naughty, terrible part of me kinda hoped he was. He shot me a mischievous smirk over his shoulder but then smoothed it out until his face was the picture of innocence.

"Just thought you could use a place to lie down, have another nap. Can't have you working too hard."

"I'm hardly working at all," I complained.

"Only you would bitch about that." He laughed and pushed

open a black door, marked *Phoenixcry* on a piece of masking tape stuck to it. "Here's home for the next ten hours. Merch is already loaded out to front of house, so you can coordinate with their sales department. They handle it in-house here, which is.." Finn breathed out a huff of air and turned to me. "This is a lot bigger than I thought it would be."

"You okay?" There was a look on his face when I asked that. He ran a hand through his hair.

"Just... I didn't ever think we'd get here, honestly. It was always, y'know, move around a lot, playing on street corners for change to keep us all fed, and then we got on this house show circuit and played the shittiest, dirtiest places and slept rough." Finn blinked, and I realized there was moisture on his lower lashes. "When you've had everything ripped away from you like we did, this? This feels like we're being given a second chance. Then you came along, Darcy, and everything slotted into place."

His words bounced around in my mind for a moment.

"Me? But I'm—"

He leaned and hushed me, pressing a finger to my lips. I narrowed my eyes. The guys really needed to stop pushing me around like that.

"You're just what we needed," he said, voice rough. "You think it's bad you're a witch—" He rolled his eyes when I made a noise of protest, "—used to be a witch, whatever, you think it doesn't work for us? It works for us." His hand came up and then he was cupping my chin, and leaning down. His blue eyes were large as his face came in close, and my heart was suddenly thudding in my ears and my throat, right down to the tips of my fingers. Was he—were we—

Bang!

The door kicked open and we jerked apart.

"That's the table, there's chips!" Finn pointed at the far wall as if he was explaining to me where everything was in the room. Looking over my shoulder, I felt my gut clench unpleasantly.

Jake Tupper stood in the doorway, frowning at us.

SIXTEEN

Darcy Llewellyn
@DarcyLuvsDonuts

Eat. Sleep. Drive. Merch. Merch. Merch.
Sleep. Drive. Drive. Sleep.
#whydidithinkthiswouldbeglam
#itsamazingthough #bandlife

13 Retweets 35 Likes

Q 7   ⇄ 13   ♡ 35   ✉

"Gunner," Jake said with a tip of his head, and looked at me. "Llewellyn. I'm glad you're on the tour. You keeping these guys in line? They're not giving you a hard time, are they?" The way he paused over the word *hard* made my nerves frizz with tension. Had he seen us doing whatever? Had he seen Finn nearly kiss me? I didn't need to know. I didn't want to know.

Sometimes it was just better not to wonder.

"They're easy to work with," I said with a shrug. "Although I'm not looking forward to finding out who snores."

"I bet you snore," Finn countered before shifting in front of me, as if he wanted to block off Jake's line of sight to me. "You need something, Tupper?"

"No, I just heard that Darcy was here."

"Yeah, she's here, but we've got some show stuff to talk over. So if you don't mind?"

Jake looked frustrated at Finn's not-so-obvious-but-obvious cock-blocking. Gratitude was the only thing that I was feeling. Jake Tupper was persistently annoying. Were indie rock stars really that thirsty? He should've had a thousand girls hanging off of him. Why was he bothering me?

"Well," Jake said, and went silent, leaving without another word. The door shut behind him and I let out a breath I'd been holding.

"He's a fucking creep."

"Sharp observation there," I replied. *But you're the one who brought me here, to this empty green room, and almost kissed me,* I didn't say. Except it wasn't creepy. I was anything but creeped out by Finn's behavior. I think in a way, that I was probably, somehow, encouraging it. He hadn't heard me protest and I hadn't stepped away.

The thought had been tripping around in my brain, just out of reach, since Charlie had first mentioned it.

"Don't freak out... small packs are usually a group of males and a single female mate."

Don't freak out, he'd said. Little too late for that. Every time

I closed my eyes I thought of *it*. I'd slip into Bad Idea City, Population: Darcy Llewellyn.

Because every time I closed my eyes? It wasn't just Cash pressing me into the couch, his mouth on the curve of my breast the night at Candy's show. Finn was there, his hand steady on the back of my neck as he whispered in my ear how bad he wanted me, how bad they all wanted me. Ace, eager to please, would tuck his fingers into the waistband of my jeans and peel them down my hips.

Who was I kidding? Charlie'd be on his phone, and Eli would stand in the corner, glaring and growling. Then my family would burst in, human hunters at their heels, and the next thing I'd know, it would be the experience of watching the men, the guys, I was starting to fall for, get cut down before a black bag got pulled over my head.

The road through Bad Idea City always turned into the roaring freeway right to Nightmare Valley right after it.

"Darcy?" I jerked when my name called me back. Finn's expression was concerned. "You vanished on me, sweetheart."

"That's not a professional nickname."

"I'm not a professional guy," he said with a shrug. "C'mon. Let's go check out the stage, and take some pictures for Chrissy back at music HQ."

THE GUYS BARELY GOT A SOUNDCHECK, not even fifteen minutes, and I could tell that Cash was pissed. The sound crew only partially mic'd his drums, because the 'big guns' were going to be brought out for the headliners later that night, so we didn't get the full sound system treatment. Charlie had to remind him to keep his cool over it, because one day *we'll be playing stadiums, and these guys'll wish they treated us better*. It was more than obvious that we were on the tour because of Jake and his unhealthy obsession with getting in my pants or whatever. The guy was there every time I turned around. It was a damn good thing we had our own tour van, even if it was smaller than the fancy Prevost bus Jake and his friends in Glory Revolution were on. The thought of sleeping under the same metal roof as Jake was enough to give me nightmares, and I was already having a few bad dreams.

But the looks on the guys faces when they peered out from backstage at the crowd made it all worth it. I'd deal with ten Jakes to see them that happy, like they weren't even thinking about the future of their pack or the hunters trailing them. It didn't matter, none of it, when the size of the crowd got to them.

Finn sought me out, right before they went on stage.

"Good luck kiss?" he asked, in the shadow of a large stage riser which was shoved behind the curtain for the show.

"Are you kidding?"

"Not really."

I leaned up to kiss him on the cheek. My lips brushed his skin and I shivered, hesitating before I pulled away. His eyes glittered in the dark as he watched me settle back down on my heels.

"That'll keep me, next time aim a few inches over," he said, and sauntered back to just off the the stage, grabbing his wireless microphone off the table and checking that it was off. I watched him go, my belly fizzing with nerves. The van was calling me, but I didn't want to go. Earlier the guys had rounded on me in our small green room and said they'd decided for me that it would be better if I hung out in the tour van while they played, just in case there was another *incident*. And yeah, it was probably better if I did that.

Except I wanted to test my own resolve. Could I resist them, the call of their music, if I was mentally prepared?

And, the stupidest part of me, wanted to know, would I regret it if I wasn't able to? It was becoming clear that if we hadn't gotten interrupted, that things would have gone a lot further between me and Cash back at that house party. I didn't think I'd have a single bit of regret over it.

I closed my eyes, ducked between two rows of curtains where I couldn't be seen, and waited for the first scream of guitar. It hit me moments later when the house-lights went down completely. There were no cries from the crowd yet as the boys stepped out on stage.

Just wait, I promised the audience. They might've not been overwhelmed with what could only be called some sort of crazed sex hormone like I did when I heard the guys perform, but the audience was still going to be assaulted by some powerful music played by an amazing band. The drums started up, then the bass, and Finn's voice echoed through the room.

I grabbed onto the curtains behind me and held them tight, waiting for the swamp of emotions to overtake me. I couldn't see them, which I hoped would help.

There, in my chest, the first flutter of heat as my heart

started thudding in time with the 120 beat. It wasn't as strong as before, and I could still breathe. I closed my eyes tighter, and just listened.

Dirty Secret was their opening song this time, and when they got to the second chorus I could hear the audience start to clap along. Someone had started a clap, and it spread across the audience, thudding along with Cash's bass drum. Getting out from between the curtains, I rushed to stage-side to watch. Opening bands almost *never* got an audience to clap along, and definitely not for the first song in their set either. The way the guys played was working for the audience, winning them all over.

My toes lined up with the glow-in-the-dark tape on the floor that marked where we'd be visible to the audience if we stepped past it, and I stared at the band. Ace was closest to me, on his knees, back arched, the bass strings vibrating and blurring as his fingers worked them through an athletic performance.

He turned his head and saw me there, for a moment his hand hesitating as his lips parted into an 'o' of surprise. Then he jerked up onto his feet and lunged forward, out of my view. I'd have to step out onto the stage to still be able to see him. The music was so loud; I hadn't even put in ear plugs. I could just see some of the audience. They weren't reaching up and grabbing at Finn like the girls at the house party, but they were pressed right against the barrier, watching with open mouths and cellphones up.

Cash went into his trash-can ending, signaling to the audience that it was time for the song to be over and their turn to perform by clapping for the band. Finn stomped his foot and pulled the microphone away from his face, up into the air, theatrical in every inch of his body as if he was born for it. I stepped back.

The magnetic pull of the band was still there, but knowing it would happen helped me brace for it. I could deal with that. I wasn't going to fling myself out onto the stage, and probably not at them when they got off the stage.

Progress. It comes in small steps, but I was going to be grateful for whatever I was given.

Ace walked up to Cash, and someone brushed past me. It was Paul, carrying Ace's second bass, this one tuned down for one of their songs that was in a different key, drop-D, I thought.

The audience kept clapping. It was so loud, and Finn's voice barely cut through it to thank them, before announcing,

"We are Phoenixcry, and tonight, Redding, we are gonna have an awesome time! Get those phones out, let's party!"

Cash held his arm up, and went into the count-in, shouting out the time as his sticks struck the drums. I watched his arms, fluid and flowing as they licked out. My gaze followed them up to his shoulders, and then his face—

He was staring at me, eyes narrowed and almost glowing in the shadowed light that didn't quite hit behind the drum-kit where he sat on his throne.

Guilt nipped at my heart. He'd thought I was out in the tour van. I lifted my chin and crossed my arms over my chest to show him how unaffected I was by the music. He tossed his head and glanced back over the audience. Ace must have told him I was there.

Well, no big deal, right? I was fine. Big girl, handling herself. They could just suck it up. I dug my heels in, mentally anyway, and stuck it out, watching the audience get worked up. It mirrored my own feelings, as my chest grew tight, and my nerves were tingling with each new song. By the end of their set, the audience was reaching up to Finn, and I was breathing hard, white-knuckled and determined not to leave but knowing I should go hide out in the green room, or better yet, the tour bus.

"Darcy." Jake appeared at my left side with no warning, and I jumped. He caught me, one arm on my shoulder, to steady me. I pulled away without thinking. "Their set is almost done, but I thought you might like to join me for a pre-show drink in my dressing room?" he asked. "I'm not on for another 45 minutes."

"I can't." The excuse popped into my head immediately, and it wasn't even really an excuse. "The guys are doing a signing at their merch booth right after the show, and I need to be there." Jake frowned.

"It'll only be—"

He was cut off by the last song ending, and the roar that swelled up from the crowd. As it died off, a bemused expression crossed his face.

"They're doing well, huh?"

"Yeah," I said, and bit my lip. "Thanks for inviting them."

Jake watched me with a guarded expression.

"I'm a nice guy, Darcy, but I gotta say, you're throwing off a lot of mixed signals," he said after a moment. I had to bite my tongue, and was about to ask him what he meant, when he shook his head. "Good luck at the signing." He turned and left. I guessed he was going back to his dressing room. He might've gone, but he'd left a gnawing worry eating at my insides.

Did he think I was interested in him? Nothing could be further from how I actually felt. The only guys I wanted to be close to were the ones currently thanking the audience and telling them they'd be back at the merch booth in ten minutes. I didn't have time to think about it though, because Ace was racing off stage.

He whooped and grabbed me up in his arms, throwing me in the air.

"Ace!" I gasped, but he caught me easily, his muscles flexing around my waist.

"Holy shit, did you see us?" he asked. "Did you, Darcy? You did, cause you were supposed to be in the van, but you stuck around. Eli's so pissed, but who cares, did you see us? They loved us." He talked a mile-a-minute and I laughed.

"Put me down." Kicking my legs, I wriggled. "Seriously, Ace."

"But holy shit, holy shit, it was amazing, it's never been so good, not ever."

"Shut up, Wesley," Cash drawled as he came off stage. Ace dropped me on my feet and glared at Cash.

"Don't call me that."

"Why, that's your name," he said with a hitch of his shoulder. I looked between the two guys and ventured the question,

"Seriously? Your name is *Wesley*?"

Ace's cheeks went pink.

"Why do you think I go by 'Ace'?" he growled.

"We said *shut up Wesley* one too many times to him, and now he's sensitive about it," Cash explained with a snort.

"You guys are rude," I replied, and tucked my arm into Ace's. "C'mon Ace. Let's go to the merch booth and find all the girls who totally prefer bassists to crappy drummers."

Ace grinned down at me, and tweaked my nose.

"You're my favorite manager," he said.

"I'm your only manager."

"Details." He waved his hand, as Cash watched us.

"So, no unwanted side effects?" Cash asked, and I felt my face grow a little hot under his scrutiny.

"Nope," I said, because the little tremble of heat between my thighs wasn't exactly unwanted. He didn't need to know that though. Cash paused and then,

"Good," he said. "Mind if I join you at the merch booth, Wesley?"

"I do if you keep calling me that," Ace said through gritted teeth.

"Don't be a rude jerk," I interrupted their fight.

"Who's a rude jerk?" Charlie came up, slipping his hand around my other arm. I didn't shrug him off, and instead revelled in being close to both men.

"Cash," Ace answered for me.

"What about Cash?" Finn asked, trailing Eli, joined our group just off stage.

"Ugh, it's nothing," I said. "C'mon, I have to get you guys to the merch table. We want those t-shirts to sell." I also wanted to get out of there before Eli could corner me and ask me what the hell I was thinking. Getting him out in front of the public again would prevent that.

I was right.

As soon as I brought them out onto the venue floor behind the mech booth, there was a flood of girls and guys waiting for them, with records in hand, and t-shirts, waiting for them to be signed. I held back against the wall and watched, skimming the crowd for a moment *just in case*. Nobody looked out of place. There was not a single audience member that looked suspicious to me. Tension leaked out of body; tension I didn't realize I'd been holding onto. Would every show be like this? Me, getting caught up in the music and then panicking that I hadn't done my part in keeping the guys safe from a potential hunter, or hunters? I relaxed slowly, and let the feeling of buzzy satisfaction bubble away inside my stomach.

They'd done amazing that night, and I was so proud. *This is what being part of a real family is like.* Before I'd left home, Willa pulled me aside and gave me a long talk, girl-to-girl about the realities of the road in the conference room at XOhX.

"No matter how much you try to stay removed, they're gonna be your family by the time you get back, Darcy. You guys are going to fight, and make-up, and go through the most

amazing, tough, incredible time, more intense than you've ever been through. But if you get through it you'll be a family."

She hadn't known it then, but I was pretty sure she was about to be right in the deepest, most intimately possible way. When Finn looked back at me over his shoulder, and gave me a wink that went right to the soft spot down between my legs, I knew she'd been right. Whatever was happening between us all was creeping up on me, the tension winding around me and inside me, and soon it was going to snap.

I just had to be able to handle it when it did.

SEVENTEEN

Load-out was sometime after 1 AM. I leaned against the side of the van and tried to hide the yawns which were threatening to crack my jaw right off.

"Tired?' Finn asked, his voice hoarse as he ambled up to me.

"Mmm, yeah," I said, hiding another yawn behind one hand.

"We've got a three hour drive tonight," Eli called from the back of the trailer where he was passing gear up to Cash.

"Fuck that," Charlie said, crossing over to us from the loading-bay doors. "Darce, I got our cash-out and sheets here." Finn tucked himself in next to me beside the van as Charlie held out a plastic accordion folder for me. "Sorry, they forgot we had a real manager now."

"It's okay," I said with a shrug. "Willa said she let the next venue know that I'm the one they're reporting to, not you." Charlie shoved his hands in his pockets.

"What am I going to do with all my free time now that I'm

not handling the excruciating, day-to-day details?" he asked the sky, looking upward. Finn nudged me and when I glanced at him he grinned at me with a wink. I knew that wink by now. That wink meant trouble, but luckily not for me.

"Maybe work on your fretting," he offered. "You totally screwed the bridge in *Dirty Secret*." I felt Finn's hand slip behind the small of my back, and curve around my waist. Charlie made an annoyed noise.

"I fucked up the bridge? Who forgot the words to the last chorus in *Hopeless Beautiful*?"

"Ah, yeah, that was my bad," Finn admitted with a shrug. "I was distracted. Someone was hiding backstage, and her scent was all over the place, driving me crazy."

"Oh come on," I said, giving him a shove. He laughed and stepped away as Charlie eyed us both. "You're not seriously blaming *me*."

"Can't help it if you're a distraction, Llewellyn." Finn went to grab me, and I stumbled back with a yelp.

"You guys are irritating." Charlie crossed his arms over his chest, although the expression on his face wasn't one of annoyance. Finn paused in trying to catch me and looked hard at his band-mate and pack-mate.

"Irritating? Seeing something you're jealous of there, Gage?"

"Ha," Charlie scoffed and turned on his heel. "It's hard to be jealous of someone who hasn't even made it to first base. Talk to me when you actually make a move." He walked off with a snicker, to help Ace as the younger wolf crossed the long swath of loading-bay with three instrument cases.

"Asshole." Finn watched Charlie go. "It's not like he's doing anything either..." he trailed off when he saw me looking at him. "Sorry. I guess we talk about you like you're not here, sometimes." It was impossible to stay mad at Finn. Between his baby-blues begging forgiveness, or the slight sheen of a blond stubble along his jaws, I was gone.

"Try all the time." Charlie had been right though. Finn hadn't made much of any kind of move, although we both knew where things were going, and I had a feeling the rest of the guys were waiting on Finn to take the first step before *they* threw their hats in the ring. That thought was terrifying and electrifying all at once. Was I seriously thinking about all of them? And me? Together? I'd moved so far past the realm of 'appropriate contact with werewolves' that I couldn't even see the line anymore. I was tired of second-guessing myself.

"I'm really so—"

I never would find out what Finn was 'really so' about. I lifted myself up on my toes, and gripped the front of his shirt gently, before pressing a slow, soft kiss to his lips. Finn went still against me, his breath stopping, as if he worried if he moved that I'd bolt. When another moment passed and I was still there, his arms came around me and he turned us.

My back hit the side of the van, the cold metal leaching heat through my clothes. But the front of me was warm, so warm, as his lips slid over mine and he groaned, deep in his chest.

I heard the soft whistle and a smattering of clapping, but I ignored it in favor for letting myself get lost in the slow heat of Finn's kisses. He pulled away with a ragged breath, caging me against the van between his arms, blocking me from turning my head to look for any of the other guys, as if I'd want to. Their low murmurs were carrying over to us, but I knew deep down they were just giving us time to be, to explore this small thing that was blossoming. There was a frantic energy among them, like Finn had to be the first one to cross the threshold, tentative and unsure. They'd been through so much... it made my heart ache for them.

"You're killing me," he whispered, his thumb coming up to smooth over my lower lip. "I never know what's going on in your head."

"Good." I gave him a cheeky little smile that melted when his brow furrowed. "No, no," I said gently. "I was just teasing." His eyes darkened, and his expression shifted.

"Oh you think that's funny?" He crowded me closer against the van, until I almost couldn't breathe, trapped between metal and two hundred-something pounds of muscle and sexy determination. "You like teasing, Darcy?" His thumb trailed over my lower lip again and dragged down over my jaw, to the soft hollow at the base of my throat. "You're gonna get what you give, sweetheart. I can tease too, and I promise you, you don't wanna play that kinda game with someone like me."

My eyes searched his face as his thumb tucked under the neckline of my shirt, pulling it down. The lace edge of my bra showed, and his breath hitched.

"What if I like to live dangerously?" This was it. I was standing on the edge of who I'd been: a care-free mundane with a past she was leaving behind. The next moment was going to push me into a new world, a new path, that I could never come back from.

The only problem was that I didn't care. Before she'd passed, my grandmother, another lightning witch like me had pulled me aside and told me to always trust the feeling inside of me. *"That's the source of your powers, Darcy, no don't shake your head at me, girl. You may be no good at casting now, but I promise that one day, the lightning will come, and if you've learnt to listen to your heart, you'll be able to call on it and control it. The fates wouldn't have you any other way than how you are now, your silly mother and father be damned."*

"Is that what you think?" Finn's hips rolled into mine and I gasped. I could feel the hard length of his cock, firm, against my belly through our clothes. "You think you like danger?"

"Uh huh." I struggled to keep it together when he rocked his hips again, a smirk sprawling across his lips.

"I think you don't even know what you like," he said. His head bent down and he pressed a kiss to the side of my neck. My eyes fluttered shut and I clung to him. "How many guys have done this to you? You shiver every time I come close, and I think it's 'cause you're not as sure about what comes next as you'd like to pretend."

Bang!

The metal underneath me vibrated as someone slammed the two back doors on the van shut. I peeked over the top edge of Finn's arm and saw Eli standing there.

"Get off her," he growled. "Are you a fucking idiot?"

I felt Finn tense, and he shifted his weight, forcing his hips in tighter against me. The guys were silent, Ace, Cash, and Charlie filtering around us as if I wasn't being pinned up against the van and the two twins weren't showing down.

"Don't tell me you're gonna make me stop *now*. You know this has been simmering for weeks. This isn't stopping—"

"Shut up and listen." Eli marched over to us and grabbed Finn by the shoulder, pushing him away from me. Cold air rushed against my front.

"Hey," I snapped. Eli looked over his shoulder at me. "Stop talking about me like I'm not here. Seriously, I'm sick of it."

Eli made a frustrated noise.

"That's not—"

"Yes it is. You keep talking around me like I'm invisible, or like I can't hear you." I shoved my hand against his chest, pressing in close and getting between him and Finn. I felt a hand ghost down my back, and for a moment it was like I was being sandwiched up between the two of them. A shudder of heat ran down my spine and coiled at the base of it, humming through my blood. *Not now,* I ordered my rebellious body.

Eli's lips parted, and his pupils dilated. He looked like he was *inhaling*... he pulled away abruptly.

"Get in the van," he ordered us both, and without another word or explanation, he stalked around the van to the driver's side. I gave Finn a look and I could tell that he was trying not to laugh.

"Uh," he said, dropping his voice down, "don't feel bad. It's not you. I mean, it's you, but not what you think. It's just that, please don't get mad, seriously, cause normally we don't tell girls this cause they freak out if you even hint that they smell."

"Do I smell?" I hissed, not wanting to do an under-arm check in front of him but suddenly feeling very self-conscious.

"Not in the way you're thinking. C'mon, get in." He helped me into the van. Charlie and Ace were sitting in the middle seats, courteously leaving the back bench for me and Finn. I could hear Cash up front, murmuring to Eli, low and quiet.

I tucked away the plastic accordion folder with our night's cash-out. Somehow I'd managed to hang onto it even through everything that had happened, and figured that was an additional point towards me as a competent band manager. Never mind that I was quickly starting to fall for my 'clients'.

"We're gonna need to stop at a bank to do a deposit drop," I said to the back of Eli's head. He stiffened but nodded. I fell into my seat with a sigh, Finn settling in next to me. My stomach shivered as we pulled out of the loading-bay lot. Would every roll out effect me the same way? Everything about tour was exciting and new.

"Every person has a unique scent. And that changes, depending on how they're feeling," Finn explained with a shit-eating grin on his face. "You, well. Heh."

"Oh god," I whispered and covered my face with my hands. "No. No, no."

"It's not bad." Finn's arm snuck around my shoulders. "It's very... it's sweet."

I peeked out at him from between fingers.

"Really?"

"Yes, really, what, no-one's ever told you that before? I mean no human or witch has the senses like we've got, but still." His fingers teased along my arm, sending little tremors of electricity. Eli's interruption hadn't changed the rising feeling inside me, the tight feeling that I wanted to desperately snap.

"No, no one's ever told me I smell good when I'm turned on. I've not really..." I turned my face away, hiding a flush. Sure, I'd had a boyfriend, it was almost expected I'd have one, especially as a child of a council family. It was almost demanded that we marry within our rank, to another council family offspring, or someone well-heeled and well positioned enough. My boyfriend at the time, Creston, had always *wanted* more from me than the few heated kisses we'd shared, but I'd known I wasn't ready. Maybe my sister was an easy pushover, and cause she'd married his older brother, Creston thought I'd be as easy to push around too, but the harder he'd pressed the issue the more I'd shut down.

"Really?" I felt Finn's eyebrows raise more than saw them. I didn't have to look, I could hear the skepticism in his voice. "Like you're all, pure, untouched, virginal? Really?"

"Is that so hard to believe?" I asked finally getting exasperated enough to look up at him. He shook his head.

"Nah, you've been resisting me plenty hard," he said. "I was surprised, that's all. You're not exactly a prude but—you know it doesn't matter right? Not to me, not to any of us."

My cheeks were burning hard. This was not a line of conversation I was ready for, although if I couldn't handle talking about it, how was I going to handle it when we finally had a quiet, uninterrupted moment and things went beyond a few kisses? I knew that's where we were going to end up, and I wanted it, so badly I ached.

"I guess my sister scared me shitless when she told me how bad her first time was," I admitted. "So when my boyfriend at the time wanted to have sex, I wasn't uh, that excited about it."

Finn pressed his lips together, looking less than impressed.

"It doesn't have to be bad," he said, and he nuzzled the top of my head in a move so affectionate, it made me wish I could crawl into his lap. "It doesn't have to hurt. Not always, not every girl anyway."

"Done a lot despoiling of virgins?" I asked. He chuckled.

"A few. It happens when you've lived for over half a century," he said his word slowly, and he must've been expecting me to react badly to the fact he wasn't some sort of vestal virgin.

"Mmm," I said, closing my eyes and resting myself against his shoulder. "Well, at least I know I'm in good hands." I felt him tense under me, but honestly, even if he wasn't a long-lived werewolf, he was in a band. And band guys slept around. A lot. It didn't bother me.

After a long moment, Finn murmured into the top of my head,

"I'm gonna show you, real soon, what kinda hands you're in."

EIGHTEEN

I slept forever it felt like, and barely noticed when someone moved me gently, tucking me under a blanket after the tour van stopped moving. There were soft whispers in the night, low murmurs, the guys talking. All of the noise was at the edge of my dreams.

I woke up to warmth of sunlight splashing across my body, the smell of coffee, and the scent of the grass beyond it. A cool breeze filtered in, bringing the fresh air and rousing me. Sitting up, I noticed the side door to the van was open,,and Charlie sat in the driver's seat, his feet up on the dash, reading on his phone and drinking a coffee. The van was empty other than that.

"What?" I asked as I knelt and stared out the windows. We were parked at the edge of a lakeside beach, the sand reaching down pale and pebbled fingers to the water. A long line of darker sand marked where the tide lapped as it rolled in.

"The others are washing off," Charlie said, pointing down at the body of water we'd camped by. It was a largish pond, more of a lake. I saw them then, four heads, all wet, their hair plastered down against their skin. Eli stood up in the water, droplets cascading down his back. He shook his head, blond hair sending off a mist of water and fluffing up, messy and disheveled. Finn, beside him, laughed and tackled him. They went down with a splash.

"Don't tell me you guys wash off in lakes and streams, like some kind of raw mountain-men," I drawled. Charlie raised his cup of coffee to me, not looking away from his phone.

"You can take the wolf away from a heartstone, but you can't take the—" He paused. "Never mind, that doesn't make sense. Ignore me. You sleep okay?" He moved back to me, sitting on one of the middle captain chairs. He reached out, tousling my hair. His fingers lingered for a moment. "We were worried the music would do stuff to you again."

"No, I was okay. I mean, I felt, well, something, but not like the house party."

He looked relieved at my answer.

"I'd have thought that guys would be really into something that made chicks desperately want them," I said, and immediately regretted it. Charlie scowled as he put down his coffee. His glare was a terrifying expression on his normally cheerful face. But when he spoke, I knew he wasn't mad at me. He leaned forward toward me.

"Any guy who takes advantage like that is a dog, and I don't mean like us," he growled. "When I take you, Darcy, and I'm gonna because this thing we've all got going on, it's happening, whether any of us want it to stop or not. When I take you? You're going to want me, every inch of me, because I've gotten you so riled up you can't stand it. Riled up the normal way, with my lips, my tongue, my teeth. My hands all over you until you're begging for some relief. Got it?"

I couldn't breathe. Not because the images his words had conjured up were too much for me to handle, but because I was hungry, my body was hungry, for more.

"I—"

"Yeah, you. I'm being polite, letting Finn ease you in because he's no slouch in the sack, and he'll be good for you, gentle even, but when you want playful, you want rough? Charlie Gage'll set you right, and make sure you know the meaning of good, old fashioned, American fun. Plus, I think you're still shit-scared of what being with all of us means."

"No, I'm not," I said. He raised his eyebrows, skeptical.

"Uh huh." He grabbed his coffee and took a long sip.

"Really, I'm not."

"I'll believe it when I see it," he said. I stood up and took the two steps over to him, plunking myself down in his lap. This close, I noticed his brown eyes had gold flecks in them, and he hadn't shaved that morning, the dark line of shadow rolling along his upper lip and winging along his jaw.

I leaned in and kissed him. His arm was around me in an instant, and I could feel the cool outline of his phone on my hip. I couldn't help the smile that curved against his mouth, he had a serious technology addiction. He groaned into my lips, pulling me tight into his chest.

"I'm not convinced," he breathed the words out hard.

"Need more proof. Scientific, empirical evidence." He kissed me back, his coffee disappearing and his hand splaying wide against the back of my neck. When my fingers braced against his chest, and my nails scraped down to where I could feel his nipples were hard under his shirt, he dropped his phone. Excitement thrilled through me, and I felt powerful, for the first time in maybe ever.

Sure, maybe they were without their heartstone now, and not as strong as they had been when they'd had it, but they were still werewolves. Charlie was strong; I could feel the wiry thick muscles under my fingernails as I scratched at him, and I was controlling him, making him want me so bad he couldn't think.

We parted, breathing heavily. He stared at me, blinking hard.

"I'm a good man," he insisted. "Finn's first. You can't take us all at once, it'd be too much; it'd overwhelm you."

"You guys keep making decisions for me, and I'm gonna walk," I threatened although I didn't mean it.

"Bullshit. You're wrapped up in us, Darce, you own us. We're yours right back. You know it in your heart." He leaned in close, inhaling me deep, his nose sliding along my neck to my ear. His teeth grazed my earlobe and a whimper escaped my lips. "You've changed, it didn't take long, but your scent changed too. You smell like us, like pack." I gasped when he bit, softly at first, then a little harder. It hurt for a moment, and I whined. He let go and kissed and licked at my ear until I was shaking in his arms.

"This can't last, us, this is—it's wrong, not allowed," I said, but my protests were hollow.

"Then walk," Charlie said, sitting back, his arms loose around his waist. "Go. I won't stop you. Call up your family, have them come get you. You keep fighting this, acting like you're not ours, and we're not yours, but you made up your mind when you came on this tour. You chose to save us, Darcy, and in doing so you stitched our fates together."

His words dropped into my mind like stones in a still pond, sending ripples and movement everywhere. I stared at him, and lifted my fingers to my lips. The skin was swollen from his kisses.

"I know," I whispered. "I know. I just didn't want to say it."

"You're scared to get attached," he said, holding me close. "I get it. You lost your family, you don't talk about it, but I see it in your face. I think the only person you've probably opened up to since you left home was Max, right? Kept yourself locked away in isolation so no one could ever hurt you again. What did they do?"

I shook my head. That life was done, and gone. I'd shut the door on it.

"Darcy, baby, you're gonna have to tell me eventually. Or Finn, or Ace, he's hard to say no to. Fucker always gets the last piece of gum because he gives me those damn puppy eyes." Charlie's words startled a laugh out of me, that was edged with tears. I wiped at my eyes, my heart not able to handle the back and forth of being turned on to melting into tears. He was right. I hadn't loved anyone other than Max, and she was different. She was safe. A mundane with a boyfriend, and a normal dad, and a normal life, she'd been safe for me to befriend and entrust. But the guys? It was terrifying loving them, but it was happening whether I wanted it to or not.

And I wanted it to.

Charlie looked at me expectantly.

"I don't want to talk about it," I said. "I'm good, really. It's fine."

"That's crap, but I haven't had enough coffee to argue with you," Charlie replied, but he cradled me against his chest. I tucked my head against his shoulder and sighed, letting his warmth sink into me. I'd noticed the guys all seemed to run hot, hotter than humans normally did. "You gonna trust me someday, kid?"

"Stop calling me kid and I might. It's weird."

Under my ear, I could hear Charlie chuckle.

"Alright, babe, I'll banish it from my vocab."

My eyes sank shut as a breeze wafted into the van and played with some of the hair around my face. We sat there for a long time, Charlie taking slow sips of his coffee, his hand crawling up and down my back.

"My boyfriend was a guy named Creston Hailward, his family is on the council," I said after the sun had moved a good few inches down my legs. Charlie made a soft, soothing noise, and his hand cupped the back of my head. "It's the usual kind of story. A guy doesn't understand what no means, or if he understands he just doesn't listen—"

Charlie stiffened.

"He didn't?"

"No, I fried his balls," I said, trying not to smile. That part of the memory was a proud one at least. He'd pushed and argued with me, telling me I'd owed him a good orgasm since I hadn't let him touch me anywhere under my clothes the whole time we'd been dating. It wasn't that I didn't want him, because Creston had been the hottest guy I knew, but more that I wasn't ready yet. Something had been holding me back. Now I knew that it was because I hadn't loved him, not really. How I'd felt for him was like a candle compared to a volcano when I placed my feelings for him next to how much I cared for and wanted the guys.

"You fried his balls. Huh. Remind me never to piss you off. I'm kinda glad you're with us, if we run into any trouble. Hunters'd think twice about taking on a witch." He shook his head. I bit my lip. It wasn't like I could actually take on a human being armed with a weapon who wanted to kill someone. But he didn't need to know that, especially if me being a witch gave him comfort. I imagined the snide look on my father's face if he'd heard Charlie. My father would have laughed and said something like *She's no good for anything to do with magic.* I brushed the thought away.

"Yeah. I let him think he was getting a handy, and then gripped the jewels and—well, his family was pretty pissed. Called it assault. They're on the council like I said, like my family is." Charlie shifted under me as I talked, and I could tell he wanted to say something but he kept quiet.

"They wanted me stripped of my power," I said quietly, "although joke was on them, I might as well have been already."

"What?" Charlie sat up a little. "What does that mean?"

"Well, if you're bad, like really bad, they, the council, they can do something, I'm not sure what, but it drains all the power out of you. You're left a husk. Like a mundane, except you know what it was like to be filled with energy, your powers. I've never seen it done, but I heard it drives witches crazy." I shivered at the memory of wondering if they'd actually do that to me. The dread stole over me for a moment until I shook it away. That moment, and my family, were in the past.

"That seems like a pretty stiff punishment."

"He had pretty bad burns, I guess."

"Still," Charlie's chest bounced for a moment, chuckling. "Shit, I bet his face was something else. But what did you mean, you might as well?"

"I'm not very good at spells," I admitted after a moment and pulled back from him to give him a brief smile. "Like, as in terrible. I can't cast them."

Charlie frowned.

"At all?"

"Not even the littlest. I'd call myself a bad witch, but everyone would think I meant as in as in badly behaved, but no. I'm just really terrible at magic. I can't do it. The most I can do is, you know, command with my voice a little bit, or spark somebody if they scare me or I really want it bad."

Charlie was looking at me as if I was crazy, and I saw a flicker of what looked like disappointment in his eyes. It was gone in an instant, I thought I must have imagined it.

"Well. That's that then," he said, looking past me. "We

should get on the road. We've got another five hours of driving before we hit the venue." He gave me a gentle push and I got up, surprised at how quickly he shut the door on our conversation. Then I saw Eli and the rest of the guys making their way up the sandy bank toward us.

It was sweet that Charlie had wanted to stop talking about what had happened between me and Creston, at least before the rest of the band got back to us.

I got out of the van to stretch my legs, and Finn swaggered up to me, enveloping me in a huge, wet hug as I shrieked.

He kissed me, his lips tasting of fresh-water and his own, subtle flavor underneath it.

"I dreamt of you," he said when we parted. The weight of the other guys' eyes were on me, but this moment was for me and Finn.

"Yeah?" I asked, my heart squeezing hard. "Good dreams?" He gave a dirty little chuckle.

"The best," he said, and bent down to nip at my ear. "You smell like Charlie."

"Sorry," I moaned.

"It's good. One day you'll smell like all of us, and you'll be home."

I felt my cheeks flush at that thought. Home. I looked over at the van where Ace was rifling through his backpack, and Cash watched us with a smothered longing in his eyes. Eli and Charlie were on the other side of the van; I could just see them through the windows.

"That sounds really good," I whispered.

NINETEEN

Being on the road suited me. There was an energy that hummed up through the tires on the highway, and I found myself scribbling in a journal for the first time ever. Max had made me take one, telling me that I'd want the memories from my first major career move.

She was probably right. We'd been texting back and forth, although she was definitely more subdued than normal. I missed the old Max, my Max, but felt selfish because I knew her heart was breaking when mine was blossoming.

Finn stayed in the back of the van with me, even when Charlie grabbed a guitar in the front and strummed to new tunes. I could feel that Finn wanted to sing, write lyrics, do something, but he felt bad about leaving my side.

"You're acting kinda broody," I said as we pulled into another venue a few days later.

"I'm not grumpy," he protested. I snickered.

"No, like, broody as in brooding. Like you're a chicken and I'm an egg you're trying to hatch."

The look on his face was priceless, half offended, half grouchy.

"It's true," Ace said as he ducked out of the van when we rolled to the stop. "You stare at her like a love-sick puppy."

Finn made a sputtering noise and glowered down at me. He ducked to whisper in my ear, pinning me against the inside wall of the van.

"I'm going to show you brooding later," he promised. A shiver of heat in me answered his words, and he smirked, pulling away.

Charlie made a soft clucking sound from the front and Finn gave him the finger. I caught my breath and pushed past him.

"Work now, fun later."

WE WERE FALLING INTO A ROUTINE. The guys would unload while I'd go check-in with the venue manager. We were still getting dicked around on our soundcheck at every venue. I'd tried bringing it up with Jake Tupper (and I didn't tell the guys I'd talked to Jake alone. They hated him but kept it together for the sake of the tour), but he'd only talked down to my breasts about how Phoenixcry had better be grateful to get any soundcheck time at all instead of just a line check.

Except half the time, all we got was a line-check, where the sound crew let the guys do a quick plug-in and strum before bringing up the house lights and letting the audience into the room. The guys barely had time to get backstage before the low rumble of the crowd swelled inside the venue. Frustrated, but with nothing that I could do about it, I spent time snapping pictures of everything and loading it up on the social media.

Doing great kid, keep it up. Gonna make a photog of you yet, Chrissy texted me one night, after I got a clear image of the crowd bracketed by Finn's denim-clad legs as he wailed through the ending of their finale, a haze of fog drifting through the air. The guys were happy with my work, and I never told them the real, secret reason to my dedication over documenting the tour: if a hunter showed up, and tried to attack the band, I'd have a better chance of IDing them after if I had pictures of the audience. Photos of kids, teens, and college students like me filled up my phone night after night. When I couldn't sleep sometimes, I'd scroll through the photos, trying to find faces that showed up more than once. Nothing stood out, and I'd often fall asleep with my phone still in my hand.

Every day was melting into the next, and even though the scenery was changing around us as the north faded into the south, time seemed to stand still. The only way I knew that we were moving forward at all was how many days Instagram said it had been since the first tour picture of Finn's arm wrapped around me. Things were heating up between us, and I kept flicking my phone open and scrolling to that picture, feeling the butterflies fluttering around in my stomach at the sight of it. Everything had changed since then.

"You're obsessing," Charlie said to me outside a rest stop in Arizona.

"What?"

"You're staring at that picture. Why not go for the real thing?" His eyes shifted off me and over to where Finn was drenching his head with water from a spigot at the rest stop. He and Eli had been bickering all morning and they'd gone on a run to 'work off their frustrations' which was wolf-boy code for go somewhere private and punch each other until they got over whatever the hell they were mad at each other about. It wasn't the first time, and it wasn't the last.

"Do you guys smell like wet dog when you do that?" I asked, motioning to Finn with the hand that held my phone. Charlie spat out a mouthful of coffee and laughed.

"Bitch," he said affectionately. He'd picked up the habit from me when I'd called Max a few times and he heard how we talked to each other. It didn't offend me, but still I was trying to train him out of that habit.

"No no, you don't get to use that word unless?"

"Unless I have a magic lady-cave and monthly bleeding," he said with a roll of his eyes. "Yeah, I know, I'm sorry."

"You should be." I watched as Finn loped over to us from across the parking lot. "Especially cause I think he heard you."

"Charlie," Finn snarled, reaching us in a few strides. In the next moment I was grateful we were the only people at the rest stop in the remote reaches of Arizona. Finn grabbed Charlie by the shirt and hauled him up on his toes, squaring his shoulders and bearing down on the shorter man. "The fuck you think you're doing, talking to her like that."

"Easy, easy," Charlie said as he held up one hand, the other going to the fist that was holding him half off the ground. "It's a joke. C'mon Darce, tell him."

"Finn." He looked over at me and I gave him a small smile. He swallowed, and let Charlie go, immediately walking over to me. "You okay?" he asked me. His hand came up to cradle the side of my face and I had to close my eyes for a moment. His closeness was perfect.

"I should be asking you the same thing. You know Charlie likes to dick around," I whispered.

"Don't like it." Finn pressed his forehead into mine, a thing I'd gotten used to. I wondered if it was some sort of wolfy habit, or it was just Finn being Finn.

"I'm okay, big guy," I promised. "I'm a tough cookie. I can hold my own against someone like Charlie. He doesn't even phase me."

"Hey," Charlie protested. Finn ignored him and kissed me, his arms encircling me. I kissed him back, slicking my tongue over his lower lip until he growled and his grip on me became possessive and hungry. I heard Charlie's footsteps walk away, giving us a moment. He'd hover, probably, they all seemed to do that when Finn and I got close like this. A hum of need buzzed in my stomach and when Finn pulled away, I moaned in protest.

"Don't," Finn warned, his eyes glittering with heat. "You make that noise, I can't be responsible for what happens next." His threat made me want to test his restraint, because it was going on weeks now that the sexual tension had been burning between us, and the peripheral heat from the other guys was weighing down on me. It was like me and Finn were circling each other, waiting for the other one to flinch, neither of us quite willing to be vulnerable, not yet anyway.

You been takin' care of business on your own, then, girlfriend? Max had asked me when I'd explained the perpetual state of sexual anxiety and deprivation I was in.

You know it. Guys never know what to do anyway, so I learnt to provide the good times for myself. He'll probably suck.

Yeah, right. A guy like that? He knows what's down with going down. I have faith. You should have some too.

The mental image of Finn going down? That had stuck with me for days, and right then, standing in front of him and knowing that he wanted me so bad that his self control was fraying quickly, I wanted to find out if Finn Gunner actually knew what was down with going down.

I had a feeling that Max was right.

"Let's hit the road," Cash came up behind Finn, eyes on me. His body was tense, and I wondered how much it was affecting him to have us fake-out-make-out all the time. Even Ace was getting edgy, and I'd catch him curled around my sweater sometimes if I left it in the van and he got back before I did.

"Where's the captain," Finn asked, looking around for his brother. The ridiculous nickname for Eli had stuck as he guided us from one gig to the next. Of all of the guys, he seemed the least affected by my presence and the scent I had to be putting out. Charlie admitted in a quiet moment that it was nice, because I smelt like them, already, and there hadn't been a female presence, a *moderating* presence in their lives like that since Ace had been just a kid.

"Right here," Eli said, "Where's Ace?"

He got his answer in a yelp, and the sight of Ace running out from behind one of the restroom out buildings at top speed.

"Go go go go go go!" Ace yelled at us, sprinting full tilt. In a split second my guys, my indie rockers, turned into alert predators. Finn crashed into me, wrapping me up in his arms and shoved me into the van. Charlie and Cash piled in after us, and Eli dove into the driver's seat. I couldn't see anything as Finn covered my body with his. Fear thudded in my chest as the van doors slammed, and panting, Ace climbed into the front seat.

The tires squealed, and I smacked my head as we took off out of the parking lot and hit a bump.

"Ow, shi—"" I cursed as a bright split of pain erupted along one of my temples. The copper-scent of blood filled the air. Finn and Cash growled at almost identical times, and Finn pulled off of me.

"What the hell was that?" Eli asked Ace, voice low as I sat up. Finn inspected my head.

"It's cut," he said to me. "Charlie, get the first aid kit." His face swam in front of me and I felt nauseous for one moment, my head throbbing.

"I think I'm gonna be sick." I reached out and Cash grabbed my hand.

"No, you're not, look at me, sweetheart." He brushed his fingers under my chin and lifted my face. "You got any healing magic?"

"I wish," I grumbled, his warm fingers soothing some of the ache in my skull. Cash shot me a disarming smile, and crept up closer. He wrapped me in his arms, holding me steady as we pulled onto the highway.

"Are you kidding me?!" Eli's astonished tone made us all look to the front. I felt the drip of blood as it slid down the side of my face. Ace turned back to glance at me, guilt on his face.

"Uh."

"You wanna tell them what you scared the shit out of us for?"

"Not really."

"Ace," Eli growled. Ace threw up his hands.

"Okay, okay, geez, sorry. It was a rattlesnake. Uh, I'm sorry." He glanced at me again, and bit his lip. "Really sorry. She gonna be okay?"

I rested against Cash's chest, trying to slow my breathing to help with the pain.

"She's gonna be fine," I said, my voice doing funny things, drawing out real slow.

"Sweetheart?" Cash's voice broke through the lines criss-crossing my vision.

"I'm fine," I said, or I'm pretty sure I said. I blacked out after that, so I don't really know.

"MISS LLEWELLYN. MISS LLEWELLYN. *DARCY*!"

The dark parted and Eli was looming over me, his crystal-blue eyes narrowed, two fingers on the pulse in my neck. His skin was rough, working-rough, probably from playing guitar and loading equipment in and out of venues all the time. I shuddered in response to his touch and closed my eyes again.

"I wanna sleep," I said, because sleep sounded like the absolute best thing in the world right then. Better than ice-cream. Better than sleeping in and bacon in bed and chicken n' waffles. Better than I thought Finn would be when we both finally gave up keeping away from each other. I bit my lip just thinking about it, his heavy heat covering me as he pressed me down, down, down

Eli snapped his fingers and my eyes popped open from where they'd flagged shut.

"Stay with me," he said. "You'll be fine, you just need a few minutes, and you're definitely not going to sleep." Beyond him, Cash and Finn hovered. I could hear Charlie talking to Ace, but their words were blurry and I didn't care about them right then.

"How do you know?" I asked, my words belligerent and sloppy. Sleep sounded so amazing. "You a doctor or something?" Eli's face split into a brief, shadowed grin.

"More like I have practical experience."

"He patched more than a few guys up in the field," Cash offered.

"Oh no, you guys are not doing that old war-dogs story-time shit," Charlie called. "Just cause some of us never were possessed with a sense of self-sacrifice to serve our country doesn't mean you can rub it in that you were."

Finn and Eli exchanged twin smirks, and I had a feeling, sleepy and swimmy as my mind was, that this was some sort of bone of contention and if not right then, sometime soon, Charlie was going to get his ass hard-core trolled.

"You're so serious," I said to Eli, reaching up to pet his face. "'Cept when you and Finn decide pranks are a good idea."

"I don't know what you're talking about," Eli said solemnly, but he took my petting and didn't avoid my hand on his cheek when Finn snickered.

"She's on to you, brother," Finn taunted.

"Alright, she's fine, just can't sleep. Ace, no more freaking out over rattlesnakes," Eli ordered.

"Aw, but, I didn't mean to."

"It's okay Ace, " I reassured him as I rolled over on my side to be able to see him properly. His eyebrows looked like they were permanently fused together in an expression of worry. He got down on his knees.

"I feel like an ass."

"You kinda are but you're our ass. Help me up?"

Ace gave me his hand and Eli slid his arm under my back, helping me to sit up.

"How big's the cut?" I asked, reaching for the side of my face. Eli tapped my hand gently.

"No," he scolded me, sounding completely mother-hen and

not at all like his normal scowly, rumbling self. "It's just a small cut, but head-wounds bleed a lot. You'll be fine, just take it easy."

"I'm gonna take on manager duties tonight," Charlie said. The guys moved back to their seats, Finn helping me into mine.

"I can do up my own seatbelt," I told him as he tried to do it for me, and he gave me such a look that I let him, rolling my eyes. The throbbing in my head was still there, and I wanted drugs. "I can do tonight, Charlie, you don't have to. Does that first aid kit have any painkillers?"

A bottle of water and two pills appeared as if by werewolf magic, and I swallowed them down. I closed my eyes.

"Don't sleep," Finn muttered to me.

"Not sleeping, just hurts to keep my eyes open," I said softly. A weird feeling of homesickness enveloped me. My mom may never have been the greatest when it came to comforting her one daughter who should've been a boy and couldn't even cast a basic magic spell, but the times I got sick she was always there with a cool cloth for my forehead and a story. My throat got tight and my eyes damp. I kept them shut, not wanting to let any tears leak out. Finn nuzzled the top of my head, and a soft, subtle rumbling sound started up. I froze and looked up at him, the light hurting my eyes. "Is that you?" I asked. A flush of color rose in his cheeks and the rumbling stopped.

"Yeah," he said, glancing away.

"Is that a thing? Like, do werewolves, are you purring? Like a cat?"

He scowled.

"It's not like a cat."

"It's like a cat," Charlie called back to us, breaking the unwritten rule of the rest of the van pretending like they couldn't hear us talking/making-out/whatever in the back. I covered my mouth with one hand as a laugh burst out of me.

"You guys are like big cats."

"We are not like big cats," Finn glared and pulled back.

"No, come back," I said, tugging on his arm. He gave in without a thought, wrapping around me, and I settled against his chest with a sigh. "It was nice."

"Yeah?" he asked, and relaxed under me. After a few moments, the soft, deep rumbling purr in his chest started again. It was soothing, like a big cat, but better, because he was warm and also crazy sexy, and a good kisser. He chuckled.

"Did I just say that out loud?"

"I'm a good kisser, huh?"

"No kissing her until she's more awake, interim-manager's orders," Charlie interrupted again. Finn grunted and grabbed his water bottle, chucking it across the van and pelting Charlie right on the back of the head. Charlie snarled for a moment, but when he caught my eye, he softened. Whatever he saw, me curled against Finn, defused the situation immediately. Finn's hand stroked up and down my back. I sighed. Tonight was going to be interesting, and I wasn't sure how I felt about being benched.

Darcy Llewellyn
@DarcyLuvsDonuts

Follow ⌄

PSA: Guys in bands want you to love their music, not their butts. I mean, you can love their butts. But just don't touch without asking first, mmmkay?

14 Retweets 38 Likes

♡ 5   ⟲ 14   ♡ 38   ✉

Phoenixcry
@PhoenixcryMusic

Follow ⌄

@DarcyLuvsDonuts **You can touch our butts anytime, babydoll ;D** #managergirlsocute #weareokaywiththebutttouching #touchmahbutt

13 Retweets 38 Likes

♡ 13   ⟲ 13   ♡ 38   ✉

Darcy Llewellyn
@DarcyLuvsDonuts

Follow ⌄

@PhoenixcryMusic **please keep Charlie away from the Twitter account for 24 hours.** #boys #srsly

5 Retweets 14 Likes

♡ 11   ⟲ 5   ♡ 14   ✉

TWENTY

I was back to normal, mostly, when we pulled up in front of a low, purple-painted club. It was smaller than the last few venues we'd played at, but the guys piled out without remarking on it. I hadn't spent much time, if at all with Glory Revolution, but Jake was prone to fits of temper if a venue didn't live up to his standards. My guys? They were just happy to be on the road and playing. The pure joy of performing for an audience radiated out of them even when we were tired and had no clean socks. Obviously they'd seen worse than crappy dressing rooms with toilets that rocked off their bolts when you sat on them, and green room food that was basically a bag of chips and a bottle of water each.

And the guys? They ate a lot. More than the per diems would cover. I put it down to their preternatural appetites to their supernatural natures, and started stinting myself a little to pad the communal food budget, since the guys would buy groceries together and share. That was the other thing that was making me fall more for them, putting me dangerously close to that *family* thing that Willa had mentioned.

Phoenixcry stuck together. Sure, they fought, snarling at each other, and there'd been more than one night that devolved into fisticuffs (Finn wanted to go after Jake for wolf-whistling at me, Eli had warned him to leave it alone in one instance) but they took care of each other. Nobody went without, if there wasn't enough then Eli and Finn cut back, then Cash after them. The youngest got priority, and they never ate anything I had bought no matter how hungry they were. It was enough to melt my heart, a part of me I'd thought was long-frozen.

"You lost in your thoughts again?" Finn asked me as he helped me down from the tour van. The bus that Jake shared with Glory Revolution was parked right next to us. There wasn't enough room in the lot for more space, even though the guys usually preferred to stay away from Jake and his buddies. He was a dick, and his band wasn't any better. Glory Revolution were okay as far as I could tell. "Thinking about how hot I am?"

"You wish," I teased Finn and he grabbed at his chest, faking a broken heart. He really was a big goofball, like Ace, but flirtier and less panicked by rattlesnakes.

"Gunner."

Finn stiffened at the sound of Jake's familiar drawl. Jake came around the side of the van and saw me there and stopped short. His gaze went right to the bandage that was half-hidden by the fall of my hair.

"You get hurt?" Jake asked.

"Just a bump," I brushed it off. It wasn't any of his business anyway. "You guys all loaded in?" Jake ignored me though. He turned to Finn.

"She hit her head," Finn said before Jake could open his mouth. "She asked you a question."

"You know why I brought you on this tour, Gunner? You and your moody bastard of a twin brother?" Jake's snapped each word, and he squared his shoulders as if he was honestly thinking he might equal up to Finn. Jake wasn't a slouch in the muscles department, but Finn was stacked, pound on pound of hard, well-earned muscle. I knew. I watched him do pull-ups every chance he got in playgrounds when we stopped for a breather. Jake didn't have a chance.

Given the way he was eyeing up Finn, he didn't really care. I stepped in close to Finn, my hand brushing the back of his lightly to remind him how badly we needed to be on this tour, to stay safe, to grow the band, to be together.

My heart skipped a beat in my chest. We were an 'us', even if we'd never said it out loud.

Finn grabbed my hand and squeezed it and I relaxed. He had this handled. I trusted him. He'd never endanger the pack. We were safe.

Eli came out from behind the van, arms crossed over his chest as he leaned up against the side of the hood.

"Is there a problem, Tupper?" he drawled, scraping the heel of his boot over the ground. Jake's eyes flicked from Finn to Eli, then back to me.

"What's going on? Why aren't we loading in?" Cash

sounded annoyed as he emerged from inside the trailer, one drum balanced on his shoulder.

"Jake was just checking to see if we need any help loading in," I said sweetly, lifting my head to meet Jake's gaze. His eyes broke from mine and looked at where my fingers entwined with Finn's.

"This shit is heavy," Cash said, his voice barely above a whisper.

"I think we're good here, aren't we Eli?" Finn asked, his voice soft and dangerous.

"Looks good to me," Eli replied, his tone more relaxed. "Looks damn good."

Jake made a noise of frustration in the back of his throat, glared at me, and spun on his heel to stalk off, taking his bad attitude and his artfully ripped, expensive, jeans with him.

"Asshole," Finn murmured as he pulled me into him. I went without protest, curling into the cage of his arms as his fingers ran up and down my hands and wrists, as if to warm his skin.

"Yeah, well, he's the only reason we're on this tour," I said. Eli scoffed.

"There's not a lick of truth in that." He pointed at me. "You're the only reason we're on this tour."

"Cause he wants in my pants?" I asked. Finn grumbled, and held me tighter. Eli's expression softened.

"Because you said yes when we asked. We'd be nowhere, if not for you."

I couldn't help the grin that spread across my face.

"Aww, Eli, are you softening up on me?"

He rolled his eyes.

"Let's load-in, slackasses," Eli called as he rounded the back of the van. "Especially you, Cash."

"Hey, what? I've been? Oh fuck no," Cash said, but before he could set his drum case down and go after Eli, I whistled, sharp. His head jerked up and he looked at me.

"Load in," I repeated Eli's words, but with a slight touch of thunder. My head was pounding, and that somehow made it easier to call on the echoing power that was hidden away, inside of me somewhere. Cash's eyes went wide and he shivered in response, before nodding

"Yes ma'am," he said.

"That's my little manager." Finn tousled my hair. I swatted at his hand; he was going to mess up the carefully plaited braid I'd done up that morning since my curls had decided to turn wild and unmanageable.

"You guys aren't weird about me doing that?" I asked, "Like I feel guilty. I shouldn't be ordering you around."

Finn sighed and shrugged before he picked up a box of gear and started walking. I followed with my backpack that held all our paperwork.

"If he really didn't want to listen, he wouldn't. Cash likes you, too much, probably, for his own good."

"I think I'm insulted."

Finn laughed and shook his head.

"I think maybe, some of us, like Cash, enjoy being bossed around a little," Finn admitted after being quiet for a few moments. A little thrill of heat raced down my back.

"Oh really? And what about you?"

Finn shot me a look out of the corner of his eye.

"Well, sweetheart, if you have to know, you wanna boss me around, you go ahead. But don't forget that the tables are gonna turn eventually, and when they do, I've got nothing against making you beg for mercy."

I had to remember to breathe. He nudged me with his arm.

"C'mon, now who's holding up load-in?" he asked.

TWENTY-ONE

Darcy Llewellyn
@DarcyLuvsDonuts

Follow

If you're at the @PhoenixcryMusic show tonight along with the @GloryRevBand, then come say hi! I'll be at the merch booth slinging shirts! Free stickers to the first 10 people! #yay #merchgals #livemusic #newmusic

7 Retweets 20 Likes

♡ 12   ⟲ 7   ♡ 20   ✉

The merch booth was in a cramped corner of the room that night and there was only space for me behind it. I couldn't be backstage, waiting for my guys to pile off, sweaty and excited after their time on stage. The fog machine kept misting through the air, curling and swirling from an AC that was on high as the venue was prepped for three hundred kids that were about to enter it. Ginny, the merch girl for Glory Revolution was arranging the t-shirt display. A new shipment had come in earlier that day for all of us. The guys had a fresh, heathered lilac shirt that was so soft under my fingers, the band name emblazoned on it in a weathered gray. I planned on stealing one later to wear to sleep. I hadn't packed enough clothes for the tour, even with our frequent laundry stops.

"Your guys soundcheck okay?" Ginny asked as she flipped open her cash box and started counting through her float. We had a little more time for this show, and I was relieved. Doors were pushed back because the local nightlife laws were more lax in the area.

"They keep just getting line checks, and it's killing me. They're rocking it anyway, but..."

Ginny nodded.

"I feel you, I feel you so bad, girl. They're so good though. The nights you're not at the booth, like, when they're on stage? Oh my god, the girls are going nuts over them. They outsold Jake last night, but don't tell him that."

Shara, the other merch girl working Jake's stuff leaned over Ginny's shoulder.

"Do not tell him," she hissed. "He keeps asking if you guys are doing shit or what, and I've been telling him yes. He's got an ego the size of a planet."

I swallowed hard.

"Yeah," I muttered. Jake's attention on me, and his ego problem, were definitely causing me a few sleepless nights. The rest of my difficulty sleeping had to do with the fact I was sharing a van with five impossibly attractive, deadly sweet guys.

"How are you handling it in that tiny van with all that dick?" Shara asked as she pulled out a cardboard box of t-shirts and began sorting them by size. "I would have murdered at least half of them by now."

"Oh, they're really great actually. It's like the nicest road trip I've ever been on," I said despite the fact I'd never been on a road trip before. Witches spent most of their time spell casting, talking about spell casting, surveying the human world from their fancy chateaus and oversized mansions, and engaging in back-stabbing politics. They didn't do road trips. I bent down to give Shara a hand since my display was finished. Ginny shot me a smirk.

"I don't know how you keep your hands off of them, like, holy shit, the Gunner twins? So hot. I wouldn't mind a twin-sandwich with them," she said.

"You're such a slut, but I love you," Shara laughed and rolled her eyes.

"Doors!" called one of the security crew. We shoved away the last of the merch and stood as the crowds were let in. There was a high-pitched shriek, and a group of girls ran to the front of the stage, where the barrier was belly-high and they could hang onto it in case a real mosh pit broke out.

"They always do that, I swear. It's getting old," Ginny said as she took a long sip from her water bottle.

"More like you're getting old." Shara elbowed her in the side and held out her hand. "Pass that here."

"You thirsty?" I asked. "I've got a cooler under my table

with extra water bottles." Shara and Ginny exchanged a long meaningful look.

"Ours isn't—it's y'know," Shara paused and searched for her words.

"Fire-water. You want some? Makes the night go a hell of a lot faster." Ginny held out the bottle.

"Oh no, I'm good." I shook my head. Ginny narrowed her eyes at me but I didn't have to explain further when a pair of girls came up to the merch table, holding tight to their wallets. The guys weren't getting paid much per show, being an opening act meant we got the dregs of what was left over, but the merch sales were 100% ours.

"Hey guys, see anything you like?" I put on my best smile to greet them.

"Are you Darcy?" one of them asked, as her other friend giggled.

"Um, yeah, I am. Can I help you find something? We just got in these—"

"Like, Darcy-Darcy, as in Darcy who tours with Phoenixcry?" the first girl asked, eyeing me up and down.

"Yeah, that's me." I looked over at Ginny who's carefully groomed eyebrows were making graceful arches up her forehead.

"Okay," the girl said before looking at her friend and snickering. She turned back to me. "You're a slut!" she yelled, and ran off, dragging her friend. They disappeared into the thickening crowd, as I stood there, jaw dropped.

"What the hell was that?" Shara asked as Ginny took another swig from the spiked water bottle.

"Uh oh, I think I know," Ginny said, wrinkling her nose. "There's a bunch of gossip accounts on Tumblr and Twitter, spreading shit about this tour. Mainly Jake fangirls. Sorry Shara, but he's an asshole and so are his fans."

Shara sighed.

"As long as you keep supplying the booze, I can keep pretending I don't hear you."

"But what does that have to do with me and Phoenixcry?" I interrupted them, a burning acid feeling crawling up the back of my throat. Shara and Ginny exchanged another pair of looks. Ginny sighed.

"Look, you seem really sweet, so like, I'm just gonna tell it to you and then you can figure out where you go from here," Ginny said. She fished her phone out from her pocket and opened her Twitter app. She handed the phone over to me. "Scroll down."

My heart in my throat the whole time, I saw picture after picture. They were all of me, candid photos. Me unloading with the guys in the band, me hanging around backstage. Pictures from behind me as I stood there, the lights flashing around me. There was a picture of me dozing off in the green room, Finn's jacket draped over me. Then another one while I slept, closer, just a hands breadth away from my face.

And underneath, a caption.

She sleeps like an angel, never knowing how much she means to me. Soon, sleeping angel, soon.

"What the fuck," I whispered and looked up at Shara and Ginny. Shara winced.

"So like, Jake does this thing..."

"Oh you're kidding me," I said. "That's him? He's taking photos of me, while I'm sleeping?!"

"Don't freak out," Shara said, but I was the very definition of freaking out. He'd violated my privacy, taking photos of me when I had no idea, and the whole time during the tour he'd been posting them.

"Is that his official account?" I was going to get his ass blasted by Willa. At the very least, I was going to complain to her, and she'd deal with him, I knew it in my heart.

"No, it's like, a secret one, but some of his fans know about it, like the long-term ones that have been around since he was playing coffee shops," Shara said, looking guilty.

"Willa's gonna have your ass if she finds out. Chrissy is going to kill you for not telling her he's doing this, you know how protective she is over the social media strategy," I pointed out. Shara's face transformed from ashamed to annoyed.

"You're not going to run to them and tell them I knew about this the whole time," she said, stepping toward me. Ginny threw up her hand.

"Whoa. Ladies? We have a show to deal with," she said, pointing out at the crowd. "Just cause those walking wallets haven't come over here yet doesn't mean they're not going to. Shara, you should have said something, but you didn't. Neither did I. Darcy, yeah, Jake is a total freak, but at least now you know."

I gulped down painful feelings, like knives, and turned back to my merch table. They weren't my best friends by any stretch but I had liked them at least. I had trusted them, a little bit. I popped out my own phone and tapped in Jake's little secret twitter username.

There was one more photo, that I hadn't seen before, that made my heart clench and my stomach curdle.

It was a picture of me and Finn. His arm was curled around my shoulders, his eyes closed and a relaxed smile on his face.

Underneath was a single word.

Heartbroken.

TWENTY-TWO

After the show, Eli took one look at me and said we were gonna spend the next day away from towns and cities. We had two days off in a row while Glory Revolution did radio dates and a TV appearance, and Jake had to go into studio in Sacramento to record a quick demo for the label.

We were on our own for at least seventy-two hours and I couldn't have been more grateful. The rest of the night with Shara and Ginny had been painful, although I kept it to myself when the band came out after their set.

I don't know how Eli knew something was wrong, but he did know, and as soon as he noticed, so did the other guys. I didn't blame Finn, or Ace, for not seeing it first, even though I was closer to the both of them. The post-show merch table hang out and signing was always crazy, and Finn especially had to be 'on' for the new fans they'd made that night.

Watching girls cling to him, touch him, as he hugged them and laughed at their jokes, didn't do my mood any good. At first I lied to myself, pretending like I was worried that one of those underage girls was a blood-thirsty hunter. After a few minutes where not a single fifteen-year-old pulled out a knife and stabbed Finn in the chest, I had to be honest with myself. I was feeling flickers of jealousy.

Truth was, I had no right to be jealous. I knew, even if he hadn't said it, that his heart was mine. His touches had told me, his kisses had promised me. So I kept quiet, but tried to smile as we loaded out.

"Not now," I said when Ace asked me what was wrong. He frowned but nodded, not prying.

The stars were out later that night, not a single cloud in the sky. We pulled off at a local federal park, away from people. As Eli turned off the engine, the quiet seeped into the van, and nobody spoke. Then Ace sighed, and tumbled out of the front passenger seat. Charlie laughed and went after him. Cash reached over and brushed my cheek with his hand, and followed, sliding the van door shut after him.

I hear the click and rasp of Finn's seat-belt as he undid it. There was the hushed noise of moving fabric as he slid closer, and his warmth enveloped me.

"What happened?" he asked. I shrugged my shoulders helplessly. How to explain it? We'd been caught out, people, fans, knew about us being together, but it hadn't reached him yet.

"Jake." It's all there was to say, really. Eli rumbled a low growl.

"He touch you?"

"He didn't have to." I pressed my face into Finn's neck.

"I knew we should have done something about him. I fucking knew it. Eli, this tour—"

"It's worth it," I interrupted what Finn was about to say. "It doesn't matter. Jake's a creepy stalker, but it doesn't matter what he says about me, as long as you guys don't care."

"What's he saying about you?" The darkness settled all around us as the cab lights died, and I could barely make out the outline of Eli's body in the driver's seat. His shoulders were tense.

"He's been taking pictures of me, kinda surreptitiously like, and posting them on Twitter. Captioning them. He got one of me and Finn hugging, and at the show two girls came up to me and called me a slut. I don't think it's that big a deal, it was just the one incident..." I trailed off when I realized Finn was so tense that his muscles felt rock-hard against me.

"We're gonna take care of him," Finn promised. "Eli, call Willa."

"Finn, no I don't want to make a big deal out of it!" I stood up, pushing away from him. I needed space. It felt like the tour van was closing in on me.

"Sweetheart." Finn was on his feet in a second. "He's dangerous."

"I know that!" I took a deep, gulping breath. "I know that. I didn't mean to yell I'm just—" I rubbed a hand over my face. "I thought, and it was stupid, I thought that when I left my family behind, my world behind, that this kind of back-stabbing, creepy behavior would stay there."

In the dark, Finn's face pulled down into a slow, sad smile.

"Witches are people. People are fucked up. Your family, whatever happened with that, they weren't fucked up because they were witches."

"I beg to differ," I grumbled. "Please don't do anything about Jake, not yet?"

"How far does it have to go before you want us to step in?" Eli rumbled, and I turned. He'd stood as well, stretching his legs slowly. He leaned against the driver's chair. "What's your line, Darcy?" He'd dropped the honorific use of my last name and it felt weird, as if he was challenging me. Like using my first name only, he was finally addressing *me* and not just his idea of who I was.

"I don't know," I admitted. "I'll know it when he crosses it."

"Far as I'm concerned he's already crossed it," Finn said, and he reached out a hand, brushing it along my shoulder. "Sweetheart, if he hurts you, I don't—I couldn't stop myself from...=..."

"I'm going for a walk." Eli opened the door and ducked out of it. "I'm taking the guys with me." I could hear him, crunching off across the gravel road, to where Ace's laughter echoed back to us even through the closed doors of the van. Silence roared up between us once more, so quiet I could hear my own heartbeat in my ears.

"Sweetheart." Finn's hands slipped over my hips, and I looked up him. He bent down and kissed me. I met him part-way and shivered as he held me tight, his thumbs tracing over the bare skin above my waistband.

"Please, let's not talk about Jake Tupper anymore," I said when I pulled away to breathe.

"Whatever you want," Finn murmured, pulling me back in for a kiss. "You tired?"

"Not really."

His teeth glinted as he smiled.

"Good." He tugged me back toward the bench, his arms wrapping around me. I leaned up to kiss him and his teeth grazed my lower lip. His tongue flicked out, licking into my mouth, my fingers running through his hair and pulling him in close. He groaned when my nails scratched down the back of his neck and he pulled away to catch his breath, still holding me tight. "My brother's a good man."

"Why do you say that?"

"You don't think he is?" He smiled down at me and pulled away, fumbling behind the bench seat for the lever that would turn it into a bed. My belly squirmed as the mattress came down, and Finn spread a blanket down over it. I swallowed hard, but went with him when he pulled me onto it as he sat down.

"That's not what I said, I just don't know why you-*mmph*!" He kissed me silent, tongue licking up into my mouth in another second as soon as I parted my lips to moan.

"Giving us time," he whispered, breathing uneven. He groaned and pulled me tight into his side. "I want you, sweetheart, so bad. Fuck." His hand trailed over the neckline of my shirt, and cupped my breast in his fingers. A shiver rolled through me in response, and he smirked in the rising moonlight that filtered in over us. "You like that, babydoll?"

"What's with the nicknames?"

"They're sweet, like you." He nuzzled my ear and flicked his tongue over the lobe slowly. My eyes slid shut. We'd been building up to this for weeks, and now that it was happening, I was suddenly nervous.

"Finn," I whispered, uncertain. He froze and pulled back, frowning down at me.

"I'm going too fast," he said, and smoothed the back of his hand over my cheek. "I'm sorry, sweetheart. Just when it's you and me, I get carried away and I shouldn't. You okay? I'll stop."

"No. Please don't. I'm just…"

He lay down next to me, and with a sigh, rolled me up on top of him.

"Ladies first," he said, with a crook of his eyebrow. "You touch whatever you want." He rested his fingers on the small of my back, warm, reassuring. "I'll stay right here. Won't move an inch."

"That sounds like a challenge," I muttered. He chuckled, chest pushing me up and settling down.

"Maybe it is."

I sat up on him, straddling his thighs, and looked down at his body. He'd shrugged out of his denim jacket, and he was just in a soft, dark gray v-neck shirt. His jeans were rough and thick under my butt and I wriggled down. He grunted.

"Trying' to make this hard on me?"

"Trying to make it *hard*," I said, and laughed. He rolled his eyes.

"Don't bother, you don't need to try. I'm halfway there every time I look at you." His fingers were rubbing slow, small circles over my back, and I swallowed hard at his words. He needed to cut out the sexy talk, or I was going to melt right then and there.

But maybe that was his plan. I narrowed my eyes.

"You trying to get me to cave?"

He smirked and said nothing. Bastard. I leaned down slowly and kissed him, just a soft brush of my lips over his and then firmer. He sighed, but kept his word, staying still as I kissed over the stubble on his jaw, my teeth nipping sharply at his neck until he made another noise, this time a low gasp. His fingers tightened up over my back as I tugged at his shirt, trying to get it off him. He obliged, muscles going tight as he sat up and hauled his shirt off, over his head before laying back down.

A smooth expanse of golden skin over chiseled muscle greeted me, and made my hips dip down against his. I muffled the moan that was trying to escape me.

"You objectifying me there, sweetheart?" Finn shifted his head until his hair fell in his eyes and I wanted to kiss him again.

"I'm not gonna lie, that's pretty much what I'm doing," I admitted, my hands slipping over his shoulders. I dragged my fingers down his chest, listening to his hiss of breath as he exhaled long and slow. My nails caught on his small, flat nipples and he jerked, but stayed still otherwise.

"Having fun?" he asked through gritted teeth.

"The most," I whispered and squirmed, pulling out of my t-shirt and letting it flutter to the ground. Finn's eyes tracked my movement and I felt a flutter of heat, right above where we were pressed together, when he licked his lips.

"Can I make a request?" He nodded at my bra. "That can come off, now, preferably. Why wait, sweetheart? It's gonna get warm in here."

"That's crap," I said to his flimsy, transparent excuse to get me out of my bra. It didn't stop me from whimpering anyway as his hands slid up my back, teasing right along my bra strap. "Wanna help out?"

"You only had to ask." His fingers twisted, and my bra straps fell loose over my shoulders. His eyes glowed in the dusky light, and his fingers drew down the straps until they caught in the crooks of my arms. He let out a slow breath and sat up, shifting underneath me until I straddled his thighs. I felt exposed in the best way, his hands going to wrap around each of my breasts, a look of intense concentration on his face.

"You okay there?" I asked, wanting to tease him for being so focused, but I was finding it hard to think of the right words to say in the correct order.

"Was gonna ask you the same thing." His thumb swept in an arc, brushing the peak of my breast, making me shiver. My thighs flexed, tightening on his legs, and a smirk spread across his face. "I think you're good, though. I think you're about to get even better."

I rolled my eyes at his ego.

"I'll believe it when I see it."

He chuckled and the sound went right to my core.

"You gonna keep talking, or let me make you feel good, sweetheart? Cause we can talk all night, if that's what you want." His thumb and finger pinched lightly over my nipple and I inhaled sharply. "That's what I thought. You tell me if anything doesn't feel good."

That's not possible, I thought, my eyes slipping shut as his head bowed and he pushed my breast up to meet his lips. My fingers dug into his shoulders, the muscle indenting under my tight grip as the soft, wet heat of his mouth enveloped my nipple. He growled, pulling me tight, up to him, his tongue teasing me until my breathing sped up. My nerves fizzed in my belly, and I squirmed, wondering if this was what he wanted too.

"I'm being selfish," he said against my skin, taking a moment to breathe over the damp flesh. It prickled, tingled, and I bit my lip to keep from whining. "I keep thinking how fucking glad I am that no one's done this with you before, that I get to show you how good it is." He chuckled and shook his head. "You're so beautiful, and perfect, you gotta know that, right?"

I felt my cheeks flush at his praise and he cocked his head, as he looked up at me.

"I—well—"

"Don't tell me you're feeling insecure, sweetheart," his voice was husky. My breath hitched in my throat.

"Not exactly, it just feels like you're doing all the work and I'm—" I shrugged one shoulder. His hands hadn't stopped moving, stroking along the curves of my breasts, before fanning out along my ribs below.

"What, this can't be all about you? You know how much you do for us?" He sighed and pulled me over, until I lay down on my back. It felt better, to be laying down, and I relaxed into the bed.

"My job? I'm just doing my job."

"Uh huh, well right now, it's my job to make you feel good, and more than that, I want to." He moved over me, his weight pressing me down into the firm surface that cushioned me from below. "So you stop thinking so hard about what you need to do for me, because all you need to do for me is tell me if I'm not making you perfectly, amazingly, completely happy."

"That's a lot of adverbs," I said, nervous laughter bubbling up in my throat. His eyes narrowed.

"If you're sassing me, I'm not doing this right," he growled, and his fingers dragged down my belly, over the soft curve of it. I sucked it in, and he pinched me, just lightly.

"You're beautiful," he said, "every inch. I'm gonna show you." His mouth followed his hands, more wet kisses peppering over my skin. It made my breath catch and my hips lift up into him, a building heat in my core demanding attention. When he mouthed at the edge of my jeans, I let out a hiss of breath. I felt his lips turn up into a smirk, and his index finger traced the rise of my zipper. I could feel the light pressure slip down, down over the fabric, a sharp line of fire following his touch. The breath stilled in my chest, all my awareness on his one finger, teasing me through my jeans, making me ache.

"Gonna get you out of these." His fingers flicked open the button of my jeans; he was pulling them down the next moment and I wriggled my hips to help him. His hand scooped under the small of my back and then my pants were gone and it was just me, him, and my underwear.

A flood of nerves made me feel like I had to cover myself, but he caught my hands as they crossed over my belly.

"You okay?" He stroked his thumbs over the soft spot on my palms.

"Feeling underdressed," I admitted, eyeing his body. He raised an eyebrow and moved away from me, shucking himself out of his jeans. They joined my pair on the floor of the van. A pair of tight, black boxer-briefs hugged him low on his hips.

"Better?" The bench-bed dipped under him, and his hand slid along one of my bare legs. The heat of his skin was soothing and I relaxed as he cupped my thigh. I nodded, feeling more like the playing field was level, although he was all hard edges where I was soft curves, and a few more pounds than I'd have liked. I pushed away those thoughts though when his fingers crept closer, closer to where my thighs touched. "Gotta let me in sweetheart or we're gonna be staring at each other for the rest of the night."

"Sounds like a good plan to me," I joked, but bit my lip after a moment and slipped my knees apart. His eyes slammed shut.

"Fuck, sweetheart, you smell so hot." He moved over beside me, his chest pressing into my side as two of his fingers cupped the heat of my pussy through my panties. "Right here," his words buzzing in my ear. My focus was down where he was touching, the slow rub of his hand, and the way my hips demanded to move. I obliged, rubbing into his hand, the warmth turning into a desperate heat.

Finn's tongue slipped out, teasing along the skin of my jaw, startling a cry from me.

"Feels good, doesn't it? You feel amazing. Your skin is so soft, Darce. I bet your soaking wet, I can feel you right through your panties. You want it? You want me to touch you?" His filthy words should have made me blush but instead I reached down and grabbed his wrist pressing his hand up higher where I wanted it. He chuckled. "Perfect girl, I like you when you tell me what to do. You want more?"

I bit my lip and nodded. His fingers slipped under the fabric of my underwear and I moaned, turning my head away. It was too much, I felt so exposed. My breath stuttered in and out of my lungs as he stroked my wet center, his fingers dragging through the folds. I was still clinging to his wrist, my grip tight, tighter. The tips of his fingers slipped over my clit and I cried out.

"Right there," my voice broke as he did it again, a slow, soft curl of pleasure building inside of me.

"Got you, Darcy," he said, and he kissed me. "Gotta keep you quiet, can't let the guys get too jealous of all these sweet sounds you're making for me."

"Can't promise... I won't..." my words disappeared, the shuddering, shaking feeling inside of me breaking open and I cried out again, the small of my back lifting off the bed as everything at the edge of my awareness whited out and all that mattered was his fingers insistently teasing me, stroking my clit over and over. What I wanted was just out of reach, and it felt like the tight, desperate feeling inside of me was never going to—

His body rolled fully on top of mine, his mouth finding the soft spot on the column of my neck. I felt the light graze of his teeth over my skin, his fingers teased one more long, slow stroke over the rise of my clit and I was gone. I shuddered into an intense orgasm, my fingers scratched hard into the skin of his wrist, and a scream ripped out of my throat.

His hand slipped over my pussy, pressing down flat, the pressure soothing the sweet burn that always followed when I'd made myself feel good, like he knew what I needed before I could even think to ask.

Feeling shaky, I opened my eyes only a crack at first, my heart racing. Finn gazed down at me, a broad, shit-eating grin on his face. I threw an arm across my eyes and whimpered.

"Oh no, sweetheart, don't you dare hide from me." His fingers wrapped around my wrist and he peeled my arm away from my face. "You're beautiful, and perfect, and a helluva lot more words I don't have the sense to find right now." He kissed me, mouth sweet on mine, and I squirmed, feeling the trembling after effects of what he'd done to me as my thighs shivered.

"That was pretty great," I admitted, my cheeks hot. "It's different when someone else does it for you, and I," I shrugged my shoulders. "It felt for a minute like it wasn't gonna happen, and then it did, and I, uh, like, wow."

Finn licked his lower lip and stretched, almost lazily, beside me, before his arm came down and he cuddled me into him.

"If it didn't happen, well, I woulda worked until it did." He nuzzled the side of my face and sighed. "Just want to make you feel good over and over. You sound so beautiful when you come."

"Please don't. Do we have to talk about it?"

"Not if it makes you feel bad," he said, "we don't have to do anything that makes you feel bad."

"Oh it doesn't make me feel bad, just weird. I'm not used to someone—"

"Giving a fuck about you?" His words were flat and I blinked at him. "We've gotten a bit of a picture of what you've lived through, and you haven't said much but you don't have to." He tapped me on the nose and I flinched. "I look at you and I feel like nobody's ever loved you much in your whole damn life, maybe aside from your friend, Max. Maybe that's why..." he trailed off and looked away before sighing. "Feels like it's gonna take the five of us to give you the love you deserve, because there's not a girl alive who's sweeter, and nicer, and smarter than you."

"You forgot beautiful." I stuck out my tongue and he laughed, kissing me hard.

"You're right I did." His eyes half-lidded and he smiled, stroking the side of my face. "I feel like I can have you, knowing the other guys are right there, waiting to take care of you if I can't. That doesn't scare you, does it? All of us, you being ours? We keep wondering if you're gonna ditch us."

I thought about it for a moment. Maybe at first it had been shocking, but I was in college. It wasn't like this was the first time I'd heard of people having more than one partner, and there was one girl in my program who had a girlfriend and a boyfriend. I shrugged.

"I forget sometimes that things have changed since I was a kid," he said, sounding older than he looked.

"You reminiscing? You know Charlie hates it when you reminisce," I teased to get him out of it. I could still feel the press of his hip into mine, and the firm length of his cock, hard in his briefs. The evidence of him needing me that badly made me shiver.

"That's because Charlie is an irreverent asshole, and I don't much want to talk about him right now." His fingers ran up and down the length of my arm. "You feeling sleepy?"

"Not really." My whole body was awake, and the the way he was touching my arm made my nerves jump and tingle, waking up a slow heat between my thighs again.

"You feeling good?"

"Finn, stop worrying about how I feel," I said, pushing up on one elbow and kissing him hard. I arched my hips into his, and he groaned. "You always worry about how I feel."

"Maybe cause if I don't then who's gonna." His hand wrapped around my thigh and he pulled it up until my knee brushed high on his ribs.

"Got four other names on my list, at least," I whispered, breath catching when I felt him pressing up between my thighs. Apparently my body was more than okay with this turn of events, acting like it hadn't been satisfied five minutes before. I wanted him, the hollow ache inside me demanding more.

A low growl started in his chest, and he pressed me down, flat on my back.

"I'm sorry," he said, his fingers stroking over my hip.

"What?" His words confused me and I yelped; his fingers tightened into the side of my panties and the fabric gave way, ripping he pulled. "Finn!"

"You said to stop worrying," he kissed me when he paused, "so I'm not gonna." I whimpered as he pulled my panties away from my damp skin, fully naked in front of him and not even caring about it. I wiggled my hips, wrapping my fingers around his shoulders.

"Please, I want..." I wanted him, but it felt too intense to say it.

His eyes closed and his hand cupped my warmth, fingers slicking back and forth through my folds for a moment. I felt the pressure of his finger teasing a circle over my entrance, and then the low, sweet burning feeling of pressure as he slipped it inside of me. I held still, staring up into his face, watching his expression, trying not to move my hips. I wanted to shift, rise up to meet him, but I was a little nervous to at the same time.

"That hurt?" he asked, eyes opening as his finger tested me, slipping in and out in a slow thrust. I shook my head, because it didn't, not really. He eased in a second finger and my breath hiccuped in my throat. It felt *good*, so good. So much that I couldn't help but roll my hips, rocking up into him as he fucked me with his fingers. He bent to kiss me, mouth hot on mine, and then he was gone his fingers slipping out from inside me. I cried out and tried to follow him. He soothed me with a firm press of his mouth on mine, and I heard him shifting out of his boxer-briefs. I swallowed hard and looked down his body where his cock jutted out from his hips, hard and swollen. He reached down over the side of the bench-bed and there was a soft crinkling sound. There was the silver flash of a condom wrapper before he was stroking the latex over his cock, before shifting between my legs.

His eyes never left my face as I slid my thighs up to hug his hips, anticipation building inside of me, terrified I wouldn't feel anything and that it would suck and I'd have to pretend it was good, or that it would hurt, really bad, even though—

"Stop thinking, sweetheart," he said, his voice husky and hoarse as he slid one hand under my butt, lifting me up as if I weighed nothing. "I've got you." He kissed me, once, and then his cock was between my thighs, pressing into me. There was a moment of panic fluttering in my chest before it gave way to elation as he slid inside me. It stung, but only a little bit, and I tried not to squirm. The feeling would go away, probably, and the warmth of him was more than enough to distract me. Pleasure, sweet and tinged with an edge of desperation, grew in my belly, as he took a deep, shaking breath and lowered us both to the bed.

He was still for a long moment, and he smiled

"Needed a moment," he admitted, with a shaky chuckle. "Haven't been this worked up..." He shook his head and then muttered softly, "Shut up, Finn." I wanted to tease him for talking to himself, but his hands pressed me down into the bed and his hips started their slow, steady pull away from me. I felt a shuddering, needy pleasure inside of me grow with each press and pull of his hips. His cock was thick, firm, opening me up and I clung to him, burying my face in the side of his neck as he covered my body with his. It was so real, and I was grateful that I'd waited for the right guy, the right group of guys, to be this close and vulnerable with. Finn was perfect, he was everything.

I melted under him, relaxing and letting it happen, the pleasure building inside me with each roll of his hips. The stinging sensation was gone, and all that remained was a shivering feeling of being filled up. He kissed the side of my face, then my ear.

"You feel amazing," he murmured, and I shivered. "You're mine, all of you, gonna make you feel so good." His hips hitched and my knees squeezed his waist.

"Already did," my voice sounded breathy and light in my ears. He snorted and pulled back the shift of his cock inside me. One hand splayed across my belly, keeping me flat on the bed, the other cupped my breast.

"If I have it my way, not a night goes by without me making you feel good from here on out." He smirked when I moaned, his hips never stopping in their easy, lazy thrusting.

"You're gonna kill me with sex," I protested, but when he arched his back and bent down to catch my tight nipple in his mouth, I figured there were probably worse ways to die. He was kissing and licking my breast, his teeth scraping over my skin every so often, and the threat of him nipping me made me bear down on him, clenching hard until he groaned. He pressed his face between my breasts, breathing hotly against my skin, and his hands both fisted in the blanket on either side of me. I heard him growl, low and hungry, and his hips picked up speed. The fluttering feeling inside me turned into pulsing need, and I squirmed, trying to lift my hips to get more of it. The hand of his on my belly, holding me down, slid down to where we were joined, bracketing his cock as he took me.

"Please." I needed more. His tongue licked a hot stripe up from my breast bone to the dip of my throat, and he kissed there, tenderly.

"Greedy girl," he teased, although his words were soft, and his thumb slicked down between my folds, stroking me over and over. It didn't take long, a light nudge with the pad of his thumb, and one hitch of his hips, and I screamed, my throat raw as he sent me, shaking and shivering into climax.

His teeth scraped against my throat again, and he groaned, long and loud, his hips churning hard between my thighs. His hand slipped over my hip and he grabbed my leg, holding me still as he fucked me hard into the sheet. I felt the shudder roll through his muscles, and he bit me, the slightest clamp of his mouth on the side of my neck. I shivered, feeling worn out, as my body went limp under him. We stayed there for a long moment, his hips stilling between my thighs, then he pulled his face away. His thumb came up to rub the side of my neck, soothing the spot where his teeth had bit into me.

A low rumble started up in his chest, and he stretched out over me, covering me completely with his body, the light minty scent of him turned heavy and thick. My eyes slid shut and I sighed.

"Like a big cat," I whispered. He snorted.

"Nothing like a cat," he shot back, but he snuggled me again. There was a creamy feeling between my thighs and I wriggled, making him hiss out a breath.

"Hang on," he muttered and pulled away from me, pulling his cock out of my body. I felt a mild twinge, and the overall feeling of being satisfied, very satisfied, but that was it. My first time had been *nothing* like I thought it would be. Finn cleaned himself up and was back beside me, tugging up one edge of the blanket to cover me up as his arms wrapped around me tight. I burrowed into him, feeling sleepy and perfect. He was perfect. Everything was perfect. I never wanted to move again. The soft rumble of his chest made every inch of me relax, and I just listened to it, his breathing, and the breeze outside as it rustled through the park's greenery and foliage.

This felt like home should feel, although a part of me longed for the other guys, and...

"I'm hungry," I said. Finn squinted at me in the dark.

"What? But you just—"

"I want cookies. Chocolate chip ones, like right now." It was like I was starving, and I realized that I hadn't eaten much that night after Shara and Ginny had put my good mood in the dumpster. Suddenly I knew why Max kept after-sex snacks for when Craig visited. Post-coitous hunger was a real thing. Finn sat up, and I followed, pulling the blanket right up under my chin. "Please tell me we have cookies."

"Um..." He scratched the back of his head. "I don't think we do."

"Oh."

He watched me for a moment and grinned.

"Let me get dressed and get the guys. We'll all go get cookies."

I felt my cheeks turning pink.

"Oh, god they're going to think I'm weird, and they're gonna know about us, and they already know about us, obviously, but," Finn's fingers landed on my lips, shushing me. He gave me a gentle, but stern look.

"It's okay. You're not weird, and I should've known you stinted yourself. You haven't been eating enough on tour as it is. Let me get the guys, and we'll go get cookies. Okay? Whatever you want. Cheeseburgers, you name it."

I thought for a moment.

"A cheeseburger kinda sounds amazing right now," I agreed. He smiled and leaned in, kissing me softly.

"I love you," he murmured. "Beautiful, crazy girl." He pulled away and grabbed his jeans, stalking down the aisle of our little tour van. I barely had time to appreciate the tight curve of his ass because I sat there, staring after him, my heart trembling in my throat.

"You what?" Had he really said it? Had he even meant it?

He flapped a hand at me, as if it was no big deal that he'd just confessed some serious feelings. It wasn't like the same hadn't been simmering in my chest for days at least. I loved him. He loved me. Was this real? He yanked on his jeans.

"Get dressed," he said, "we're going on a cookie hunt."

TWENTY-THREE

Darcy Llewellyn
@DarcyLuvsDonuts

I've never seen a more beautiful sky in my life. #everythingsamazing #countingstars #darknightsbrightlights #glowingheart #maybeitsreal

14 Retweets 39 Likes

♡ 13 ⟲ 14 ♡ 39 ✉

I didn't bother to get back into my jeans and instead decided on leggings and an oversized sweatshirt. I felt different, my skin felt like it was glowing almost, and I wondered if it would be like that every time or if it a side effect of being a 'newly despoiled virgin'. I was putting the bench seat back up, and folding the blanket when the sliding door on the van opened, and Ace ducked inside. He eyed me up for a moment, hesitating, and came to me and pulled me into his arms for a tight hug.

"Ace?" I felt him put his chin on top of my head, and his grip grew tighter. "You okay?" I asked, my face smushed into the front of his shirt.

"Just having some feelings," he said. "I guess I'm a little jealous, maybe, just wanted to be close to you." He sighed and pulled away. "You okay?"

I nodded.

"Pretty great," I admitted. He smiled and booped me on the nose. What was with these guys and the nose-touching? Wolves. It had to be that.

"He took care of you." It was a statement rather than a question.

"Mhmm. I'm—it was good. I'm good." I sat down at the back as Charlie crawled in, an odd expression on his face.

"Well that's just not fucking fair," he said, gesturing around the van. "It's gonna smell like your scent, all sweet and... tasty and we have to just—" Ace elbowed him hard.

"Shut up," Ace said, "you're joking around but you're gonna make her feel weird." Charlie shot me an apologetic look, but I didn't mind. My whole body was buzzing. They could've said *anything* and I wouldn't have cared right then.

"Sorry, kid," he said.

"Don't call me that," I replied mildly. Eli got in the front, and Finn stepped up into the van, heading back to sit by me. Immediately his arms were around me, and he pulled me into his lap. Eli started up the engine and threw the van into gear.

"Where's Cash?" I asked, sitting up. Eli's eyes met mine through the rearview mirror.

"By the highway. He went for a run," Eli replied.

Ace whistled, and grinned at me over his shoulder.

"Somebody got himself all worked up," he explained. Charlie snickered, and Finn just hugged me tighter before letting me settle in my seat. The headlights of the van bounced over the gravel road as we drove out the way we'd come in. I shot Finn a grateful smile, my belly rumbling. I really was starving. I reached into my bag for my phone and send Max a quick *omgomgomg* text message and then Ace pointed.

"There he is!"

Cash was looking up at the stars, his shirt slung over one shoulder as he stood on the side of the road. His skin glowed in the light from the van, and he squinted at us, shading his eyes. There was a slick of sweat down his front as Eli pulled to the stop and Cash started walking toward us. His shoes spit up gravel as Charlie leaned over and opened the van's sliding door.

"Good run?" Charlie asked, as Cash hauled himself inside.

"Yeah," Cash said, his gaze finding me in the back. He stopped for a moment, visibly swallowed and sat down with a grunt, slumping down in his seat. Finn's hand wrapped around mine and he squeezed my fingers. He leaned in close, lips brushing my ear.

"He's not mad at you."

"He's kinda acting it," I whispered back. Finn hesitated and sighed.

"He still feels guilty for how he behaved at that house show. Cash takes things hard. He's not having an easy time forgiving himself."

That made sense. I'd have to pull Cash aside at some point and let him know it was really okay. I was good and, especially, I was good with him. I snuggled into Finn's side as we got onto the highway.

"So it was cookies?" Eli looked back at us through the rear-view mirror.

"And cheeseburgers," Finn called out.

"Aww yes!" Ace turned to me and gave me a thumbs up. "I could eat like five right now."

"When could you not?" Eli asked with a snort and a rare smile. It transformed the profile of his face, and when Ace muttered,

"I fucking love cheeseburgers."

Eli shook his head and looked to the road ahead.

I WAS SURROUNDED by food wrappers, and Ace lay on the floor, one hand on his belly, groaning.

"It hurts so good," he whimpered. Charlie snickered and poked him with one foot. Ace swatted at him.

"Want my last cheeseburger?" Charlie asked.

"Yes," Ace said at the same time as Eli said,

"Don't."

Ace grabbed it anyway, and stuffed in into his mouth with a satisfied groan. We were back at the campsite, enjoying the soft breeze as it came through all of the open windows and doors of the van. I stood up, brushing cookie crumbs off my lap. "Where's the outhouse?"

Cash got to his feet.

"Let me take you, it's a bit of a trek." He hopped out of the van and held out his hand to help me down. When our fingers touched, my fingers tingled with electricity. He must not have felt it because he didn't say anything when I pulled away. We set off to the outhouse. It was clean, thankfully, and when I emerged I stretched my arms up to the sky.

"I love how you can hear all the crickets, and the night birds," I said as I came up next to him. He was sitting on the top of a picnic bench, looking up at the stars.

"This is how I grew up," he said. "Not a lot of lights, out in the woods. It was nice. I miss it sometimes."

"You still could be out here. What makes you need to be performing, and touring?" I sat down next to him. He let out a long breath.

"The guys. I wouldn't be anything without them, and life wouldn't be worth living," he said. "We're nothing without each other. We're pack. This is the only thing we have left of our old lives, our old selves." He closed his eyes for a long moment and smiled. It was beautiful and relaxed, and I was relieved that he was finally having a moment where he felt like he could let his guard down around me. "And this way, we can do what we love to do, for as long as we're around to do it."

I swallowed down a lump of feelings that had formed in my throat. I wanted to say that it was 'unfair' that their heartstone had been destroyed, and that over time, they would weaken and age like a human instead of continue on like the werewolves they really were. But 'unfair' seemed like an understatement.

Before I could stop myself, I found myself closing the space between us, wrapping him tight in my arms, and pressing my face into his shoulder. He made a small noise of surprise, and his arm slowly, so slowly, curled around my shoulders.

"I'm sorry," I whispered. "I wish I could do more than just manage the band. Just, more."

"It's okay, Darce." His fingers squeezed my shoulder. "We're happy, we're doing what we love."

"Yeah but it's fucking shit, is what it is." I pulled away to look at him. The starlight fell on us both, highlighting the sharp angles of his face, the fall of his dark hair where it was tucked behind his ear. His blue eyes were almost black. "Is this going to be your lives? Riding around in a tour van, hoping that these hunters chasing you don't cotton on to the fact you guys are wolves? You think they're not going to notice the magic in your music if they stumble across one of the shows?"

"Darcy—"

"No, listen. And then what, you guys just lose what makes you, *you*? What happens when you can't do whatever it is you do with your music anymore? Maybe you don't know much about how it works, but it's magic, and it's a form of a spell, sorta, and with time, if you're the source of that magic, and it fades inside of you." I was so upset I was trembling, and Cash frowned.

"I hadn't really thought about that," he admitted after taking a deep breath. "You figure that one day, we're just gonna stop being able to..."

"Oh you'll be good musicians, of course, you're amazing already, but what makes you werewolves is dying, you don't have a heartstone, right? So it kinda makes sense that as your ability to shift, to heal, to live a long time, when all that fades, so does the magic in your music." I bit my lip after a moment. "Sorry to be the bearer of bad news. I guess it feels like you guys are just running from a problem that's never going to give up. The hunters might, they might leave you alone, but this? This is inside you, around you."

"What are we supposed to do?" Cash asked, his voice rough. "This isn't a hunter, we can't rip this open and spread their blood across the ground."

I flinched at his raw words. He raised his eyebrow and I felt defensive.

"What?"

"Seems like you forget who you're sharing a van with sometimes," he said. I snorted.

"Hardly. You guys are always growling or rumbling at each other or—"

"Or staring at you like you're the prettiest thing we've ever seen?" He raised his hand and stroked it down the side of my face. "Did you mean it when you said you wished you could do more?"

"Obviously," I whispered. "Anything."

His breath caught in his throat.

"Anything? You **swear** it?" The words sounded old in his mouth, ritualistic, and I recognized the weight of his power in them, demanding that I answer. I didn't even bother to fight it.

"I swear it."

His eyes lit up and he stood.

"Good," he said, and grabbed my hand. "Come with me."

"Where are we going?" I gave him my hand and he tugged me up off the bench.

"Where the guys can't hear us."

"Uh," My shoes crunched over the gravel as we crossed the site that we were camped in, leaving the van behind us. "Cash? Are you okay?"

"You remember what I told you about the heartstones, how we need them, and without them, we're basically not a pack anymore, and slowly we lose our ability to shift, to heal, to exist as who we were?" He searched my face as we came up to the edge of a slowly moving creek. Water glinted off the surface, the glassy eddies swirling under the night sky. When the breeze picked up I could smell the greenery, the damp smell of water-reeds sticking to the back of my throat.

"Of course, we were just talking about it—"

He grabbed my arms and I fell quiet.

"You can change that," he said. I frowned.

"What?"

"You. You're a witch, and you can change that. Here." He pulled up my hand. "You're a lightning witch. The energy lives inside of you, a living storm, and in that storm is the ability to create life, to fix us."

I shook my head.

"Cash, no, I'm not—"

"Yes, you are. You've sparked me enough times, and I hear it in your voice, when you get mad, or you tell us what to do and you're not fucking around. There's thunder in you, echoing in the back of your voice, demanding I listen and if I don't there'll be hell to pay." He was breathing hard as he spoke, and I knew if I put my hands on his chest I would be able to feel the frantic beat of his heart. He thought I was a powerful lightning witch, able to call down storms at the snap of my fingers. What would he think when he found out I couldn't? That the storms had never answered me, no matter how much I'd begged and pleaded with them as a small child. I'd stopped trying in my teens. It was easier not to try than to be disappointed again.

There was no reason for me to not tell him. The danger of the guys posed me was gone, the bonds we were building as a motley pack, five wolves and a witch, meant that I was safe. I knew they'd never hurt me, no matter what.

"You don't understand, you don't know Cash."

"No, Darcy, you don't know. There's one kind of witch that can make a new heartstone, and it's you."

"What?!" I pulled back from him in shock. "I can what?" The rise of dread in me threatened to swamp over any of the lasting warmth I'd felt from being with Finn that night, and the ache between my legs faded as I stared at Cash.

"You can *make* a heartstone, if you want to bad enough. How do you think we got them in the first place? Witches made them for us, helped our packs grow." Cash didn't pull me back to him, but from the way his fingers clenched, I could tell he wanted to.

"I don't know how," I said instantly. His brow furrowed.

"You can find out. Your family—"

"Not a fucking chance," I shut him down right then. My family was nothing to me. The pack was my family now, I knew it deep in my bones, in my heart. They were where I was supposed to be, and my family couldn't help me. They wouldn't help me, even if I'd asked. And I wouldn't ask them, not if I could help it. Going back to them? It was hard to even imagine what would happen if I did.

"Darcy—"

"*No!*" I put every ounce of my power into the word, and he stumbled back, eyes wide. We stared at each other for a moment, me breathing hard, him hardly breathing at all. "No, I can't," I whispered. "Please don't ask again."

Cash lifted his hand out to me and then dropped it to his side. His eyes glittered, and this time I realized he was angry, not surprised.

"I'm not letting this go."

"That's great, but it's not happening."

"This is our lives," he snarled, stepping toward me. It was like he'd slapped me. He might as well have. How could I explain to him I wasn't what he thought I was? I swallowed hard.

"I'm not refusing because I want to, Cash. If I could help you, I would, you know I would."

"Do I?" he asked, and he crossed his arms over his chest. "I'm not so fucking sure." All my intentions to tell him the truth right then fled from me and I hiccuped a noise, small and dismayed, in my throat. His face softened, he must've realized he crossed a line. He reached for me.

"Fuck off," I snapped, my face suddenly wet. I wiped at my cheeks with the side of my wrist. Finn's scent lingered there and I felt sick. I wanted to retreat to the safety of his arms, but if he knew, if Cash told him what we'd talked about, would Finn even want me? "I'm going to the van," I said.

"Darcy, wait."

I didn't wait. I spun on my heel and stalked, stumbling, over the hard gravel. The van emerged from the darkness, promising warmth inside of it. It was a warmth I thought I'd earned. Had I even though?

When I'd left home, I'd left the struggle to control my weak powers behind me, or so I'd thought. Now for the first time in almost four years I *wanted* to cast magic. It was killing me, that there might be a way to save the pack from their inevitable fate, and I couldn't do it. I pulled out my phone from my pocket and shot Max a text message.

GUESS IT'S true what they say. You can't run from your problems. They find you, no matter what. Miss you, Maxy.

I WIPED the last of the tears from my face, and resolved to not say anything to the other guys about the conversation between me and Cash. With any luck, they'd be too blissed out on cheeseburgers to notice he hadn't come back with me.

TWENTY-FOUR

The Sacramento venue had showers, clean and pristine, and it felt so good to wash off the frustration and hurt from the last few days. I'd spent the rest of our time at the park faking it and pretending like I was fine when I wasn't. The hollow ache in my chest followed me around wherever I went, and not even a long hike with Finn to the edge of canyon could cure it. Cash stared at me darkly every time I looked at him, so I stuck to Finn's side, and let his arm around my shoulders shield me.

The water sluiced down my skin and I reveled in using as much hot water as I wanted. We had a solar shower that we'd hang on outside of the van to rinse off, but it wasn't the same thing. It was one of the rare moments I was jealous of everyone on the bus with Glory Revolution and Jake—at least they had a proper shower to use whenever they wanted. Baby-bands like Phoenixcry took what they could get though, and we were just lucky we had a higher-end tour van and not some sketchy mini-van that overheated every time it went up a tiny hill.

Stepping out into the chilly air of the bathroom made my skin goose-bump all over and I remembered last night when Finn had spent some time learning all the places on my neck that made me shiver. His touch was near to the only thing that could chase the bad feelings taking up space in my heart, away. I braided my hair to cut down on any fly-aways, 'cause curls and the road were a bad mix, and joined Ginny and Shara at the merch booth.

"Your guys sound checked during your shower," Ginny said. "They sounded good." She checked her watch. "You mind watching my table while I go have mine? Jake keeps bitching we leave long hairs in the bus shower and doesn't want us to use it anymore."

Shara rolled her eyes.

"Guy's a grade-a asshole," she said.

"I'll watch your table, but you'll probably be back before doors anyway," I said, shifting over to stand between the two tables. Ginny squeezed my shoulder and walked off, determination in every step. Shara watched her go then turned to me.

"I'm really sorry," she said, "I was a dick the other day, and you didn't deserve it."

"I don't understand." Sure it had hurt like a stab right to the chest, but she had just been honest with me.

"I should have told you when I first saw those pictures go up," she gulped a deep lungful of air and then bombed through the final words, "and if you want to tell Willa I knew, that's fine, I'll take whatever she dishes out."

I stared at her for a long moment, and then felt tears welling up in my eyes. I blinked them away, not wanting to start sobbing in the middle of the venue right before a show. I missed Max, so bad. She was barely responding to my texts, and I felt selfish demanding so much of her time when I knew she was suffering.

"It's okay." I got control of my rebellious emotions and gave Shara a brief smile. "I don't want to get you in trouble, or anything, I don't even think I'm going to say something to Willa."

Shara's eyebrows hiked up.

"You're not?" she asked. I shook my head.

"The band comes first, and I just have to not be in places where Jake can be a creeper. That shouldn't be so hard, right?"

Shara snorted and responded with a weak smile before sorting through some silicone wristbands on her table.

"Just be careful," was all she said, and when I opened my mouth to speak again she gave a sharp jerk of her head to tell me she wasn't going to discuss it anymore. I buried my frustration and fussed with the Phoenixcry merch, straightening it over and over until every shirt was folded crisply on the table. I stripped a few CDs of their plastic wrap to get ready in case some kids wanted them signed, which they always did. My nails slicked thought the cellophane; I was getting practiced at the move after all the days on the road.

One of Glory Rev's members walked up, eyeing their table since Ginny was gone and looked at me and Shara.

"Gin out?" he asked.

"Shower," I answered. "Can I help you?" I didn't know him super well, and I thought maybe that he might have been the bassist. The big band stayed far away from us, although I didn't blame them. They had important stuff to do, I figured, lots of radio drops to be recorded on the fly, so that their new single could be introduced by them over the air, and other label-related stuff.

"Darcy, right?" he asked, ignoring Shara as she bit her lip and eyed him up like he was a chiseled piece of rock candy. He was alright. Good looking, with a shock of black hair, and an easy smile; he might have impressed me pre-Phoenixcry. Now, he was just another guy. Nice to look at, but didn't stir anything south of my waistband. He held out his hand. "Aaron. I've heard a lot about you. Do you have a sec?"

I glanced at my booth and then at Shara. She made a shooing motion with her hands.

"I'll watch it," she promised. Aaron smiled at her and started walking away. I gave Shara a confused look, but tagged after him. We crossed the expanse of the floor; this venue was open with no seating and no mosh-pit.

"I just wanted to grab you while things were quiet, cause I've been hearing from all the venues about how easy you are to work with."

"Oh. Oh? Really? That's cool." We walked to the edge of the stage, Phoenixcry's gear set up on it and ready to go. They'd be in the green room, having their pre-show amp-up together. "Thanks," I said lamely as he leaned against the edge of the stage, his arms crossed over his chest. I couldn't get a good read on him.

"Look, I'm gonna come right out and say it. I heard you're doing an internship at XOhX, and that's great, but we've been watching you and I think you'd be a good fit on our team. After this tour is done, we're getting picked up opening for a stadium tour—" His words whited out in my ears as I stared at him, eyes wide.

A stadium tour? For a moment, I imagined it, coordinating merch and backstage tour management on a larger show, and I trembled. That's what I'd always dreamed of. The closest I'd gotten to a stadium show had been sneaking rock CDs into my room and listening to them on low so my parents couldn't hear. The only music allowed in our house was classical, which after 19 years of it, I was a little over.

"So yeah, what do you think? Our tour manager says you've got a good head on your shoulders, and you'd be working directly with him as his assistant. You're not in this to be a groupie or get close to the bands, and you sling merchandise better than anyone I've seen. You've got a real connection with fans when they come up to you. That's something, Darcy, and we don't see it often. Somehow you manage to be extroverted and not make it all about you." He uncrossed his arms, hands wrapping around the edge of the stage as he leaned forward.

"I..."

"Ginny's not cutting it for us," he said flatly. I frowned and glanced away, back to the merch booth. Thing was, maybe she wasn't super focused, but Ginny still worked hard. Plus she'd had my back a few times when I'd needed help dealing with a creepy fanboy who thought it was cool to paw at the merch girls. My answer was going to be no either way, because I wasn't leaving my guys no matter what, even if I was still half-mad at Cash.

You can either be a broad or a bitch, Darcy. Willa's words echoed in my head and I gave him my best, most diplomatic smile. His shoulders sagged; he immediately knew.

"I'm really sorry," I said.

"We can get your internship switched," he said, although his rueful smile said he knew it was hopeless.

"That's not the only reason I'm sticking with my guys." I shoved my hands in the back pockets of my jeans. "Although I appreciate the offer. That's pretty, wow, I feel like an idiot turning it down but..."

"Phoenixcry is something special. Jakey keeps trying to play it down, but we all know they're going somewhere fast. But," He pulled out his phone. "What's your number?"

"You call him Jakey?" I asked, amused. That probably pissed Tupper off to no end. I gave Aaron my number and my phone buzzed at my hip.

"You change your mind about world tours, just call me," he said with a wink. "We'll figure something out that works for you. Maybe you don't need that internship and could jump straight on the payroll."

A pang of FOMO in my gut sounded off but I shook my head. A paying job? Still, not worth it. Plus, I'd worked hard for my degree. I wanted to finish it.

"I really believe in the band I'm working with, but I am so appreciative of the offer," I said. If Aaron was extending some sort of olive branch to me then I needed to take it, not just for a future job but maybe, just maybe I could wrangle something good for Phoenixcry in the future.

"One more thing," Aaron said as I turned to go back to my merch table. "Is Jake giving you a hard time?" His eyes were half-lidded as he surveyed me. My heart skipped up into my throat.

"No," I lied.

"Mmkay." He stood up and stretched. "I'm gonna go do my hand warmups. I'll see you later, Darcy. You and the guys are welcome to hang on the bus if you want."

"T-thanks," I said, and trying not to float, I walked back to the table. Shara was giving me a *look*, like she was about to burst with questions but didn't want to be a total pleb about it.

"Jake won't even let me talk to them," Shara hissed at me. "What did he say, what did he say?" She apparently was giving up on the not looking like a pleb thing. I cut her some slack and grinned, but froze for a moment. If I said anything about Ginny. Fuck.

"He asked me if me and the guys wanted to hang on the bus tonight," I said. "He likes them, and thinks they're doing good."

Shara's eyes narrowed.

"Really? Oh my god, Jake's going to shit a cat." Her frown turned into a smirk. "Good." She looked so pleased that I had to laugh. I collapsed on the chair behind the table with a sigh.

"Is it doors soon?"

"Mmm, yup. Prepare yourself, here come the fanboys."

I heard the yell of 'DOORS!' A fog machine shot out haze from the front of the stage, the lights glistening and shooting through the thick air. A prickle of nerves ran over my skin, like it always did when the crowd started to come in and I had to fight between watching out for someone who didn't fit and seemed dangerous, and doing my job as manager and merchant girl. With a sigh, I got to my feet.

Sometimes it felt like the nights were starting to melt into each other, but in a good way. Shara offered me her water bottle but I shook my head. Last thing I needed was to get tipsy and set some Phoenixcry merch on fire by sparking up.

My phone buzzed and I pulled it out, checking it quickly. It was Aaron.

I forgot to say you're a class act. Loyalty is everything in this biz. Take it from a road warrior.

My cheeks flushed hard and I tucked my phone away, unable to keep the grin off of my face. I wanted to text Max but it felt like bragging. She'd even stopped commenting on my Insta photos and we hadn't Snapchatted each other in forever. I was at the point I didn't even want to send her a filtered image, I just wanted to *see* her. (True trust and love, in my opinion, was sending someone a pic of you without cat-ears hiding half your face.) I sighed and as the pulse of the house music rolled out and two young guys started walking toward the merch area, I put a big smile on my face. Work first, feelings later.

Darcy Llewellyn
@DarcyLuvsDonuts

You can be a broad or a b$tch. Pick one, and stick to it. This gal here is gonna be a broad forever. #musicindustrychicksbeforedicks

8 Retweets **22** Likes

◯ 11   ⇄ 8   ♡ 22   ✉

TWENTY-FIVE

Half-way through Phoenixcry's set, Finn stood on the edge of the stage, arms outstretched. I saw the wave of hands from the audience, reaching back to him, and he grabbed fingers, squeezing hands, sharing the love in his heart out with everyone there. It was hard to watch, knowing what I did, knowing that at any moment, we'd turn a corner, and *they* would be there, hunters, cutting the guys down when they were defenseless and unable to shift or fight with their full strength. Sometimes it was a far away worry, but for some reason that night it was nagging at me.

It made me wonder, already the guys in the pack were so strong, what would they be like if they were still close to their heartstone? The thought made me shiver. The power in their music would likely be stronger too. As it was, even being steeled against it, their magic still hit me like a sledgehammer. It was constantly leaving me feeling a bit drunk and wobbly until I got myself under control after the first song. My family would have been disgusted with me, and that thought made me want to throw myself into the music world, the werewolf world, even more. I'd thought my family had just been bad to *me*, but with each day I spent with Phoenixcry, on the road with people who actually cared for me and appreciated me for who I was I realized that the real monsters in this world were my family and witches like them.

"They're so good," Shara said next to me. The merch booth was quiet, and Ginny had gone to get us snacks from the bar, on her. That was good because my wallet was squeaking from how empty it was.

"Mmmhmm," I said, letting my gaze wander over to Cash at the back. He had his hand on one of his cymbals, holding it to still the vibrations after their last song ended.

"So, we don't normally do this," Finn said, raking a hand through his hair and taking a quick swig of water from a bottle. When someone reached for it, he laughed, and squirted it over the crowd. The resounding shriek echoed through the room. He grinned and stepped up on one of the stage risers. He sounded slightly breathless as he spoke, and I knew his adrenaline had to be running on high-speed. He said performing felt like falling, in the best way, when he was on stage surrounded by his pack and connecting with a willing and excited audience. "So we don't normally play new stuff until we've had a while to practice it, cause that's just not how we roll, but we wrote a song today, real quick in the green room. When something comes together so quick like that, you know it's going to work."

He lifted his head, eyes squinting against the light, and I swore for a moment he was trying to look to the back of the room where I stood. My heart beat double time in my chest.

"So what do you think, you wanna hear it?" Finn's question was answered with an enthusiastic cry from the audience, but he stepped back and shook his head. "I dunno guys, I don't think they really wanna—" He was drowned out by a roar that shook the rafters. Shara grabbed my wrist.

"Oh my god, he is so fucking good. Are you two like a thing or is he single?"

"Uh, what?" I looked at her. She grinned and winked at me.

"Dunno, you just seem close."

I held my breath for a moment, but Finn saved me without knowing it.

"Hit it, Cash!" He yelled, and any answer I could have given Shara would have been drowned out. The drums came to life, Cash's arms flicking out, their movement fluid and almost elegant. Ace jumped up on a low riser, shoving his bass into the crowd as he bent into them, locking into the beat Cash set with his drums.

I could hear Eli and Charlie, Eli's lead guitar skating close to Charlie's rhythm and before pulling away from it in a way that made my heart soar and the breath catch in my throat. Finn stepped up, pulled the microphone to his mouth, and the world dropped away from me.

"*I've never said those three words so fast, 'n now I can't let that moment pass,*" he sang, eyes closed for a long moment. "*I'm in my head, reliving every kiss, and the worst part is, I can't say sh-,*" the curse word vanished as he tugged his microphone away at the last moment, his own subtle nod to the all-ages crowd. Another breath, and more lyrics, building up in a crescendo of emotion inside me. The swell of his voice almost cracked on a high note. Anxiety built in me, like I was afraid he would break and drop the note, but he reached out and a fan grabbed his hand and he seemed to hold the words. His eyes opened and he smiled down at her. I could barely see the top of her head. He let go of her to pull back from the crowd. His back arched, his shoulders dropping, and I saw him inhale.

"She's got the sweetest of hearts, it's the deadliest of sins. She's got everything," he sang, stealing my breath, because I knew he was singing about me. Eli stepped up to a back-up mic, his fingers flashing along the fretboard as he sang the repeats. I grabbed the edge of the merch table. It's one thing for someone to tell you they love you, it's another for them to sing their heart right in front of you, stripping themselves bare and vulnerable, telling everyone in the room that you were the only thing that completed them. He'd written this song for me. They, the pack, had written it for me.

"Now I'm in her hands, and she's pulling my strings, she's my everything, my everything, everything..." He trailed off and fell back, Charlie stepping to the front of the stage as the song shuddered into the post-chorus. The lights flashed and dipped, flickering off his skin, licking at the stubble along his jaw, as his dark brown hair got in his eyes. He shook it away, and stepped back in time for Finn come back in front for the second verse.

I had to look away. It was too much. My fingers trembled and I felt like I was going to be sick.

It wasn't fair. What we had, this small thing that had taken root under my heart, would never be forever.

"I need a minute," I said to Shara, and pushed past her,

going out the back door. The hallway to the lobby was empty, and I pressed my face against the cool, painted cement brick that made up the wall, my eyes closed. "Get it together," I whispered. A flash of light lit up my vision through my eyelids, and I cracked my eyes open. I stumbled back. Lightning flickered along my hands, up my wrists; thin webs of blue light hummed in the dim light of the hall. They crackled and popped when I lifted my hands so I could see them better. In a panic, I shoved my hands, palm-first against the wall. The lightning disappeared with a soft *phut* noise. Terror ate at my belly, coiling around my spine and made me freeze for several long moments until I heard laughter. Looking up, I saw a couple come out of the doors, leaning against each other. I dropped my hands, and my head, and steadily walked past them, determined not to make eye contact.

"There you are," Ginny said as I came back. There were two bowls of nachos balanced on one of the folding chairs. "You okay? Shara went to get you water, real water, not our fire-water."

"I'm fine, just felt weird for a sec." Globs of cheese ran, thick and congealing over the nachos and my stomach turned over. Ginny pressed the back of her hand to my forehead to check me for a fever.

"Tour crud," she said, "it gets us all. You should go to the green room, lay down."

"Here's the water." Shara appeared, bearing two bottles of cold water. I took one and twisted the cap off, gulping down half of it to drown the queasy feeling in my gut. Finn and the guys kept performing, having no idea I was going through a panic attack at the back of the performance hall over them. I closed my eyes as I felt the cold water trickle down and settle in my stomach.

"Better?" Shara asked when I looked at her. She shared Ginny's worried expression.

"I still think you should go lay down. Don't stress it. We've got you covered." Ginny held out her hand and I undid the money belt around my waist, passing her the small, black apron.

"Don't tell the guys," I said, "just come get me when their set is over?"

Ginny sighed.

"Okay. But that doesn't give you long."

"All I need is twenty minutes, tops." *To retch back up all that water I just drank.* I didn't add that though. They probably still wanted to enjoy their nachos and not think about me puking. Ginny felt my forehead again and frowned. "I'm good, just need a quick cat-nap." There was a burst of applause and I flinched, and gave them both an ironic, weak little salute before walking swiftly to the backstage exit. I flashed my backstage pass to the security guard there, and in a few moments I was in the muffled quiet of the green room. The other bands preferred to hang out on their tour bus before their sets if they weren't by the merch tables or signing autographs, so I had the whole room to myself.

I sank down onto the couch, guilt and shame weighing me down there as I stared at the floor. How long could the guys run until the hunters caught up with them? For six months? A year? Forever? I toppled over and curled up. If I'd paid more attention when I was younger, if I'd tried harder, maybe I would've been able to cast the spell to create a heartstone. It was probably complicated magic, but I would have been able to try at the very least.

A few hot tears leaked from my eyes. My powers had never been very strong, and now they seemed to be going haywire. I tried not to think about it.

But if I'd been any good at magic, would I even have run away from home to begin with? Frustration mounted inside of me. I couldn't even feel pathetic and useless without my brain playing devil's advocate. One of the guys had left their hoodie slung over one arm of the the couch. I reached for it without thinking, and pulled it over myself. Cash's scent hit me hard. I doubled over, pulling it into my face, and the tears came to me then, fast and hot. I cried it out, the immense grief of finding a place, a home, and knowing that it was going to be taken away because how long before I was found out by someone my family knew? How long before the hunters tracked us down? How long before the residual power of the heartstone, singing in my pack's bones faded away and they lost everything that made them who they were, including the ability to fight and heal?

Misery gripped me tight and I let it, until the pain bled out and I lay there, staring at the ceiling, Cash's hoodie pulled right up to my nose. I closed my eyes. It was better, maybe, not to think for a little bit.

TWENTY-SIX

The brush of cool air on my cheek woke me. My eyes cracked open, salt-crusted and dry. Finn hovered over me, his expression worried. Shara and Ginny had sent him, or he'd figured it out and come on his own. Either way I was grateful.

I sat up before he could ask, and held my arms out. He came to me, pulling me into a tight, warm embrace. I shivered but didn't have the energy to speak.

"What's got you so worked up? Shara told me you weren't feeling good," he said, breaking our silence. Several more minutes passed, and his hands stroked my back.

"Just thinking about stuff."

"Sounds like the wrong kind of stuff to be thinking about."

"I miss Max," I admitted. He pulled away and shrugged one shoulder.

"Well, when we loop back down you could see her, I know it's not much, but sweetheart, you rarely mention her. I didn't realize you were so upset about it."

"It's just, she broke up with her boyfriend before I left, and now here I am, on some glamorous tour, or what everyone thinks is a glamorous tour because they have no idea that it's really just a lot of hard work, and I feel bad about messaging her. It feels like a humble brag. 'Oh I wish I was there at school with you instead of touring the country.' Ugh. I don't want to say that to her." My teeth clicked shut. "Rambling, sorry." Finn sat back and stretched his arms above his head, pulling me in to rest against his side.

"You'll never talk as much as Ace, so don't worry about it."

I rolled my eyes.

"Nobody talks as much as Ace."

He snickered at that, and started playing with my braid, teasing the end of it against my collarbone. I shivered.

"I think Max would probably wanna hear from you even if you're rubbing it in that your life is going more smoothly. When we left to go fight in the war, me, Cash, and Eli? I'd never felt anything so painful as leaving the rest of our pack behind, and I would have given anything to be able to message them in an instant." He let out a long, sad breath. "We went charging off to war, thinking that it was us making the sacrifice. We came back to half of our pack gone." He rubbed a hand over his face and then shook his head. "Charlie would be bitching about me telling sad-warrior tales."

"You can talk about it, I don't mind. I've been having a serious case of the 'sads' for the past few days. How do you put up with my sulking?" I held my breath. Maybe he hadn't noticed? He turned to me, his fingers reaching up to tuck under my chin, his thumb tracing over my lower lip.

"I'm not gonna pretend like you weren't in a mood while we were camping, doing something that was supposed to make you feel better, but I figured you'd tell me if there was a problem I needed to deal with." A smile tugged at his lips. "Was that wrong? Should I have asked you right out?"

I thought about it for a moment, I shook my head. I hadn't been in a space to even talk about it. In an unreasonable pit of sadness, I'd needed to wallow for a bit. Finn's fingers took an interesting path, over my shoulder, skating down my arm, to slip over my stomach. Cash's hoodie was on the ground, I must've shrugged out of it in my sleep. Now I was just wearing a soft band t-shirt, and he played with the hem of it for a long minute.

"I know something that would make you feel better," his words pooled like molten lava in my belly and I took a slow, shuddering breath.

"What, your dick is a magical anti-anxiety?" I asked, startling a laugh and a grin out of him. Despite my snarky comment, he turned to me, bringing his lips down to mine to give me a soft kiss.

"Let me take care of you, sweetheart." His next kiss turned demanding, and I went with it. He pulled me into his lap. My short black skater skirt let me straddle his hips easily. The friction between us made it hard to forget that the only thing between me and him was his jeans and the thin fabric of my panties. He seemed to know it too, his hands rubbing along my thighs, thumbs digging into the muscle in a way that made me shiver and groan in response. His kiss was all teeth and tongue, making me squirm. This was what I needed, him, to forget everything and exist in the moment. I let my hands scratch down his back and he grunted, tensing under me.

His knees locked and I was airborne, as he stood, holding me in his arms. I exhaled a soft yelp and clung to him.

"What're you doing?!"

"Making you feel good," he growled, hands wrapping under my thighs. I clung to him, wrapping both arms around his neck.

"Someone's gonna find us," I whispered.

"Not if they can't get in the door." He took steady steps across the room, and I shivered as he pressed me up against the closed door to the green room, trapping me between it and his body. The inside of my thighs rubbed against his denim-clad hips and I squirmed. He sighed, pressing his forehead to mine, our noses barely touching. "I want you to remember that there is nothing more important to me than making you feel good. You're sad? I'm gonna make it better. You're hurting? I'm gonna make it better." His eyes opened, inches from mine. The fairy lights, strung around the ceiling of the room, reflected back at me in the deep blue of his eyes. "Anyone hurts you, and I'll fix them too. But you gotta tell me, sweetheart."

I bit my lip. Max was always complaining that Craig never

opened up to her, even though they'd been going out forever. How'd I get so lucky that this hot guy, along with several other hot, talented guys, wanted me to *talk* about my feelings?

"Promise me, Darcy," he said, looking serious, even as his thumbs rubbed up and down my bare thighs.

"Promise," I murmured, and closed my eyes.

"Good," the word brushed over my lips and he kissed me. "I'd hate to have to punish you for not telling me when something's wrong," he said, playfully, as he nipped at my lower lip. A shiver ran through me at the heat in his voice.

"Uhhhm, punish?" My cheeks were hot, and I snuck a peek at him from under my lashes, barely opening my eyes. The smirk on his face taunted me, and I squirmed in his grip. He huffed out a breath, grinding his hips into mine, making me moan and rest my head back against the door.

"How's about you don't be a bad girl, and I don't have to teach you a lesson? Seems easier that way." He dropped a hot kiss at the base of my throat.

"But what if the lesson was, um, good," I mumbled, because it didn't sound like anything he was saying implied that this 'punishment' or whatever would be something I wouldn't end up liking. His tongue slid out, and he laved over what parts of my collar bone he could reach before it disappeared under the boat-neck of my shirt.

"Rewards are better," he assured me. His fingers squeezed my thighs and he pressed me hard back against the door. "Lemme show you."

I inhaled sharply when he pulled away, falling to his knees, the tight muscles in his arms flexing to keep me where I was. He looked up at me, chuckled and planted a kiss on the inside of one of my bare knees.

"Finn, I'm gonna—"

"I won't drop you," he promised. "Relax and let me make you feel good."

"You're holding me against a door, what do you mean 'relax'," I hissed at him. He shrugged and deftly worked his shoulders under my legs. I locked my knees around them and tried not to panic.

"You work too hard," he said, nuzzling the inside of my thigh. I felt the scrape of his stubble over my skin, and it prickled, making me shiver. He crowded up against me, laying a path of kisses up my thigh. I squeezed my eyes shut and tried to pretend I wasn't several feet off the floor. My skirt had been pushed up my legs. I could feel his fingers holding me, and then, the light pass of his breath, over the thin cotton of my panties. The dull, warm pressure of his mouth made me gasp and tense. "Relax," he said again, and I willed my muscles to go slack. I sank down a half-inch, but he held me tight, and kissed the mound of my pussy with a groan.

"I've never—" My face was hot, my neck was hot, all of me was a five alarm fire, because I'd never done anything remotely like this, and I knew I'd probably like it because it was *Finn* and he seemed damned determined to make me feel good at every turn.

"You've got a lot of firsts to get through, and aren't I damn lucky that I get to be the one who's here for this one." He looked up at me from between my thighs, the wicked smile on his face turning my insides to jelly. His thumb traced a line of fire on the soft joint where my thigh met my body, teasing the skin there. He nosed at my underwear again, sighing out. The hot flood of warm air made me moan. "Shouldn't be selfish, keeping all of you to myself like this, but…"

His thumb hooked into the crotch of my panties and pulled it aside. My cheeks were flushing with embarrassment, but the noise he made at the back of his throat told me there was no part of him that was displeased with what he found. He kissed me again, no fabric in the way, and I grabbed onto the back of his head for balance, my fingers digging into his thick, blond hair.

"Good girl," he purred, and licked me, one long, slow stripe. It felt warm. It felt perfect. It felt like it wasn't enough. My hips rolled and he held me up, letting me move into him as he licked me again, teasing through my folds into the most intimate part of me. The soft, wet pressure was good, so good, and maybe he was right, maybe I just needed to relax. My eyes drifted shut and I let myself feel. The brush of his tongue over me, the squeeze of his hands on my thighs, the scrape of his five-o-clock shadow; all of it was building a curl of heat inside of me. When his tongue slid over my clit, slow and deliberate, I moaned and pulled his head closer to me, begging for more without using words.

He gave it to me, his tongue flicking back and forth, slow at first and speeding up as my body shifted and rolled into it, needing more.

I felt empty, a hollow ache like I needed him inside of me to come. I didn't know how to ask for that though, it felt like I was being selfish, needing *more*. I shivered, on the edge, for a long minute before he pulled away with a short, soft lick against me. He shifted his arms, letting me down off of his shoulders. My shoes hit the ground, and my skirt fell back into place, although I'd need to fix my underwear if I wanted to go anywhere and not be squirming as I walked.

I tried not to be disappointed, because he'd been so good at making me feel amazing, and maybe orgasms every time weren't going to be a thing for me. Some girls struggled with that, right?

Finn took one look at my expression and chuckled.

"You think I'm done with you?" he asked, and pulled me down. "Just needed my hands free for this, is all." A whine escaped from me as he laid me out on the carpet, his hip jammed up against the door to keep it shut. He pushed my skirt up my thighs and bent down, licking over my hip, and down between my legs.

"Oh god," I whispered, before pressing a hand over my mouth. The dampened fire inside me roared to life, and my thighs squeezed at his shoulders. I wanted it so bad. I needed it so, so bad.

His fingers joined his tongue, stroking my wet flesh, and I felt the pressure on my entrance as he slipped one finger into me. There was the faintest twinge in my muscles, but that disappeared quickly. The push-pull of his finger was what I needed, and my hips rocked up.

"You didn't think I was gonna leave you like that, did you?" He mouthed at my clit, sucking it gently. He was using the right pressure, just enough, and as his finger dragged out to thrust in again, I moaned. "You're mine, all of you, and if you need this, as much pleasure as I can give you, you're gonna get it. Every time, sweetheart, every damn time."

His words were pushing me further and further up the tight climb toward oblivion, and I reached for him, needing something to steady myself as I teetered on the edge. His hand came up and he laced his fingers through mine, holding onto me.

His tongue slipped over my clit, and I cried out, the shaking in my muscles exploding into a bone-deep shudder as I came. His finger stilled inside me, thick and exactly where I needed it, and he kept giving me slow, opened mouthed kisses over my pussy until I whined, the pleasure turning from *perfect* into *too much*. He pulled away, not before settling my underwear back over my tender skin. He sat up between my knees.

Love fluttered in my heart, a trembling emotion that needed to be protected, as I gazed at him through my half-opened eyes. My pulse was slowing, and a tired, wrung-out feeling was crawling through my limbs. I wanted to sleep for a week. He gathered me up and, as if I weighed nothing, got to his feet and walked me over to the couch. He curled around me as he laid me down, a soft rumble in his chest making me relax even more.

My eyes cracked open. His cock, hard and insistent, pressed against the small of my back as he spooned me. I reached back for his hip, my fingers grazing along his waistband. His hand caught my wrist and he moved my arm to curl it against my chest.

"Don't have time for that," he rumbled into my neck as he nuzzled against me, a giant wolf in a man's body.

"But you're, um, you're sorta in a state. That has to be uncomfortable."

"Not everything's gotta be about other people, Darcy, sometimes maybe it's gotta be all about you." He kissed my cheek and stroked the spot with his thumb. His eyes glittered in the low light of the green room. "You feeling better now?"

I nodded, vigorously. He grinned and kissed me slowly. I could taste myself on his lips, earthy, almost like the ghost of raw honey and something else I couldn't quite place.

"You wanna go back to the van?" he asked. My eyes opened wide and I sat up.

"You're not at the merch booth," I said, "the fans, sales, autographs!" He followed me and shrugged.

"Some things are more important than money, or stuff like that."

I was about to protest but he kissed me again, arm scooping around my shoulders and pulling me in tight to his chest.

"You give me a choice between what's out there, and what's right here in this room, in my arms? I'm gonna pick this, any day, any time." He sounded so serious and looked so intense that I swallowed down a knot of argument that was waiting to be let out.

"Okay," I whispered. "But maybe now? Now can we go to the merch booth?" His eyes slid down my body, and a smirk so devious crossed his face that I wanted to know what it was for.

"Sure," he drawled, "let's go see my pack-mates, let them sense you all over me, get the scent of how good you smell, and drive them crazy."

Oh. I bit my lip and he lifted a hand to stop me, soothing the skin with his thumb.

"You keep eating yourself," he commented.

"Nervous habit, it's hard to stop," I admitted. He chuckled and stood, pulling me with him.

"Let's go torture the guys a little bit. If they wanna be noble and not take what's in front of them, letting me be the first to gentle you into this, then they'll pay the price for it." He winked at me. I had to shake my head. Finn could be a bit bratty sometimes, but I liked it.

"Thanks," I said, as we walked toward the door, his arm around my shoulders for a few last, precious seconds. Once we were outside he'd have to keep his distance so it didn't look inappropriate. Jake had already enough fodder for his creepy little Twitter account, I thought darkly.

"Making you feel good is everything I want, is everything the guys want," Finn said with another one of those full body, devil-may-care shrugs that just seemed so *Finn*. "That was easy. Keeping you safe, and the pack safe, that's another story."

"Right," I said as he opened the door and motioned for me to step out. A germ of an idea was rolling around in my thoughts, picking up steam.

They needed a heartstone. Only a witch could make one. Maybe, just maybe, it was time for me to step up.

"I need to make a call," I said to him. He blinked.

"Okay?"

"I'll meet you out there." I gave him a push and he went, grinning.

"Bossy," he said with another wink. "I like it."

 **Darcy Llewellyn** @DarcyLuvsDonuts Follow

You ever feel like no matter what, you'll never be enough? #vaguetweet #whatever #wishingonastar

13 Retweets 36 Likes

8   13   36

TWENTY-SEVEN

"You've reached Daria Hailward. Leave a message."

Hearing her voice again was like being nineteen, wearing a witch's version of a prom dress (layers and layers of fine black chiffon over more chiffon), with the remnants of my coming-of-age gift in my hand. The black pearl necklace had been my grandmother's passed down to me from my mother on that special occasion. Creston grabbed it from my neck when I pulled away from his wandering hands, and sent pearls scattering all over the floor.

"But he's such a nice boy, Darcy," my mother had said. "Are you sure you didn't break it yourself and are just blaming him?"

She hadn't believed me. My father hadn't either.

Daria Hailward, Creston's bookish sister, two years younger than us, had been the only one who had believed me. But back then, she was my closest friend in a witching world that didn't understand girls who were different. Neither of us fell into the pattern; she wasn't glamorous and I wasn't good at magic. And she'd been living under the thumb of Creston's hidden cruelty her entire life.

We've all had that one guy, at least, who never listened when we said 'no'. That guy who pushed, pushed until we couldn't speak, the words freezing in our throats as he pawed at us, tears biting in the corners of our eyes. Maybe we knew him well. Maybe we barely knew him at all. Maybe we'd never seen him before that night. None of it mattered, because in those moments, he was a stranger to us even if we'd known him all our lives.

Creston was that guy for me. In the end though, it wasn't him trying to get my pretty dress off of me, or ripping my necklace, or telling me I was a tease, or storming off when I sparked him right in the balls, that hurt the most.

What hurt was my parents refusing to believe that he, a Hailward, would do such a thing. Even though they'd advocated for me with the council, and it had been decided that I *wouldn't* have my powers stripped, my parents still didn't believe me.

That betrayal had sent me out the window of my bedroom, a few things in my bag, running away to accept a place at a university in a city across the country from where I grew up. The only thing I'd left behind that I cared about had been Daria.

"Daria," I said into the phone, my voice rough. "It's Darcy. Call me back. Please."

I closed my eyes tight and tried not to remember how his fingers had snagged in the chiffon of my dress, dragging ladders in the fragile fabric. His body against mine, pressing into the wood-panelling of the council's ballroom. His breath, hot with alcohol he never should have been drinking in the first place, on the side of my face.

The shame in my mother's eyes at my accusation, and the disgust in my father's, when I'd come to the council and told the heads of each families what Creston had done. How my father stood, yelling over me, pointing to the door, telling me to *get out, damn you, insolent child!*

He had a way with words, my father. My mother stood behind him, pale as a lily, and said nothing. When I refused to move, my father jerked up his hand, and the red lightning of his powers came up, wrapped around my wrists, and dragged me from the room.

My knees still ached with ghost pain every now and then from the scrapes they'd earned that day. I fought him every inch of the way, my own power no match for his. But then my entire life under his roof had been a study in being outmatched, outpowered, outnumbered.

Max tried to get me to read Harry Potter once, but I couldn't stomach it, the pain was still too real and hot in the back of my mind. Maybe I didn't grow up in a cupboard under a set of stairs, but cages can come in all shapes. Mine was lined with silk and velvet, and my family looked at me with just as much disappointment and disgust.

My phone buzzed in my hand, and my heart leapt into my throat. Her phone number flashed on my screen. My trembling fingers accepted the call and I lifted the phone to my ear.

"Hello?"

Silence greeted me.

"Hello?"

I heard a soft breath.

"*Holy shit*," she said. I closed my eyes.

"Daria."

"*Darcy Evangeline Llewellyn. You missed my coming-of-age. It was nice. I wore purple. Mother was scandalized.*"

I brought my hand to my mouth, and suddenly my eyes were burning with tears. It'd been so long. I took a shaking lungful of air.

"*Dar, you okay?*" she asked, her voice turning worried.

"Yeah, Dar, I'm okay."

I heard her laugh at the nickname we'd called each other. We weren't remotely identical, her skin freckled and mine clear, her hair black and straight, where mine was lighter brown and curling, but our names were close enough we'd pretended we were the same person, split into two bodies.

"*Well you're doing that almost-crying thing. I mean, it's been years. I don't even know what you look like anymore. Mom made me throw out all the pictures cause...*" She sighed. "*I missed you. Then I was mad at you. Now I get it.*"

The aching maw in my chest gave an unpleasant pulse.

"I can't say I'm sorry. I'm not. I had to go."

"*Like I said. I get it. It sucked, and holy shit your dad got crap for months about it. A Llewellyn, leaving the fold? A council brat, cursing out the whole council? I mean it was pretty freaking spectacular."* There was a smile in her voice. *"Do you still suck at magic?"*

"Do you still not know the difference between foundation and concealer?" I shot back. She laughed, and it patched over the ache in my heart.

"Who needs makeup when I can just cast a glamour? Creston says it's false advertising, but I barely use it, which horrifies Mother. She says that someone so talented should be more interested in putting on a pretty face than I am."

Same old Daria. One of the best illusion casters that the council had ever seen, and she was more focused on reading history books than making the impossible come to life.

"How is Creston?" I asked, hating how I hesitated. But I needed to know.

"Still pissed. Still has the scars on his balls. I don't know how you managed that, also, don't ask me how I know either. It's not cause I looked, I swear."

I laughed out loud. It was like no time had passed at all from when we'd last talked.

"I have a favor to ask you."

"I don't have any money. At least not yet. Oh. I didn't tell you? I'm getting married."

"What?!"

"Ugh, yeah, in a few months. You're not invited, so don't worry, although I don't think they would know where to send the save-the-date card."

"Married to who?"

She hesitated for a long moment and a sinking feeling came over me.

"I... well. Slade Noble."

She'd named the head of the council. The Noble family could be traced back right to the beginning of the council. They'd never gone without holding a seat.

"That's an honor," I said, not able to keep the strangled tone out of my voice.

"You can say it. He's thirty years older than me."

"Uh. Do—do you..."

"Love him? That's a joke. No. But he needs an heir, and he figures that someone young enough will give him lots of time to get one." There was a flat tone in her voice that chilled me. She sounded so resigned. Like she'd already made up her mind about her future, about what was happening, and she wasn't going to do anything to change it.

She didn't sound like my Daria.

"I guess congratulations?" What could I say?

"You're not going to convince me to run away? Where did you go anyway? No, don't tell me. Then I can't tell them."

"Do you want to run?" I asked, pouncing on that small idea. She could stay in my bunk while I was on tour. Max could take care of her, teach her all about life in a world that was—

"I'm not brave like you, Dar," she said, her voice wistful. *"But it's okay. He's not the partying type so I don't have to turn into some sort of engagement-throwing, crowd-*

entertaining social harpy. Why'd you call anyway? It's been a bit too long for this to just be a polite social call."

The boys. I had to focus on the boys, because right then I wanted to get on a plane, go home, and rescue her from her fate. Daria was better than Slade Noble. He was a bitter, dried up lemon of a man, who didn't deserve someone as brilliant and talented as her.

"You're the smartest witch I know—"

"Do you need money?"

"No! No I don't need money," I bit my lip to keep from laughing. She really hadn't changed. "I wanted to ask you about heartstones?"

The line went quiet, and then, cautiously, she asked,

"What did you want to know?"

"How to make them." More silence, this time for too long. "Daria?"

"Remember when I said you were brave? No. You're crazy," her voice was flat again; unamused.

"Ummm, okay, that wasn't the response I was expecting but I can work with it. I'm serious. How do you make a heartstone?"

"You don't. Unless you want to die. Especially you, because you're so bad at magic. But even I wouldn't try to make one. I don't think anyone's made one for at least a hundred years, if not longer. Why a heartstone? They're not really that powerful unless," she trailed off and I could *hear* a frown in her voice. *"Werewolves use them, need them, really, for their long lives, the ability to heal and their strength, their vocal*

powers, oh, and procreating. They shoot blanks unless they're near one at least semi-regularly." She huffed out a breath. *"Darcy you're not, you haven't met a werewolf have you?"* There was skepticism in her voice, like she thought the idea was sort of ridiculous but had to ask it just in case.

My silence told her everything she needed to know.

"I'll come get you. Do you need money? Seriously. I'll send you money. I can borrow a credit card."

"Daria, I'm fine. I don't need money. I'm good. I've got—I'm in a good place."

"I could find you if I wanted too," she threatened. I laughed.

"You couldn't find your own head if you lost it. You were never good at finding magics. What do you mean by I'd die if I created one?"

"I mean that the last lightning witch to make one died. That's why we stopped making them. It took too much out of him, and he just crumpled and died. It's sort of this whole, witching-embarrassment thing." Daria sighed. *"So are you hanging out with a werewolf? They're treacherous. Seriously, if you are, you need to get away as fast as you can."*

The thought of any of the guys being treacherous was stupid, and I snorted.

"You sound like our parents."

"Yeah well they're not totally clueless about everything."

We were both quiet for a moment, hurt hanging in the silence. She spoke first.

"Dar, I don't know where you are, or what you're into, but

trust me. It would take a crazy-powerful witch to make a heartstone, and then he or she would probably die while making it. And werewolves are dangerous, blood-thirsty, and honestly, I'm not all that sad that they're dying out. They've killed more humans than I can count, and quite a few witches too."

I wanted to yell at her that she had no idea what she was talking about. Imagining any one of my guys as a vicious killer wasn't even possible. Ace was a goofball, more prone to bursting into stitches than hurting anyone. For all Eli was growly and grouchy, it always seemed to be in an effort to protect us. Charlie would never murder anyone because the risk of him getting blood on his phone was too great and he loved that piece of technology like it was a child. Cash, there was a thread of violence in Cash, for sure, but it was more that he was desperate for solutions to save his pack.

And Finn?

Finn, who tenderly had shown me that a girl's first time could be fairly painless, who'd taken care with me as if I was the most precious thing in the world? Finn whose love was so big that his heart couldn't contain it, and it spilled out into his music, his affection for his new fans at each show? That Finn? Who hugged young women and never let his hands stray past their shoulders? He could've gotten away with it, I'd known way too many musicians who had, but he never abused the power he had like that. None of the band did. I wondered if that was why Willa put an inexperienced young female in the position of managing them. If they'd been a band of Jake Tuppers, I would have been eaten alive.

None of my guys were violent, although I had no doubt they'd resort to it if it meant keeping each other, or me, alive.

"Dar? You there? Did I piss you off?"

"No. I just—I appreciate the info. I'm sorry I never called."

"It's not okay. I mean it is okay. But I kinda figured you wouldn't. But you can, you know, any time. Just call. I'm here! Preparing for my wedding." She sighed. *"Just promise me you'll stay safe."*

I thought of the hunters possibly on our tail and smiled, even though she couldn't see it.

"I'll do my best," I said.

"Dar."

"Congrats on your engagement. I'll tell you what my mother told my sister; just lay back and think of the council."

"Ew! She did not! That's so gross."

"That's my mom."

"God, no wonder you ran away. Even Mother isn't that batshit. Okay, well, I miss you! And stop thinking about making a heartstone. You're crazy. Okay?"

"Bye Daria," I whispered, disappointment rising in me. The one thing I could have given the pack was out of my reach. If there'd been a way to do it, Daria would have known. And told me.

"Bye Darcy."

TWENTY-EIGHT

I wish I'd had the chance to mope over my call with Daria and what she told me about creating heartstones. Instead of going out to the merch table, I got scooped up by Eli as I turned the corner of the hall backstage. He hauled me over his shoulder before I could say anything.

"We're going," he said when I yelped in surprise. I shoved my hands against his back, pushing my head up as he walked briskly. Behind him the rest of the guys followed, grim expressions on their faces, even Ace, whose frown muscles never seemed to work. They each carried gear, and my backpack was slung over Charlie's shoulder. My heartbeat picked up, thudding in my mouth and throat.

"The merch," I croaked.

"Leave it, Shara is getting it," Eli rumbled under me as he adjusted me on his shoulder. I dangled like a kitten in his grip.

"What's—" I fell quiet when Eli growled. I looked at Finn. He didn't meet my eyes, turning to glance behind him every moment. We broke out into the cool night air, a crisp breeze whipping up around us. A few short strides and we were at the van. He finally let me down, and I went to get into it. I was moving too slowly, apparently. Eli shoved me from behind and I nearly fell against it, catching myself on a seat.

"Hey!" I snapped, whirling on him. He looked instantly guilty, and Finn snarled, grabbing Eli by the shoulder.

"The fuck are you thinking? You wanna hurt her? Fucking idiot."

"Guys," Charlie, the voice of reason, spoke up as he set his gear down by the trailer. "Now is not the time."

Finn and Eli stared at each other.

"Get in the car, Darcy," Ace said quietly.

"Can't I help pack up?" Cash and Charlie were loading the gear into the back already, without the usual care they took. I could hear the quiet, muffled bangs of gear going down and winced.

"Get in, please," Finn said. I swallowed and ducked into the van, heading to the back and stared out the window, my heart thudding almost painfully. Eli stood by the door of the van, eyes scanning the parking lot, his shoulders tense.

"Got it!" Cash called, banging on the back of the trailer as they slammed it shut. Eli walked around the outside of the van and got into the driver's seat. The engine turned over, sending a soft vibration through the entire vehicle. The guys piled in. As soon as the door was closed, I heard the click of the lock. I sank down into my seat and put my seatbelt on. Finn crouched in the middle of the aisle as we pulled out of the parking lot, staring out the side window at the parking lot as we left it behind. The skin on the back of my neck prickled, like someone was watching me.

Even after we turned onto the freeway, and we were ten minutes down the road, the feeling didn't subside.

"Is it safe to talk now?" I asked, my anxiety making my words sound more annoyed than they were. Finn finally stood, balancing easily in the moving vehicle. He came and sat down next to me. The guys were still tense, and he made no move to put an arm around me like usual. His next words made my heart turn to ice.

"There was a hunter in the venue."

I stared at him.

"What? How? How do you know? Did he see you?"

"Darcy, breathe," he said his brow furrowing. "We don't know. We didn't see him."

"Then how did you know?" Confusion warred with panic in my chest.

"They have a certain scent," he said wryly, the corner of his mouth turning up. "Usually it's just flat out blood, stale and dried. But the young ones, the new ones, they smell like a burnt out fire, like ash." He sighed. "This one was young, your age, probably, and didn't have a lot of kills under his belt."

"You knew it was a guy?"

Finn gave me a flat look as if to ask *seriously?*

Ace turned in his chair, and I could see how white he was under his shock of blond hair.

"There wasn't anyone weird around the merch table tonight?" Ace asked. I shook my head. Just the usual. I didn't remember seeing anyone who looked like they murdered mythical creatures for a hobby. Not that I had any idea of what that kind of person would look like.

Charlie looked up from his phone.

"Shar's got our merch on the Glory Rev bus," he said with a sigh. "Good thing or Willa would have killed us if that hunter hadn't gotten there first."

"Not funny, Gage," Ace said, slumping in his seat and sounding worn down.

"Five of us and one of them? Guy wouldn't have stood a chance even if we'd been fully human," Charlie said, sounding unmoved by the whole event. How he could be so calm, I had no idea. My heart was trying to crawl its way up my throat and my guts were making unfortunate squelching noises. My chest was so tight that each breath felt like it was going to crack my ribs.

"So... so why didn't you... take care of the problem?" I asked. All the boys tensed. Everyone, except for Eli who was driving, stared at me like I was crazy. "What?"

Finn cleared his throat.

"Sweetheart, do you know how many kids were in that venue?"

I closed my eyes as I realized what he meant.

"Right," I mumbled.

"It's okay," he said, and his arm finally, *finally*, came out and wrapped around my shoulder. His heat sunk into my tense, painful muscles and relaxed them minutely. "We're not gonna risk kids. Even kids who are in college."

"Do you see me as a kid?" I made a face at him. He smirked for a moment.

"Nah, you're all woman," he said and kissed me slowly. I sighed and clung to him, still shivering over the close call we'd had. And only thirty minutes earlier, I'd been with Finn in the green room, having one of the best orgasms of my life, and a hunter had been sneaking around in the venue.

"Maybe he was there to watch the show," Ace said, although he didn't sound all that sure about it.

"It's possible," Eli drew out the word like he didn't want to let it end. "Just one of them showing up like that? It could have been a coincidence. It doesn't matter. We've got a show tomorrow, and we're gonna get there tonight."

"Tonight?" Charlie sounded dismayed. "We're driving all night?"

Eli grunted in response. I sighed and leaned into Finn, letting my eyes slide shut.

It was going to be a long damn night.

Phoenixcry
@PhoenixcryMusic

Follow ⌄

Sorry we had to take off early tonight, guys!
When you bust a string you gotta go deal
with it! #GStringProbs #ItsFinnsFault

7 Retweets 20 Likes

♡ 7   ⟲ 7   ♡ 20   ✉

TWENTY-NINE

Finn shook me. I opened my eyes. Light was spilling into the van, as the sun peeked over a range of mountains. I squinted and rubbed my eyes. My whole body ached, and when I touched my cheek, I could feel the mark where my seatbelt had pressed into my face.

"My mouth feels like a rat died in it," I said, to Finn's quiet chuckle.

"We're stopping for a break. Stretch your legs, rinse your mouth out."

"Where are we?" I asked, wrinkling my nose as we pulled into a gas station that seemed deserted. Hopefully the pumps were on. If we'd driven straight for hours we'd be needing gas.

"Arizona, still" Eli said as he threw the van into park and got out without a word. Charlie opened the sliding door to the van, and I shivered when a rush of cold air hit me.

"I though Arizona was hot," I protested, wrapping my arms

around myself. My thin t-shirt was not enough to stay warm in.

"Deserts get cold at night," Finn said, tugging off his hoodie. "C'mere." He pulled it over my head without waiting for me to put my arms up. It messed up my curls; I could feel the fly-aways tickling at my eyes and nose, and I grumbled but allowed his warmth and the soft mint scent of him comfort me.

I stumbled out of the van on shaking, weak legs and stretched my arms up to the sky. Streams of light were crossing it where the sun kissed it, turning it from deep purple to almost white. I breathed out slowly, shaking the last panic from our after-show run.

Charlie came up beside me and bumped me with his hip playfully, before passing me a soda. I frowned at the closed shop.

"Vending machine around the corner," he answered my question before I could ask where he'd gotten the drink. "We're gonna drive another few minutes to the venue, then camp out in the lot. It's just over the next rise. You hungry?"

"Not really."

He nodded.

"Abject terror does that to some people. Great diet trick."

I eyed him as I cracked the top of my soda and took a long sip.

"Doesn't anything scare you?"

"Being scared," he answered. He pulled me in for a hard hug, his head bowed against my shoulder. "Just glad you're safe," he whispered into my ear. Before I could blink he was gone again, going over to Cash to talk to him in a low voice. The two looked at me for a moment and Cash nodded. I was too tired to call them out on talking about me so blatantly, and besides, Finn came up to me and smiled as he saw me flagging.

"Get inside, Llewellyn," he teased, "you're gonna fall asleep right here otherwise." I grumbled at him, and he helped me into the van, grabbing the soda from my fingers before I could drop it. He stole a swig, gulping down half of it. I didn't protest, and belted myself in. His hoodie was all around me, and it lulled me back to sleep. In the haze of my descent into dream-land, I felt my seat-belt go tight around me and click into place, and the hum of the engine start up.

I drifted in and out, the light from outside threatening to wake me up completely. The van jerked to a stop and I sat up with a sharp gulp of breath. Finn was already standing, stretching. Charlie and Ace pulled down the beds that pressed into the ceiling and came down at night, getting ready to climb into them and pass out for a few hours before the show. I blinked at Finn as he smiled at me. The van rocked slightly as Cash moved around, pulling the black-out curtains closed on all the windows, and Eli got into the bed that hung over the cab. Shoes hit the aisle, and a pair of jeans next as he undressed up there.

"C'mon sweetheart, get up so I can make the bed." Finn shifted me off the bench seat and I stood there, swaying with exhaustion. Normally I slept in one of the bunks, with two of the guys taking the back bench beds, and two guys slept up in the roof-top bed. But as the other guys got settled, leaving only the bench bed for me and Finn, the usual sleeping order was clearly being shaken up. I didn't think about it too hard, leaning against the side of the small kitchenette and trying not to fall asleep upright.

Out came two sleeping bags, which Finn zipped together, and he beckoned to me. I stepped up to him, trying not to yawn in his face. He eased me out of his hoodie. His hands fell to my hips, hesitating for a moment, before he pushed down my skirt. I squirmed, almost wanting my underwear to go with them. I felt sticky, and when I made a soft noise, his eyebrow slid up his brow. His fingers hooked into my underwear and he pushed them down my thighs.

I sighed in relief, and kicked myself out of my shoes, letting my panties and skirt puddle on the floor. If the other guys were watching, I couldn't tell, because they were just making getting-ready-for-sleep sounds and didn't seem to be paying us any attention. I reached behind my back and unsnapped my bra, tugging it out from the arms of my shirt. The bra followed the rest of my clothes, and I slid into the sleeping bag with a sigh. Finn's breath faltered as I moved, and I curled up tight. He tugged his shirt off, flicking his belt open. His jeans hit the floor, as did the rest of his things, until he slipped into the bed next to me in just a pair of boxer-briefs. The heat he was throwing off was delicious, and I inched closer, my skin aching to be near him. He zipped up the sleeping bag and sighed, before rolling over onto his side. I curled into him in the darkness of the tour van, light leaking in around the curtains but not enough to bother me.

I nuzzled my nose into his bare chest and he grunted, staying still. When I did it again, the soft purr in his chest started up, making me smile.

"Hey there, kitty," I teased. He growled, a counterpoint to his soft purring.

"Gonna swat your ass if you keep that up," he threatened. I wiggled against him, my skin perfectly sensitive against the softness of the sleeping bad. Sleeping bare was a treat, and I squirmed again, reveling in it.

"Sounds awesome," I answered back, the exhaustion and panic hormones finally having run their course, leaving me feeling buzzy and electrified. I closed my eyes and nosed at his chest, rubbing my cheek against it. The sprinkling of coarse hairs there felt good on my face, and I stuck my tongue out, flicking it over one of his flat nipples.

He hissed out a breath, and pulled away.

"Darcy," he said, sounding scandalized. "Go to sleep."

"Nah," I stole his own lazy drawling word, "can't. Don't want to." His eyes narrowed at me.

"Oh, is that right?"

I smirked up at him.

"Mmhm," I said. "You want me to sleep, you're gonna have to make me."

"Really?"

"Just *fuck her already*," Charlie snapped from his bunk. "The two of you, just fuck and shut up. Some of us, very obviously *not fucking,* are trying to sleep."

We fell quiet for a moment and I noticed Finn's shoulders were shaking. I muffled my giggle into his chest, not able to contain it. His mouth fell to my ear, and the low buzz of his voice set my body alight,

"Guess we should listen to him," he whispered. He shifted, and I felt him shoving his boxer-briefs down his legs. I helped, or tried to, my arms not working too well. He batted me away, and when he rolled on top of me. His weight pressed me down, grounding me. My eyes closed, my thighs parting for him. I was already wet, somehow, just being around him was doing that to me. His fingers traced over my hips, up my stomach, pushing my shirt out of the way until my breasts were exposed to him. One of his large, warm hands cupped one, his mouth teasing the other with nips and licks. I tried to keep quiet, I really did.

I bit my lip; covered my mouth; breathed as softly as I could. My eyes closed tighter when his tongue circled my nipple again and again until my hips pushed up into his belly, insistent and demanding. His hands moved down, pinning me down, and I felt the hard, hot press of his cock against me.

For a moment, a flutter of panic overtook me and then, Daria's voice in my head interrupted my focus;

"They shoot blanks unless they're near one at least semi-regularly."

I relaxed, offering up a silent prayer to shitty situations that led to magically-induced male birth-control. The next slide of Finn's cock, splitting my inner walls apart, had every thought but how good he felt in me, disappearing. My hand fell away from my mouth, and I grabbed for the edge of the bed, anything. Finn found me, his fingers lacing through mine. He pinned the back of my hand to the sleeping bag, and watched me through half-open eyes.

It was so intimate, making love in the silence of the tour van, the presence of the pack so *close* that I could feel them pressing down on us. I should have been ashamed, but it felt right. Them being close, and Finn inside me, the short, slow pumps of his hips testing my limits; all of it was perfect.

Finn's mouth found my ear, and at first I thought he was only going to kiss me. Then he started talking.

"Love you, Darcy," he said. I shivered, and lifted my hips to meet his on a deep thrust. "Gonna keep you, forever. All mine, forever." His words devolved into dirtier talk, and I shuddered, and cried out. "That's it, baby girl, let me make you feel so good." He licked my earlobe, the purring in his chest getting louder as his hips rolled. I felt so close to him, his cock filling me with each thrust, chasing the breath out of my lungs.

"Finn, please, I need," I struggled to come up with the words. In an instant, he hitched his hips, shifting his cock in me. I moaned and arched up, needing more from him. His hand snaked between us and pressed firmly over my clit. "Right there," I groaned, "please, right there."

He buried his face in my neck. I could feel the hot flood of his breath on my neck as his fingers teased over my clit, again and again, the short, sharp strokes making my hips hitch each time. My orgasm was just out of reach, just slightly, and then—

He growled and I felt his teeth close on my neck, the move more possessive than erotic, and I cried out so loudly that I saw Ace shifting to look over the edge of his bunk. My eyes caught his and we stared at each other as Finn thrust into me, holding me down. Another flush of pleasure ran up my spine and I whimpered, closing my eyes tight as I shook through the end of my orgasm. Finn bit down harder, hips jerking into me hard as he came. I swore I could feel the wet pulse of him inside me, but maybe it was just my imagination.

He stayed over me, head against the skin of my neck, teeth holding me still. I lifted my free hand, and stroked it down the back of his head. He let go of me, raising his head to look at me. His eyes were glassy, and he glanced down at my neck, wincing.

"Shit," he said, swallowing hard. He ran a thumb and I winced at the sore skin. "It's gonna leave a mark."

My heart squeezed with pride.

"So what," I said, full of bravado. Maybe I wanted everyone to know I belonged to him. His eyes narrowed and he rumbled.

"Mine," he whispered, and buried his nose in my neck again, sighing. He deflated over me, like a warm, burly, man-blanket. It was so comforting.

I was feeling a little weird down there though, and I squirmed.

He huffed out a grumpy noise and pulled out of me gently, reaching over my head to grab a box of the baby wipes that were stashed all over the tour van. Could never have enough baby wipes on a tour, I quickly discovered.

Especially if you were fucking one of the band-members in the back of the tour van. My cheeks pinked up at that thought. He passed me a wipe and I looked away as I cleaned up, feeling shy about it. He nuzzled my cheek, following me despite my desire to curl up. The more I pulled away, the more intent he seemed on snuggling me, until I finally had to sit up to get some space. He leaned up on elbow, looking forlorn.

"Just give me a minute," I hissed. He had the grace to blush and he looked away. I got myself clean and wipes stashed away in a plastic bag, before I settled down again. "I'm good."

Immediately he was on top of me, half spooning me, half smothering me. It felt good, and we fell asleep, his arm around me, and our fingers entwined.

THIRTY

Lunch was a hot cooked meal for once, in an vintage-style diner around the corner from the venue. There was a security guard on the lot so we felt okay about leaving the van in the middle of a strange city once we were awake. We piled out into the fresh air, blinking into the sun like a group of disheveled mole-people. Finn popped his hoodie on me again, the oversized garment coming down to my mid-thighs and up to my nose almost.

"Hmmm," Ace said as he leaned over me while we walked to the diner. I glanced up at him. He grinned and winked. "Nice mark you got there." My eyes went wide and I felt my neck. The soft indents of teeth were still in my skin, just above where the hoodie folded along my neck. I reached into my bag and pulled out a compact, checking it out. What I saw made my cheeks redden, and a curl of heat bloom just below my belly. Finn's bite hadn't broken the skin, but it'd bruised me, lightly, a reddened line that made me felt claimed.

Ace studied me for a long moment. "You okay with it?"

"Weirdly, yeah," I said, running my thumb over the mark with a sigh before tucking away my compact. He bumped me gently with his shoulder, and snuggled me into his side with his arm, inhaling my scent with his nose in my hair.

"We don't deserve you," he said softly. I frowned at him and gave him a playful shove.

"Stop talking like that," I ordered. He grinned.

"Yes ma'am."

It was a treat to order lunch in a real restaurant, surrounded by the guys. After the close call we'd had last night, Eli decided to break into the merch money, and ordered an entire lemon meringue pie with the egg whites whipped so high, they wobbled on my plate. Finn stayed glued to my side for the rest the day, and it wasn't unusual for me to catch him taking selfies with me in the background.

"You know Chrissy isn't going to let you put up any of those photos," I said, shaking my head as he pulled another face for the camera. He just shrugged.

"Worth it," he replied. I rolled my eyes; we had time during the day to actually sightsee for once and, even though I was tired, it was nice to walk around the downtown area to people watch. There was a pulse to the city that you only felt when you were walking around. It wasn't the same to drive through. The afternoon passed quickly, too quickly for me, because I spent most of it with my fingers in Finn's hand.

This venue was a weird set up when we arrived at it. The merch tables were in a different room from the main performance, so me, Shara and Ginny were all by ourselves for the longest time. Eventually Shara and Ginny got tired of waiting for fans to show up, and decided to go check out the bar in the main venue room. It's not like I could drink anyway.

I sat at my booth playing on my phone. Max had finally emerged from her self-imposed isolation. She was finally sending me back text messages regularly, and I wasn't as worried as I had been. She was even starting to sound like her old self. It made me homesick, which was funny to think that the dorm room with Max was more like 'home' to me than life with my family in a massive mansion had ever been.

Footsteps made me look up. Jake Tupper stood in the doorway to the merch room, his arms crossed over his chest. His gaze burned over me, sending all my instincts screaming. For a moment his face flickered and, when he smirked, it was Creston smirking out at me. I blinked and the memory was gone.

"Hey there, merch girl," he drawled as he walked over. He knew better. He knew that I was a manager in my own right, even if I was just an intern. And frankly, I'd been doing a damn good job of it. It wasn't easy to wrangle a band that had no-one to advocate for them in the form of a booking agent. Getting their sound checks, making sure the venues all had handbills, flyers, and posters for each show in advance and then actually *used* them?

Half my time on the road was spent with my laptop open, my cellphone in one hand and the band burner phone in the other, calling street team leaders to make sure the local hangouts were all flyered so that when Phoenixcry rolled into town they actually made a splash and didn't disappear under the weight of Glory Rev or Jake.

The best part? It was working. The guys were being flooded after every set with kids throwing twenties at them, lining up for selfies, and wanting to talk forever about the songs, the lyrics, the show. I got the kids to come at doors, when they'd usually come an hour later, and once inside the venue? The boys sold it, hard. Their social media was going crazy and I was getting a steady stream of thumbs-up emails from Chrissy and Willa.

"What do you need, Jake?" The words were wrong as soon as they were out of my mouth, and I *knew* it, like watching an accident right before it happens. Jake's smirk twisted into a dirty smile.

"Well now that's just what I wanted to talk about," he said, putting his hand on my merch booth, pushing away my carefully folded t-shirts and displayed merch stacks.

The hair on my arm stood up and I glanced down in time to see a thin line of white-blue lighting zip along my wrist. I shoved my arm behind my back, feeling faint. *Not now,* I begged whatever higher entity was in charge of making my unpredictable powers flare up.

Jake's eyes dragged up my body slowly, devouring me with his eyes, and it was all I could do not to slap him or curl my arms in front of me to hide from his gaze. He remained silent and I made an annoyed noise. I was so over this asshole.

"Want me to tell Shara you were looking for her?" I asked. He chuckled.

"Don't pretend you don't feel it," he said, dropping his voice down low, tilting his head as he looked at me. He was flirting, ugh, and I'm sure it worked on some girls, who had no taste and thought that Axe made for an elegant cologne.

"The only thing I'm feeling right now is nauseous," I replied, my voice flat. He frowned.

"What?"

I took a breath and a huge risk, but to hell with it. The guy was a menace. If he was willing to risk harassing me, I probably wasn't his first. If I could help it, I'd be his last.

"I know all about your freaky little Twitter account." I watched as his face went white for a moment. "Yeah. Real cute. Think taking pictures of me sleeping is romantic? It's not. It's fucked." I heard a soft crack, and felt electricity run up my spine from where my hand was pressed against it behind me.

Shit. What was making my powers go haywire? I needed to get Jake out of there.

His face had taken on some pretty striking similarities to a thundercloud. The small, sarcastic part of my brain wondered if he was a weather witch too. I knew he wasn't. Jake was pure human. Pure garbage-person human.

"You don't know what you're talking about," he said, and gave me one of his little smirky grins. "So you liked it, huh?"

"Are you kidding me?!" I stepped back from the merch table. "Are you even hearing me?

"Oh, I'm hearing you, babe. Loud and clear." He reached for me, lightning-fast, and grabbed my wrist.

It was just like Creston. The breath stilled in my lungs. My body went stiff, by bit, even as I screamed inside my head to *move, goddammit, move!* But I couldn't.

"That's right, sweetheart," he whispered, looming into my personal space. The nickname, so beautiful on Finn's tongue, was like nails raking down my skin coming from Jake's mouth. It woke me up and, with a cry, I jerked back out of his grip. I stumbled into the folding chair I'd been sitting on minutes before, and caught myself before turning. Jake stared at me like I'd grown two heads, his pupils blown wide.

"The fuck?" he whispered. Light flashed in my peripheral vision and I looked down. The lightning was back crawling all over my arms, lacing and searing hot lights of light across my eyes. I blinked and jerked my head up. He took a step back, and power swelled inside me.

"**Back off**," I ordered, and he took a shaking step back, nearly tripping as my command forced him to do what I said.

"Darce—" Ace came in through the doorway. "The guys are almost—" He stopped dead in his tracks, taking in the sight before him and snarled, turning from sweet marshmallow Ace into something dark and dangerous right in front of my eyes. He was across the room in a single breath, his hand up around Jake's throat, and a low, powerful grumble emanating from him.

Jake gulped and coughed, his hand going up to Ace's, scratching uselessly at Ace's skin.

"Let go," he struggled to breathe the word in. "F-freak, let go!"

"Ace," I said.

"No, Darcy," Ace defied me, glaring up at the taller man. He gave Jake a shake by the neck like Jake wasn't anything more than a rag doll. "You touch her?" he demanded. "What'd you do to her!?"

I walked up to Ace.

"Ace," I snapped. "Let him down." Ace looked over his shoulder at me and growled but pulled away from Jake.

"Fucking... fucking freak," Jake gasped, rubbing his neck and stepping away, bending over and coughing.

"I should—" Ace started, the threat clear in his voice, but I grabbed his hand hard and yanked him back. He went with me, as the rest of the guys arrived, looking at our little encounter for a moment before they all stalked into the room, ready to do battle. I whirled and stared down Eli. He stopped short from me and Ace, and glared at me and looked past me to Jake who was still coughing and making a dramatic show of rubbing his neck.

"Oh grow up," I spat at him. "He didn't hurt you."

"You guys wouldn't even be on this tour if not for me." Jake breathed heavily around his words and I rolled my eyes.

"I'm gonna get Aaron," Charlie muttered, and vanished. Eli was still switching from glaring at me to glaring at Jake. Finally, *finally*, Eli settled his shoulders and crossed his arm, apparently content to follow my lead. Good. I didn't have the energy to fight him and deal with Jake. I turned and stepped in front of Ace, ignoring his noise of strangled protest.

"Bitch," Jake wheezed, and I felt the guys behind me tense up again, ready for a fight. They weren't going to get one. It was one thing to manhandle Jake a little bit, that could be explained away, but a full four-on-one asskicking? They'd get kicked off the tour and off the label if that happened. And then arrested, probably. It was up to me to stop it. I put my hand on Ace's stomach behind me, and fisted my hand in his shirt.

"You're gonna leave this room," I said to Jake coldly. "You're gonna leave this room right the fuck now, and go back to the tour bus."

Jake's face twisted up in to a nasty snarl.

"You can't tell me what to do."

"Yeah, but I can," Aaron's voice rang out behind us all and I felt a tremor of relief go through me. Jake's eyes went wide as he looked past me. I didn't turn my back to look too; I didn't want to be vulnerable in front of Jake.

"Daddy's here," Charlie muttered as he came up beside me, flanking me. I'd need to talk to him later about appropriate jokes about the headliners, and calling Aaron 'Daddy' wasn't one of them. I still kept my grip on Ace in case he decided it was worth the kamikaze career move to deck Jake.

"We need to talk, Jake," Aaron said, sounding resigned. "Come to the tour bus. Now." Jake eyed me then Ace beside me, refusing to look at any of my other guys in the eyes. He hesitated when he walked by me and for a moment I thought he was going to spit in my face.

He passed me though, and the rest of the guys, and we turned to watch him go. When he disappeared after Aaron, Ace wrapped me up in a big wolf-hug, holding me tight.

"What'd he do?" Eli asked. I shook my head.

"Later. Tonight," I said.

"You should've reported him ages ago," Cash spoke up. "He's been dogging your shadow like a freak since the beginning of tour." Something in his voice set me off.

"As if it would have been that easy," I snapped. "As if I could have just *reported* him." Cash squared his shoulders, not giving an inch.

"Yeah. Yeah, it was that easy."

"That's crap," I spat, the adrenaline finally getting to me. I was shaking, my fingers trembling. Jake had seen my powers. He'd *seen my powers*. That thought ran over and over through my mind on loop, even as I argued with Cash.

"If you'd said something, it wouldn't have gotten to this point!" Cash took a step toward me, and Finn grabbed him by the shoulder.

"What, and get kicked off the tour? I'm an intern, Cash, an intern! I'm replaceable, in a heartbeat, there's hundreds of other applicants out there dying for this kind of opportunity. Just cause you guys have fully accepted me doesn't mean that the label wouldn't get rid of me if I was a pain in the ass. He's Jake Tupper!" I was shouting. I was shouting and there was a crowd of kids in the hallway, staring in at us. I felt my cheeks flush hard, and the nausea rose higher in my throat.

"Let's take this outside, guys," Charlie's voice cut through the frantic energy rolling around in my gut. I whirled and stalked off toward the exit, not caring if the guys were following me. I was done. I was maybe done *for* if Jake talked.

Cash was hot on my heels when we got into the cool night air. I took a deep breath of it, trying to calm down.

"Why were you so worried about getting kicked off tour? The only reason we were on it to begin with was because of you." Cash asked. "And besides, you know we wouldn't let that happen. We need you." There was something in Cash's voice that set me on edge again and I tried to fight it. Getting mad wouldn't fix the situation we were in. Being sensible, calming down, would.

His next words blew all my good intentions out of the water.

"We need you Darcy. You're our only chance at survival."

My stomach dropped like a rock. Of course. The heartstone. He had a one track mind, coming back to it, demanding I figure out an answer for the key to all their problems. Anger, hurt, and betrayal flashed through me.

"Right, I forgot, you need me around so I can save your pack and make you a heartstone. Never mind that I can't. Never mind that I've told you that I can't, that it's not possible. Were you not listening?!" My hands jerked up in the air, gesturing wildly, as the last, tenuous strings holding my temper back snapped. "**I can't do it!**" My voice echoed off the outside of the venue, and for a moment, I heard my power coming back at me like he would hear it, the raw force of command as it echoed off the stucco.

Cash looked like he'd been slapped.

"I didn't mean it that way," he muttered. "I just wanted—"

"Well, maybe what about what I want?" I demanded, tears welling up in my eyes although I didn't feel sad. I felt violated. I felt enraged. "I don't want to die, Cash, and guess what, that's what's gonna happen if I try to make one. I know, I called my friend." My words died in my mouth when I realized what I'd said. He frowned.

"You did what?"

"I- I called a friend," I repeated myself. He squinted at me.

"As in a witch friend," he stated. I swallowed.

"Yeah."

He inhaled deeply, his jaw flexing so hard I thought his teeth might crack.

"A witch friend who knows you're looking to create a heartstone and knows where you are."

"No, she has no idea where I am."

"But she knows you want to make one, and if she's friends

with you, she's not an idiot, so she's figured out *why* you want to make one," he grit out each word, as if they burnt him.

"It's not like that," I insisted, my anger deflating and running away from me.

"All I asked was for you to think about it, to try," he said, "That's all I wanted. And you went ahead, and made a stupid decision and ended up endangering all of us!"

"I was trying to help," I shot back, stung. "You made me feel so damn bad, saying stuff like how you guys were pretty much going to die without it, so what did you expect me to do? Nothing?"

"Don't you blame this on me." He took one menacing step toward me, and I flinched.

"Shut the fuck up, both of you," Eli interrupted us, walking out of the venue. "Do you want everyone to hear this shit?"

It was too much, all of it. I took a shuddering breath.

"I have to go," I blurted out. **"Don't you dare follow me."**

And I ran, my heart splitting into pieces with every step.

THIRTY-ONE

You know when you see an accident just before it happens? Time slows down. You can feel the hum of energy in the world shifting, warping, all around you. Your mind screams at your body to move, do something, hold out your hand, warn somebody.

But you don't.

You continue on, plodding forward, looking up too late to see the car bearing down on you. Then you're airborne, flying through the sky, the world passing beneath you, the universe above you.

If you're lucky, you fall, you get hurt, you survive.

If you're not lucky, well...

I felt like a car had hit me. That I could see it coming from far off, and I didn't do a damn thing to stop myself from walking out in front of it. Getting involved, intimately, inescapably involved, with werewolves had been me walking out into the street without looking. They'd barreled down toward me, and all my instincts screamed at my deafened ears. I'd ignored a lifetime of fear and good judgement.

Cash's anger at my calling Daria was still stinging, my realization that the whole thing, Finn, all of them treating me like I belonged with the pack, was a joke and a lie. They'd only done it for the chance at a heartstone. I could see that now that I was apart from them.

My feet took me away down an alley, and I let them, until my head caught up with my body and I realized I was in a strange town with nothing on me but my cellphone. Even my wallet was in my backpack, with the merch. I turned a corner, the thick scent of garbage around me. I wrinkled my nose and looked back. Cash wasn't following me. Small miracles. Maybe the power in my voice had actually gotten him to back off.

Max would know what to do. I pulled out my phone and called her.

"Hey Darce," her voice was like coming home. I closed my eyes and willed myself not to cry. I'd been doing enough of that lately.

"Max," I whispered.

"Oh shit, what's wrong?" There was a rustle of fabric in the background of the call.

"Are you in bed?" I asked.

"Yeah. Kinda sulking."

"Why?" I pushed aside my problems for a moment.

"Oh, I uh... I failed my last photo assignment and—"

"You what?"

"You heard me, don't make me repeat it."

"But your professor loves you. He said you were top of his class."

"Yeah well, he isn't too thrilled with the fact I've missed every other day for the last few weeks."

"Oh Max," I said softly. "I'm so sorry. I should be there."

"No, you need to be where you are, being a smarty-pants intern and rocking it hardcore with your sexy guys. I've seen the Insta, they're hot. So it's the tall smiley blond rocking your socks, huh? I'd had gone for his twin. Nice and scowly does it for me."

I let out a long, painful breath.

"I'm coming home," I said. "I, things—things aren't working out with the band, and I need to come home." There was another rustle and then a crunching noise. Was she eating?! "Max, I'm serious!"

"Yeah, I know, and it sounds pretty shitty, whatever happened. So I needed some chocolate to handle the drama. What happened?"

"Darcy?" The call of my voice made me lift up my head. Aaron stood at the end of the alley, his hands shoved in his pockets. He looked at me quizzically and jerked his head to motion behind him. "Can we talk?"

"Yeah, one second," I said, my heart beating faster.

"What's that? What's going on?" Max's voice was tinny where I'd pulled the phone away from my ear.

"Max, I gotta call you back. I think I'm about to get my ass canned from the tour. Um, I'm just gonna bus back. Do you think you could pick me up from the station in a few days? That's how long I think it'll take before I get there."

"You're what?! Uh, sure of course," Max sounded confused. *"Please call me back as soon as you can, I'm really worried about you."*

"Yup," I said, and hung up on her, trudging toward Aaron. Here it was. The end of everything. Why did I need to steel my heart against it? I'd already made up my mind about the guys—they were using me. Getting fired for how I'd talked to Jake was only for the best.

Aaron gave me a brief smile.

"Wanna walk with me? Smells like shit back here."

"How'd you find me?"

"Watched you bail on Cash. He looked pretty upset."

"That's nice," I interrupted him. If this was happening, I wanted it to happen right away. Aaron gave me a look and cleared his throat as he started walking.

"Let's go to the bus," he said.

"I'd rather you do it here, honestly," I said. "I don't, you have, like, people on the bus. I don't really want to..." He frowned at me.

"What do you think is going on here?" he asked, his tone turning gentle.

"Um, what I said to Jake, and stuff." I squirmed, shrugging one shoulder.

"I wanted to talk to you about that," he said. "The guys and I made a decision. We're kicking him from the tour. He's been a creep the entire time, and I don't know what happened to the cool dude I knew, but Jake's—yeah, Jake's changed. I wanted to let you know that you don't have to feel uncomfortable about him being around anymore, cause he's gone."

"Gone?" Shock filled me and I felt a certain bitter sadness. Of course the one person making my life miserable would get kicked from tour just as I was also leaving. "Oh. well, I mean. so I'm not?"

He snorted.

"Oh, y'know, five years ago? I would have taken his side. But I grew up, and got myself a woman who set me straight. She's on the bus. You want to come meet her?" He must have seen the hesitation on my face. "You okay?"

"I'm just feeling mixed up, I guess." There was something about him that made me want to tell him everything, even though I barely knew him. Discretion was the better part of valor, but I'd have to be up front at some point. "I think I'm leaving the tour anyway, honestly."

Aaron was sharp, and I saw that he'd caught on by the way he narrowed his eyes.

"Things not going well with the guys?"

"No," I said abruptly.

"Weeeeell," he drew out the word and shrugged. "Tour is hard. You want to kill each other sometimes. If things are that bad, why don't you crash on our bus for the night, think about it and make a decision in the morning. There's extra bunks now that Jake and his crew are gone."

"Shara?" I asked, suddenly feeling guilty. Aaron shook his head.

"Yeah, she left with him, but I think she was sick of his shit too. She's hopping on another tour with some friends of ours."

"Well that's good, I guess." I should have been running far away from the tour entirely, but maybe Aaron wasn't totally losing it when he suggested that I sleep on it before bailing.

"Okay, I'll crash with you guys. Thanks. I really, really appreciate it."

"Look, I don't know what happened, and you probably don't want to bend my ear over it, but whatever it is, you guys can work through it." He looked weary for a moment. "If you care enough about each other, you can work through anything." Watching him, I had a suspicion that he wasn't talking about me and my fight with Cash and the guys anymore. We walked the rest of the way back to Glory Rev's bus in quiet.

"I've got a set to play," he said with a wry smile. "Chelsea will take care of you." The door to the larger tour bus opened, and he hollered inside. "Chels! I got you a stray."

A silvery laugh echoed down the bus, and Aaron motioned for me to step in.

"I'll see you in an hour and a bit," he said with a grin. He turned and started walking quickly toward the venue. I walked up the steps into the bus, the door hissing shut behind me. The difference between the Glory Rev bus and ours was hard to put into words. The phrase 'I am Gucci, you are Crocs' came to mind. Lacquered wood paneling was everywhere, bringing out the deep tones in the wood grain. White leather couches formed a seating area just behind the driver's seat, and I saw a curtain that could be drawn to give privacy for the inhabitants of the main living area of the coach while the driver was up front.

On the couch, sat a long legged, thin blonde woman. She was wrapped up in an knitted blanket, and she untangled herself from it, shaking out a sheet of waist-length hair. My eyes trailed up to her face and I froze.

I'd seen her face on the side of busses, flashing on billboards, and on more than one ad spot before my favorite Youtube videos.

"Hi," she said, getting to her feet with a smile. She held out her hand. "I'm Chelsea."

"Sawyer, I know," I breathed, sounding like a total idiot and not caring. "Oh my god, I'm sorry. I didn't realize, when he'd said Chelsea he'd meant Chelsea *Sawyer*, XOhX recording alum, and top-charting billboard artist."

"That's my guy for you, complete idiot. Doesn't think he should warn you. You're," She squinted at me. "Darcy?"

I felt my cheeks go hot. She knew who I was? I felt like I was going to disgrace myself and vom everywhere. She was just so inhumanly beautiful, it took my breath away. I'd thought it was all photoshopping when I'd seen her photos. But no. She had sparkling eyes, so blue they looked violet although that was probably a trick of the light, and her blond hair was the sandy-white that made some people looked washed out but seemed to just perfectly fit her pale complexion. Even her eyebrows were white. She had to have one hell of a stylist to do that good a job bleaching out her eyebrows without burning them right off.

"That's right," I finally answered her, knowing I was staring at her like an idiot.

"Do you want anything to drink? You look like you've had a rough night," she said as she walked over to the fridge. It was triple the size of the little fridge in our—in Phoenixcry's tour van. My chest squeezed as I thought of the guys, crammed in the van. It'd had been so much like home in there with them that not even meeting Chelsea Sawyer could make the little tour van seem like the lesser of the two.

"Yeah, that'd be nice," I said. Chelsea smiled at me, and I felt a flush of warmth in my body in response. She just seemed so nice, it was impossible to not relax in her presence. She poured me a soda and brought it to me. I sat on one of the pristine white couches, and took a sip.

"Aaron's told me a bit about you," she said as she folded her impossibly long legs up under her and relaxed back into her knit blanket. "So you're my new stray, hmmm?"

"I don't know what he meant by that, but you don't need to take care of me. I'm good," I insisted. I took another sip of soda. It soothed my throat, but did nothing to fix the ragged hole in my chest where Cash and the guys' betrayal had ripped out my heart. I was still trying to figure out if Finn had ever really loved me, or if he'd just loved the idea of what I could do for the pack. I closed my eyes and sighed.

"You look tired, sweetie," Chelsea said, and I realized I was nearly dropping my soda onto my lap. She reached over and took the glass from my numb fingers.

"I'm just really..." I was tired. It was an overwhelming feeling swamping me, pulling me down.

"Let me take you to your bunk," she said, and my hand was in hers and she was leading me down the long aisle. Bunks lined the walls on either side of us, and the air felt muffled, quiet. "Here," she said, as she pulled back a pleated curtain for a lower bunk. It was just like home, back at the dorm with Max. I crawled in and sighed.

Chelsea laughed again, soft and silvery like earlier.

"We'll wake you up in the morning, but if you need anything, the bathroom is just to your left, and you can help yourself to anything in the fridge, okay?"

"Okay," I said, my eyelids feeling heavy. Grief had weighed me down, but even that was shifting away. Chelsea let the curtain drop and I heard her walk away. I squirmed to get out of my jeans, and shoes, tucking them at the end of the bunk, and sighed, crawling under the blankets. They were barely up to my chin, when the soft sound of Chelsea singing, drifted down the narrow hall to me. I couldn't quite make out the words, but they dragged me right down into sleep. I should have been worried about the guys, about my future, about hunters, about everything... but all my emotions blurred together and faded away.

Finally, I was at peace.

THIRTY-TWO

The movement of the bus underneath me rocked me slowly from sleep. I woke up in the dark, thinking for a moment that I was with Finn. My eyes opened into the faint light of my bunk, Finn's warmth missing from beside me. The scent was sterile, like cleaned carpets, no hint of mint, or the combined scents of the other wolves.

After a second of staring at the ceiling, it finally hit me that the bus was *moving*. I shoved my legs in my jeans and shot out of my bunk, stumbling into the living area. Aaron looked up from where he sat, laptop open on the couch beside him. It was light outside, just after dawn.

"The guys," I blurted out. "They—where?" They had no idea where I was. My chest tightened, a giant rubber band wrapping around it and stopping me from getting a full lungful of air.

"We agreed it was best if you rode with us to the next venue," Aaron said, his voice calm. He got up and poured a glass of water, and held it out for me. "I spoke with Eli before they left."

"They left?" I asked, my voice cracking. I took the water and gulped down a mouthful of it.

"They loaded out and hauled ass shortly after you went to sleep." He shrugged. "They said they had something to do before they got to the next venue. We'll see them there though, in a few hours. Why don't you go back to sleep for a bit?"

I looked out the window and nodded. A swirl of guilt and sadness took up home in my belly, threatening to suck my heart down into a pit of bottomless despair. Sleep sounded like a great idea. Sleep sounded like the *best* idea.

Aaron gave me an understanding, sad smile.

"You're really having a tough time, huh?" He took the glass from me, setting it on the counter, and wrapped me up in a hug that I hadn't been expecting. He squeezed me gently then chucked me under the chin. "Go to sleep, kid. You look wrecked."

"Thanks," I said, wrinkling my nose at him. I took one more sip of water before tipping the glass out into the sink.

Aaron's eyes were on me until I disappeared behind the privacy curtain that separated the sleeping quarters from the rest of the bus. The darkness enveloped me as I curled back into my bunk. Staring up at the ceiling of my little cubby, I took long, slow breaths to calm my body. Sleep was a long time coming, but it snuck up on me, stealing me away to a place where bad feelings and confusing thoughts didn't exist.

THE SOFT CRACKLE of something frying made me sit up and rub my temples. It felt like my head was trying to crack open from the inside. I grabbed my pants and squirmed into them. The grimy feeling of wearing the same things for two days clung to me as I pushed aside my bunk's pleated curtain and blinked into the light that flooded the aisle of the bus's sleeping section.

Low laughter, talk, the strum of an acoustic guitar, and the smell of bacon dragged me, hesitant, from the cocoon of the sleeping quarters. Chelsea looked up, her long blond hair tied in two thin braids down her back, from where she sat between Aaron's legs, her back against his belly and chest. They looked so comfortable that my heart ached. The rest of the band were there too. Glory Rev was a four piece band, plus Ginny, and their tour manager and gear tech, Horse. I had no idea why he was called Horse, but it seemed to suit him—he had more teeth than any human rightfully should but, despite his sort of homely appearance, he was a solid guy and had been friendly with me whenever we'd crossed paths.

"Sleep well, sweetie?" Chelsea asked as she got to her feet. She walked easily despite the rock of the bus as we drove along the highway. When I made a face, she chuckled and poured me a glass of water. "Drink all of this, then Dean will make you some bacon."

Dean stood by the frying pan, bravely shirtless, and saluted me with his spatula. He was on drums, and he had the biceps and forearms to prove it. His dark skin rippled as he flipped a pancake and winked at me. I gave him a brief smile back and drank my water slowly. It was like I was underwater, I felt so weighed down and dragged out.

Then the bus turned a sharp corner on the highway and I took a deep breath. I looked at Aaron. He was playing with Chelsea's braid ends, tickling them up her neck. I had to glance away, because it made me miss Finn too much and his warm, comforting cuddles in the back of the van.

Ginny was sprawled on one of two bench seats that made up the dining table, playing an enthusiastic game of snap with the other two guys, Seth and Evan. Horse was on his phone, muttering quietly into it. Ginny smiled up at me and patted the seat beside her.

"Wanna play?" she asked. I shook my head, leaning my hip against the counter for balance.

"I'm okay. Thanks though." My mind was going a million miles an hour. I needed to do something, get out of the bus, move, or something. We might have been traveling down the highway at 70 miles per hour, but I felt like I was standing still. "I need to make a call," I said to no one in particular, and ducked into the sleeping quarters.

Daria picked up right away. I took a slow, shallow breath.

"Darcy? Two calls in a few days, I'm getting spoiled," she joked, although I could tell she was worried.

"I-I need that money," I whispered. She went quiet for a second, and I could hear the shuffle of her sitting up.

"Why?" she asked after a moment. "Not that it changes things, I'll get you the money you need, but why?"

"I'm coming home." The words nailed my future into a coffin, and I closed my eyes as my world went sideways.

Maybe I hadn't been hit by the bus. Maybe I was the bus, knocking my own self over, flattening my future and wrecking everything. Daria was quiet, very quiet.

"Are you sure about that?" she asked, her voice wavering.

"No."

"Then you need to think about that. Really carefully."

"I can't." I needed to not think. Thinking was a privilege for the people who weren't walking around with half their heart dragging on the ground behind them.

"Tell me where, and I'll get it to you. For a flight, I'm guessing?" There was a scratching noise.

"We're in Albuquerque next," I said.

"Land of enchantment," Daria snickered. "Let me just book you a flight. So like, tomorrow?"

"Today, please. I'll be there in six hours, tops." It was really happening.

"Mmkay. You need a ride from the airport?"

I bit my lip.

"Okay. Yeah, sure."

"Alright I'll have it booked and send you the info in a minute here. Darcy, Are you sure? Like absolutely sure? Cause once you're back here, I don't know if—well, your parents were pretty pissed when you ran off the first time."

My throat tightened.

"Maybe book it round-trip. I just have questions, I need to see you, I just need a break. From everything. It's not like they ever tried to look for me anyway, so I don't—I just, I need some time. Everything's—it's all—" My throat cut off my words, and I couldn't speak.

Daria fell quiet.

"Yeah. Okay. Well, let me text you the flight information, and I guess I'll see you soon."

By some small miracle, Phoenixcry's van wasn't at the venue when we got there. It was probably for the best anyway. Aaron had grabbed my bags out of their van before we'd left the last venue the night before, so it was no big deal to pull my duffel over my shoulder, go around a corner of the venue where no one could see me and hail a cab.

I shot a text message to Max. She at least deserved to know what was going on.

I'm doing the stupidest thing I've ever done in my life.

It was a few minutes before I received one back.

Does it involve jello shots? Otherwise it's not that stupid.

It's worse than that. I'm going home. Like... home-home. I replied and sat back, closing my eyes as the cab took me to the airport. My phone buzzed and I didn't even want to look at it.

A numb, icy feeling spread through my whole body as I arrived at the airport. I went through the motions of checking in; I had to throw out a few things in my bag as I went through security because my hand cream was too big, apparently. I boarded the plane, the smell of thin air clinging to every surface, and finally looked at my phone.

Max had sent three more texts in the time I'd gotten to the airport and on my plane.

DARCY WHAT THE FUCK.

I squeezed my eyes shut.

OKAY BUT SERIOUSLY WHAT THE FUCK. THAT GIRL FROM YOUR INTERNSHIP, WILLA, JUST CALLED ME. YOU BAILED?!

I'd forgotten I'd listed Max as my emergency contact.

CALL ME RIGHT THE FUCK NOW. Her last text message, sent twenty minutes ago, left me with a sour taste in the back of my throat. I didn't have to explain anything to her. Why couldn't she be like Daria, who hadn't asked any big questions, who had just done me a solid?

I held my breath as the plane picked up speed, and took flight, sending my stomach into my spine and my heart into my throat. It was done. I was gone. This was the bed I'd made, and I was going to lay in it. There was just one more thing I needed to do...

Your account is now deactivated.

Your account will be permanently deleted in 30 days.

If you change your mind you can reactivate by logging in before your account is deleted perm

Click here to sign up for a new account.

KEEP READING FOR AN EXCERPT
FROM BOOK 2 IN THE ROGUE WITCH
SERIES

PHOENIXFALL

Available on Amazon now!

ACE

I felt listless. That was probably the best word for it. The urge to shift, like always, itched right below my skin, but I ignored it. I couldn't have shifted if I wanted to. None of us could. Eli had the driver's side window rolled down, and the breeze ruffled my hair as we drove through the hot desert from New Mexico down to Texas.

Every mile passed us, and I sank deeper into a pit of anger and sadness. Darcy was *gone*-gone. We were on our own, and the van felt so empty without her presence. Her scent still clung to our things, taunting us, making it feel like I'd turn around and she'd be sitting right there in the back, curled against Finn.

But the only thing that would be there when I turned would be Finn; his face bruised, a scowl set on his lips. He and Eli hadn't been getting along all that great since Eli decided for all of us that we'd take off after the Albuquerque gig and not wait for Darcy to show up again. His reasoning was that we still weren't sure if hunters were on our collective tails, and she'd get in touch with the label if she needed to be picked up.

Finn had disagreed. Violently. I backed Finn up, but Eli had been in a mood, and even I knew not to piss off our alpha wolf when he was stalking around like an asshole. Finn was his twin though, and apparently brave or stupid enough to challenge his brother.

It'd earned Finn a nearly broken arm and a black-eye. The black-eye would heal, the arm too, in a matter of hours and a day or two respectively. His heart, and mine? That would end up taking a little longer.

Yeah, Darcy was gone, yeah probably back to her school, because her scent had died a few blocks away from the venue telling me she'd taken transport to wherever she'd taken off to. She'd chosen mundane life over messing around with werewolves, and I had to respect that, I guess. That didn't make it any easier to lose her.

In the short weeks she was in our lives, she'd become the center of our pack. I'd expected her to become our mate, the heart and soul of our world, and she'd just vanished.

"Hey," Charlie said, nudging me. I looked up. He held his phone so I could see the screen. On it a small, fuzzy kitten rolled around with a ball of yarn. My brow furrowed.

"What?" I asked. Charlie wrinkled his nose.

"I though it would make you smile. You love cat videos."

"Meh," I said. I looked out the window and closed my eyes, inhaling the hot air and wishing it would give me a hint of Darcy, anything, any small hint of her at all. But there was nothing out there, and what was left of her essence in the van was quickly fading.

Maybe that's why Eli kept opening up the window, to clear out any evidence that Darcy had ever been with us.

Too bad he couldn't erase the marks she'd laid on us that were invisible. Finn wore them, in his shadowed eyes. He'd actually *had* her. He'd loved her, pinned her to the bed in the back of the van and made her cry his name out. My own body ached every time he'd done it, but I wasn't jealous.

Much.

"So are we getting... a new tour manager?" I asked Charlie after a half hour passed, time liquid and stretching out. Charlie shook his head.

"Willa seems to think that Darcy'll surface and, once she pays her penance, Willa will let her come back into the fold."

Up front, Eli snorted.

"Really? That's what Willa thinks?" he asked, glaring at us in the rear-view. I heard the low rumble of Finn's growl from the back, but ignored it for now. He'd been doing that, off and on, since we'd bailed out of Albuquerque without Darcy, without our heart. It was unsettling for such an easy-going, normally cheerful guy to be a storm-cloud of misery all the time.

Charlie rolled his eyes, the sound nearly audible.

"Sure Willa doesn't know what Darcy is, but just because our girl's a witch doesn't mean she isn't also human. She'll come back, and I'm just fucking glad Willa's willing to forgive her," Charlie said, sounding confident, almost relaxed about it. My skin itched more, and I nearly echoed Finn's unhappy rumble.

"For all we know, Miss Llewellyn decided to go back to her family and let them know that a group of wolves was touring the country," Eli said, his shoulders tense. Finn snarled, wordless and enraged. Movement in the front passenger seat made my eyes dart from Eli to where Cash had been sleeping, or so I'd thought he'd been sleeping.

Cash lifted his head, looked Eli square in the face, and laughed.

"You honestly think that?" he demanded. "You think *Darcy* went running back to her family to tell them that she'd been getting horizontal with werewolves? That she reported us, to them, so they could come and wipe us off the planet?"

Eli's shoulders hunched even further.

"Well-"

"Oh shut the fuck up," Cash sat forward, stretching out, although his irritation radiated out from him, in every inch of his body despite his relaxed pose. "You don't believe that for a second. I think you're fucking butt-hurt that she left us, and you're trying to come up with reasons why she did to make her into the kind of monster she isn't."

Behind us, Finn went quiet for a moment, the lack of his growling almost as unsettling as the sound of it had been before.

"Darcy would never betray us like that. She hated her family. Hated them. She knew that we, us, all of us, we were where she belonged. I think she got scared cause *someone* kept pressuring her about creating a heartstone," Finn snapped the last few words and Cash turned, glowering.

Charlie held up a hand and whistled so sharply that my ears crackled. I covered them with my hands, wincing.

"As much as this game of pass the blame is exciting, new, and fun," he drawled, "it's not getting us to our next venue any faster, it's not bringing her back to us, and it's giving me a fucking headache. Also, Willa's calling me, so shut the fuck up, all right?"

We fell quiet.

Even without Darcy, certain things were still important, like keeping our label happy. They were the money, and they gave us access to the crowds that seemed to eat up our music. The audience wasn't our pack, but none of us could deny that performing, and them responding with such enthusiasm, was a little bit like being back with our big pack before they'd all been slaughtered.

I barely remembered those times, because I'd been too young, but the other guys told me sometimes of what it was like, to be surrounded by a huge pack, the music that made up every fiber of our being floating in the air. In wolf form, or in human form, the music was in our blood and if we weren't making it on a regular basis, we all got a little stressed out.

"Thanks Willa," Charlie said with a sigh, rubbing his face. "Well... if we hear from her, we'll tell you. But our calls go right through to voicemail too."

I looked over my shoulder at Finn. His eyes were downcast, and he looked as miserable as I felt. Maybe that's why Eli was so grumpy. Elias would do anything to protect us, but most of all he looked out for Finn. As the older twin, he felt responsible or something, I guess. Darcy leaving had cut Finn open, exposed the sensitive spots inside of him that he'd forgotten he'd had.

I'm not sure when the last time Finn had been in love. Probably at good few decades, back when he was just barely out of his puppy years and chasing tail amongst other packs.

Back when there were enough female werewolves that you could chase tail and it wasn't attached to a female wolf directly related to you.

Charlie finished his call with Willa and was quiet for a few moments. We waited, patient, because that's what we were: long-lived and patient.

"She hasn't checked in at the label. Willa had to report Darcy to the professor at her college as a no-show, which means... yeah, she's in shit with her degree, and we're still out a manager. Willa put in a call to her roommate, Max, but hasn't heard back yet."

"And our Darcy," Finn croaked, his voice raw. Well, he had been screaming a lot at Eli, so it made sense. He really needed to watch his voice so he wouldn't lose it for the show later. "You forgot to say we're missing our Darcy."

Charlie let out a breath.

"Honestly, I didn't think it needed to be said." He hitched one shoulder. "Aaron texted me. He and Chelsea feel like shit because she disappeared on their watch-"

"Well they fucking should," Finn snarled each word like they were being ripped right out of his heart. "Aaron should never have let her stay on the Glory Rev bus. He should've told her to come back to us-"

"What the fuck were you going to do, pin her down and fuck some sense back into her?" Charlie twisted in his seat. Finn roared, and in a split-second he was across the van, throwing Charlie onto the floor. Eli slammed on the breaks, the tires squealing, and I lurched forward, my seat-belt keeping me from smashing my face into the back of Eli's seat.

The only saving grace, looking back, was that we were on a deserted stretch of highway. Eli's seatbelt clicked loose and he was into the back of the tour van in another second, crashing into Charlie and Finn like a boulder. I winced as the force of their bodies piling on top of each other rocked the van. Cash leaned over his seat and shoved the sliding door on the van open. The other three guys spilled out onto the hard cement, snarling and snapping at each other. I piled out after them, staring helplessly at what remained of my pack. Cash got a hand into the fray, and dragged Finn out, wrapping his arms around Finn's ribcage. Eli grabbed Charlie, who's lip was split, blood splattering on the ground below. The two fighters glared at each other, Finn lunging forward despite Cash's grip

"Stop it," Cash snapped, jerking Finn away. "Stop it you fuck-head, seriously."

Eli was muttering low in Charlie's ear. Charlie glowered at Finn for a moment then looked away. I took in a shaky breath. Cash let Finn go and pointed at me.

"You're setting a shit-ass example for our youngest," he said, slapping Finn in the chest. Despite the power behind the blow, Finn barely shifted, his weight rocking back onto his heels for a moment.

"He's an adult," Finn's voice was barely above a guttural hiss, but guilt crossed his features. I shoved my hands in my pockets, looking at the ground. They always did this. Treated me like I wasn't *enough* despite being of age, despite pulling my weight just like everybody else in the pack. Anger simmered away in my belly but I ignored it. We had enough problems without me lashing out at the guys that had raised me after my parents were cut down right in front of me. Especially Cash, I owed him my life directly.

"I don't give a fuck. You behave yourselves," Cash was barely breathing enough to get the words out, that's how angry he was. He shoved Finn again, shoulder into Finn's chest, and then stalked over to me.

"I'm fine," I said, when Cash looked like he was going to inspect me all over for damage like I was a silly pup that had wandered into a three-pack-brawl. He gave me a broody stare and I threw my hands up. "I'm fine! Fuck! This isn't the first time I've seen violence."

Cash let out a breath he'd been holding, his eyes running over my face.

"Yeah but I promised myself that you'd never... see it again," he said, his words halting. Behind him, Charlie went pale in Eli's grip, and stepped away as Eli let him go. All four of them, my pack, my brothers-in-arms, carried the guilt of nearly losing me to hunters like it was their personal burden. I knew they blamed themselves for the death of the rest of our pack, as if by being survivors they were to blame.

It was stupid. I glowered at each of them in turn. If they were going to feel guilty then I was going to use that to school them into better behavior. I didn't care if it was manipulative.

"Can we just get to the next show," I said, looking at Charlie hardest. "And apologize to Finn. That was crass. You know how much he misses Darcy."

"We all do," Cash murmured, running his hands through his hair. The dark strands stuck out at all angles.

"Sorry Finn." Charlie wasn't able to meet his eyes as he apologized, but that was good enough for me. I felt the hot melt of Eli's appraising look over me and I glanced at him. The corner of his mouth was tucked up into a smile.

"What?" I asked, defensive.

"Being schooled by you, kid, doesn't make me feel all that capable of leading the pack," his voice was wry. I made a face and he laughed.

"Get back in the van," I ordered them, and then grabbed the front passenger door. "And I'm sitting in the front this time."

PHOENIXFALL

Available on Amazon now!

WELCOME TO THE REAL WORLD. IT SUCKS. YOU'RE GONNA LOVE IT!

So that's a *Friends* quote. Because that TV show is on repeat in my house pretty much non-stop all the time, so I figured I should thank it somehow in my "end of the book author-talking nonsense". I also think it kind of makes sense with Darcy crash-landing in a mundane world after a magical upbringing.

Wow. So. This was the *book*. This was the book that stole my heart and made me finally "get" what every other truly passionate author has always talked about. I fell in love with this book. This book became my baby. This was supposed to be a standalone, one-and-done book, and then the boys grabbed me by the shoulders and demanded three books.

Then a quarter of the way through this book, they demanded five books. Five books, they said, one for each of them to woo and properly love their Darcy like she deserved. It's gonna be a long year.

So I'm sorry about the cliffhanger! The only reason it's there is because the next book is coming super, super super soon (and if you're reading this after it's published, lucky you, you don't even have to wait!!!) so I hope you'll forgive me.

THE THANK YOUS...

There's a lot of people to be thanking at the end of this book. My bestie, Gina, for sitting with me while I waved my hands around in the air and described Darcy's world, how witches worked, what werewolves were, and a whole bunch of other stuff you won't find out until the next few books. To Zephr, for being Beta o and squeaking at me, you kept me going when I was terrified. To Nicole, for being so good as to say "ha ha sure okay" when I texted you with a "hey can I put you in my book about witches and werewolves ps you are a bad-ass label manager", for not giving up on me when I totally flat out bailed on our first ever meeting, for being the best friend I could ever ask for, for cheering me up when I was really down, for commiserating with me over stupid shit-heads in bands, and for skipping the line at clubs like the super bosses we were as music-industry ninjas. To She Who Shall Not Be Named for being a terribad music industry mentor, you're cancelled, bye Felicia, thanks for showing me the kind of person I didn't want to be. Thanks to Tina for giving me the "are you a broad or a bitch?" talk. I hope I'm solidly in the "broad" category.

Thanks to Chrissy, for letting me borrow your name and for being a shoulder to lean on. To Katie for saying "hey you really love this book, I can tell, wow, it's so good, like the best thing you've ever written!!!". To Kat, my writing friend, my makeup friend, my sweetheart lovely; forgiveness is a lesson you've taught me, and humility as well.

To Erin, my PA, who came on right away and jumped into

this project and sent me a tonne of gifs and cheered me up and has been such a wellspring of positivity and organization that I just can't stop adoring you!! To Cam, for taking on this project and giving me the "down and dirty hard to hear" kind of feedback that I needed. To Dave, Rich, Ron, and Sue, my music friends and mentors who've held my hand and been there with me through the ups and downs of the music industry.

Thanks to the FTW girls, who are all amazing authors in their own right, and I am honored to be your friends and be inspired by you. To the crew at Double Dee.

TO MY BETAS, oh my blurgh. You answered a random author's call on Facebook, and gave me so much good feedback and squeeing and advice and love that it made this process that much easier. I was cracking out 10k of words a day because of your encouragement. So thank you, Alisha, Ashleigh, Ashley, Brianna, Jan, Lakerea, Liz, Megan, Mikayla, Nadine, Peggy, Robyn, Susan, Sabrina, Sarah, Shayla, Tabitha, Teresa, and Tiffany. You beauties were amazing.

To Lauren Landa for bringing Darcy's voice to life and for coming up with the coolest idea for an audio book. I treasure our friendship every day, and I am so lucky that I have you in my life. You are a gift.

To Becca Briggs, for being Darcy's face and being the most generous, sweet, kind, smart and driven woman. You are amazing, and I appreciate you letting me put you on the cover of my book. To Curtis, for your great photography and touch-up skills and knowing exactly what I needed without me really having to ask for it!

To Ciarin Shields for drawing a beautiful phoenix feather for me, and for working on the cover-art tirelessly, and for doing all sorts of odd-job graphics for me. We've crashed red carpets together, played shows on three different continents together, and you're the best touring friend and musician I've ever worked for. You're a sexy beast, and I love ya.

All my beauties over at KT's Beauties hanging out with me and sharing memes and other stuff. You guys make opening up Facebook worth it!

To my tour-cars, Wink and Hawkeye for keeping me and my musicians safe on the road, and for letting me clock the most miles anyone has ever seen on a Honda Fit ever.

To Bri, who edited this thing and has held my hand over the last year and a bit. Our chance meeting online has led to a beautiful friendship, and I'm so grateful for you each and every day, especially when you send me ridiculous Snapchats of yourself.

Thanks to every band and artist I've ever had the pleasure (and displeasure) of working with: thanks for the education, the music, and the fun.

And lastly, thanks to you. Thanks for reading my book. Gosh, I sure do appreciate it. I hope it was a good ride for you, and if it was, let me know. I'm always tooling around on Facebook, happy to chat any time I'm not writing or sleeping or on the road with a band.

Hugs, love, and all the rest,

Kit

(K.T. Strange)

STAY IN TOUCH!

ABOUT THE AUTHOR

KT Strange is a reverse harem romance author from the Great White North. After spending ten years in the music scene babysitting drunk rock-stars, she's finally ready to settle down (sorta) and write a few good books inspired by her life on the road with bands and her love of everything paranormal.

Also she is rather fond of cats.

ktstrange.com

Made in the USA
Las Vegas, NV
07 January 2022